# Carthage Prime
## Ace Evans Trilogy Book 2

by
Toby Neighbors

Carthage Prime - Ace Evans Trilogy 2
© 2020, Toby Neighbors

Published by Mythic Adventure Publishing, LLC
Idaho, USA

ISBN: 978-1-952260-09-4

Copy Editing by Julie Duke

# Books By Toby Neighbors

## Fantasy

Avondale
Draggah
Balestone
Arcanius
Avondale V
Wizard Rising
Magic Awakening
Hidden Fire
Fierce Loyalty
Crying Havoc
Evil Tide
Wizard Falling
Chaos Descending
Into Chaos
Chaos Reigning
Chaos Raging
Controlling Chaos
Killing Chaos
Elder Wizard
Lorik
Lorik the Defender
Lorik the Protector
The Vault Of Mysteries
Lords Of Ascension
The Elusive Executioner
Regulators Revealed
Third Prince
Royal Destiny
My Lady Sorceress
The Man With No Hands

## Sci-Fi

Spartan Company
Spartan Valor
Spartan Guile
We Are The Wolf
Welcome To The Wolfpack
Embracing Oblivion
Joined In Battle
The Abyss Of Savagery
Dragon Team Seven
Uncommon Loyalty
Total Allegiance
Kestrel Class
Jump Point
Gravity Flux
Modulus Echo
Zero Friction
Planet Fall
The New World
ARC Angel
Battle ARC
Broken Crucible
Lost Kingdom
War INC

## Thrillers

Charter
Jack & Roxie

## Horror

Zompocalypse Omnibus
The Other Side

For more about Toby's novels visit

www.TobyNeighbors.com

# Chapter 1

Loman Haley, Vice President of Security for Ahzco, had just settled in behind his desk for the day. Looking out the big windows of the Ahzco building, he could see the sun glistening off the polished steel and reflective glass of thousands of structures. Arcadia was a popular planet. A safe planet. A good planet for doing business, thanks to Ahzco's Corporate Defense Force.

Loman wasn't the type to bask in his accomplishments, but he was alive and still had a job—both things that had nearly been stolen from him—so he indulged himself for a brief moment. He pulled out a plain, stainless steel flask from the inside of his coat pocket. It was too early to start drinking, and it was against company policy for employees to keep hard spirits on the premises, but it was a flask just like the one that had saved his life on TROY in the Helena system. A flask and Alex Evans, Loman thought. He would check on the boy's progress in the CDF soon, but first he slipped the flask among the files in the lower drawer of his desk.

Things were starting to feel right again. His side still hurt from the laser blast that had pierced his side, but nothing serious was hurt—just some fat and skin. The wound would leave a nasty scar, but it would heal in time. The rest of the effects of the attack seemed to have subsided, and it was time to get back to work.

Just as he was contemplating all he needed to accomplish, his computer beeped with an executive memo. The worst thing about being a VP was the almost constant interruptions. The real work had to be squeezed between meetings and appointments, most of which were a colossal waste of time.

"Read it to me," Loman ordered the AI-powered computer.

"From the desk of Chief Executive Officer Ian Gentry to Vice President of Security Loman Haley. Mandatory meeting in Gentry's office at 0722 this morning."

"Is that all?" Loman asked the machine.

He didn't expect an answer. Artificial Intelligence was limited by certain protocols so as not to appear too lifelike or powerful. He glanced at the memo displayed on his monitor. It was just like Gentry to be cryptic, but Loman could guess the reason for the meeting. He got to his feet and headed back out of his office, mumbling to himself about five minutes of peace.

Everything was changing at Ahzco's universal headquarters. The board of directors had instituted a new dual head of each department. Loman hadn't heard who would be joining him yet, and perhaps the meeting in CEO Ian Gentry's office was about that very subject. The CEO was desperate to maintain what power he had, and the chair of the BOD was working relentlessly to snatch it away. Lynn Faulk was the chairwoman of Ahzco's board, but she wanted complete, unfettered control of the company. To do that, she needed her own people in charge of actually running the company's many divisions, including security. It was a classic power play, only Faulk had used the attack on Loman in the Helena system to push her agenda forward. Loman was determined to push back, but he had already stumbled into one trap. He wouldn't underestimate Lynn Faulk again, no matter how desperate the CEO was.

Most of the support staff didn't come into the offices until 0800, but Gentry's secretary was already there. She gave Loman a dazzling smile that made him feel almost giddy.

"Good morning, Mr. Haley," she said. Even her voice had been modified. It was low, almost sensual, and completely feminine. "Mr. Gentry is waiting for you. Please, go straight in."

"I will," Loman said, forcing himself to look away. He knew that the secretary was meant to intimidate or distract whoever was coming to see the CEO. She was a product of the finest plastic surgery, with no more interest in him than one might have in a total stranger one passed on the street, and yet his mind tried to tell him otherwise. It took all his willpower, but he forced himself to forget about her.

He entered Gentry's huge office and discovered Immanuel Cortez sitting in front of Gentry's neat desk. Cortez was vice president of planetary assets, essentially a corporate realtor. Loman's job was to protect company assets, while Cortez coaxed and traded to make sure every division was profitable. It was a surprise to see Cortez, and it made Loman wonder what the meeting was about; it certainly wasn't a strategy session to deal with Lynn Faulk —not with Cortez present.

"Loman, good," Gentry said as he waved to an empty chair. "We have an opportunity, and I want to move on it quickly."

"Yes, sir," Loman said, sitting down.

"The Free Trade Association is about to open a new planet," Cortez said. "My sources tell me it's incredibly rich with resources."

"Don't they always say that?" Loman replied.

"The FTA does, of course," Cortez replied. "But not my sources. They're well-placed and well-compensated. If they say it's a good planet, we should move immediately to get as large a stake as possible."

"It could be another Arcadia," Gentry said. "We don't want to share the planet with too many other companies. Skandia Seven could have been ours if we'd been more proactive."

"All right," Loman said. "What do you need from me?"

"A security team," Cortez said. "The best you've got."

"For a free planet?" Loman said. "What would be the point?"

"Word is, there's Tormenium reserves in the southern hemisphere," Cortez said.

"We don't have to tell you how valuable that could be," Gentry said.

Loman nodded. Tormenium was the elusive one hundred and twenty-first element, known by its number on the periodic table, 121. Loman wasn't a chemist, but he knew 121 was believed to be an almost magical substance. There wasn't enough of it to use in commercial products yet, but all the big companies were searching for it. The RDT department of his own division put in requests for the rare element on every quarterly report.

"They're calling it Carthage Prime," Cortez continued. "It's a level-two planet with an extreme axis.

Only the northern hemisphere's warm enough to live on. There'll be settlers in the north, but the south will be less stable."

"You mean it'll be a war zone," Loman said.

"Whoever gets the mineral rights will have legal standing," Cortez said.

"But every company with a CDF will want to take it from us," Gentry said. "As soon as the contract is approved, we need boots on the ground and ships in orbit."

"You want a full engagement on-world with no infrastructure?" Loman said. "Right now? Don't we have enough problems to worry about?"

"It could be precisely for that reason—that we've been attacked," Gentry said. "The only companies with the resources to bid with us are Zen Tech and Getty Enterprises. But if we're too busy licking our wounds, we could miss the biggest prize of the century. Do that and we're out of a job, Loman."

"Another company could knock us off the top of the mountain," Cortez said, "if there's as much Tormenium as the geologists suppose there is."

Loman sat back in his chair and crossed his legs. It wouldn't take much to divert the freighter bound for Creedence Three. He could put together a security detail to escort the freighter, but he had moved most of their available teams to bolster security on the company's other worlds. A full engagement would stretch his CDF thin.

"And if there isn't?" Loman asked. "If we spend billions on a world with nothing to show for it, we'll be the laughingstock of every company in the galaxy. Not to mention we'll be fired."

"We don't have a choice," Gentry said. "We have to commit and hold the planet. We can't sit this one out and hope there's nothing there. Tormenium is too rare and too valuable to take that chance."

"Fine, I'll get started on putting a team together," Loman said.

He stood up, and Cortez followed his example. Gentry stayed at his desk, leaning back and looking up at them both.

"This is the future, gentlemen," the CEO said, "and perhaps our legacy. Let's make it happen."

# Chapter 2

Learning to fly was more fun than Alex had imagined. The simulators were like a game, but he had quickly graduated to the Titan Trainer. The Fast-Attack Titan battle suit was the quintessential mechanized armor. It was over three meters tall, roughly the shape of a human, and had powerful weapons built into the arms and back. The suit used a variety of thrusters and repulsers to get off the ground, along with an electric minijet on the back for atmospheric flight.

Flying was difficult to master, and Alex had learned to let the suit feed into his mind all the data he needed to keep the bulky battle suit in the air. It many ways, it was like learning to walk all over again. A person rarely thought about keeping their balance, avoiding obstacles, maintaining their pace, or navigating to their desired location—they just walked. The suit did all the hard work, and what Alex was learning to do was respond appropriately when needed. He let Nyx, his controller who was far away on an orbital ship, watch over all the suit's readings like altitude, air speed, attitude, and radar. She fed him the information he needed. Some of it, such as navigation, was a transaction between the Implanted Neural Controller and his brain that he didn't have to think about. She could download the coordinates, and then he simply knew where to go. Other things, such as other ships approaching, she told him via the suit's communication system. He didn't hear her voice through the speakers near his ears, but rather as a variation of his own voice inside his head.

*Ash and Sly are forming up behind you*, Nyx told him.

"Any sign of our targets?" Alex replied.

*Negative. Wherever they are, I can't see them on the sat feed or pick them up on radar.*

"Are we even sure they're down there?" Ashton Timmons wondered, her voice crystal clear to Alex though the Titan's company channel of their com-link.

"That's what we're supposed to find out," Alex said.

"And the best way to do that," Sly added, "is to fly low enough to make them shoot at us."

*He's not wrong*, Nyx said.

"True," Alex responded, "but that's not exactly the way we've trained. We should just dive down and see if they shoot us."

"Well, cruising around and identifying possible target sights is boring," Sly said. "We're the big dogs. Why not send us in and let us do what we're made to do?"

"I'm with him," Ashton said.

Alex felt exactly the same way, but Chief Landry had hammered the team concept into them. The trio were flying Titan training suits, which had all the navigation controls but no weapons. They were bulky and awkward in the air, designed to make the operators flying them struggle —the idea being that if they could fly the Trainers, then they would have no trouble in actual FA Titans. Alex, Ash, Sly, and Newt—who was sitting this training session out as there were only three Titan Trainers—were the fliers and the best operators in the FA Titan battle suits. The rest of the company, nine fighters and one medic, would use the variety of other battle suits depending on what the mission called for. While Alex and his teammates would prefer to dive down and engage the enemy in a direct fight, their job was to identify possible targets and slowly spiral down until they coaxed the enemy to reveal their location. It was a reconnaissance mission, and as team leader, it was his job to call the shots in the air.

"All in good time," Alex said, hoping he didn't sound as frustrated as he felt. "Stick to your assigned quadrant and perform the slow, spiral descent, just the way we trained."

"Man, what a killjoy," Sly said.

"What do you expect? He's the CO's favorite," Ash said.

They banked away from Alex in opposite directions. He knew they were teasing him, yet there was a vein of truth in what they said. Alex was indeed Chief Landry's favorite, but he was also the best flyer of the group. Ashton was a daredevil and completely fearless. She loved going as fast as she possibly could in any environment, but she didn't have the ability to adapt to changing conditions that Alex had. Sly and Newt were both capable, but Alex was the best. Even in the bulky trainers, he could do things the others couldn't. Chief Landry had made him team leader A, while Oggy was team leader B. Alex was in charge of the group of Titans, while Oggy took charge of the rest of the company on the ground. Being team leader wasn't an actual promotion; it was just a way to give a little more structure to Echo Company. Landry gave the orders, and Master Sergeant Gellar made sure they were carried out, but once they were on a mission, Alex had some say in the way they did their assigned tasks.

*Does it bother you when they talk like that?* Nyx asked.

"Not really," Alex replied. "It's the burden of being a team leader, I guess. They would do the same thing in my place, but they don't have that burden, so they can voice how they really feel."

*How do you really feel?*

"Like doing something other than circling around up here waiting for something that probably won't ever happen."

They were on a training mission with no live fire. The rest of Echo Company were on a completely different field exercise. Everything was simulated, which in Alex's opinion was boring. He wanted to bank and dive, perform loops, and relish in the freedom of flying, but instead he was going slow and by the book.

*Never happen? You don't think we'll get an assignment soon?*

"Maybe, once they train us to make orbital insertions," Alex said.

*It will be ni—Wait! I've got something.*

"Where?"

*Movement, on the ground. Looks like ground-to-air missiles.*

Nyx didn't tell Alex where the ground unit was. Instead, she sent it to him and his INC translated the data. He banked to his right and started climbing.

"We must be in range," Alex said. "Titans, climb to five thousand meters."

"Copy that," Sly said. "Climbing to five thousand meters."

"I've got bogeys on the ground," Ash said. "Three groups."

*Incoming,* Nyx warned Alex.

"I see them," Alex said.

What he saw were puffs of smoke from the missiles being fired. The missiles were moving too fast to see, even with the suit's enhanced visual system.

"Evasive maneuvers," Alex reminded his team. "Mark the locations of the ground units and climb."

*Alex, I can't identify the missiles, but I have flight speed. Contact in thirty-five seconds.*

"Okay, get high, everyone," Alex said. "We've done our part."

"Great, we get to miss the fun part," Ash said. "I'm ready to kick some ass."

"When are we getting weapons on these tin cans, anyway?" Sly added.

A beeping sound began, and Alex suddenly felt the urge to escape. He was racing straight up, but the collision alarm was ringing in his ear.

*You're passing ten thousand meters,* Nyx said.

"And the missiles?"

*Still tracking you. Contact is fourteen seconds.*

"We can't outrun them this way," Alex said. "Dive! Make them work for it."

He knew it was just an exercise. There weren't actual missiles chasing them—just computer blips. Losing them would be difficult, but he wasn't going to out-climb them.

"Roger that!" Sly said.

"It's about time," Ash said.

Alex tipped his Titan over, letting his momentum slow him as he silently counted the seconds in his head. He was down to four when the suit began to descend. He maxed the Titan's power and went in a downward spin.

Gravity was suddenly on his side. He went from a slow climb to a fast dive, the g-forces squeezing him so hard he had trouble breathing. His head felt light. Even though he was upside-down, the sudden change in gravity was pulling his blood from his head toward his feet.

*You still with me, Alex?*

"Yeah," Alex managed to say, just as he pulled out of his dive.

*You're at four thousand meters.*

"Is the bogey still on us?"

*You've bought yourself a few seconds, but there's no time to slow down.*

Slowing down was the last thing on Alex's mind. He raced up and down, banking hard enough that he saw spots. The Titans were incredibly fast when descending, but he was starting to run out of space.

*Alex, you just passed fifteen hundred meters. The deck on this exercise is one thousand meters.*

"I know it," Alex said.

He pulled up, racing for the sky again, giving the suit all the power it had, but his speed slowed and the missile gained on him.

*The missile is on your tail.*

Alex dove into a spiral, then banked hard to his right. The alarm beeping, which sped up as the missile closed in on him, was a continuous tone.

*Sly's down,* Nyx said.

"I can't shake it," Alex admitted through clenched teeth.

*Stay on this course until I tell you, then pull up as hard as you can.*

"Okay," Alex said.

He was completely out of ideas, and the missile seemed to have endless fuel to pursue him with. The alarm sounded like a mechanical scream, as if the missile trailing him were a mythical banshee chasing him to his death.

*Now!* Nyx ordered.

Alex pulled up hard. The maneuver slowed him down and the g-forces almost made him pass out. But the alarm tone stopped.

*Reverse course and climb.*

Alex reacted as if the words in his head were his own thoughts. The INC gave him total control of the Titan and reacted to his will at the speed of thought. It shot up into a steep climb in the opposite direction of his previous trajectory.

"Is it still following?"

*The missiles have a slower turn rate, but we're not clear yet. Oh no, Ash just went down.*

Alex was the last of the three fliers. He felt isolated and exposed. There were no missiles in the air and no destroyed aircraft or lost lives, but the computers calculated the hits and cut off the downed trainees' communication. He was climbing for safety, but there was no guarantee he would survive.

*The missile is back on course. Contact in twenty-one seconds.*

"What's my altitude?"

*Eight thousand meters and climbing. Fuel is down to thirty percent, but it should be enough.*

"Titan One, cease your training exercise and return to base," a grim voice crackled over the trainer's internal speakers.

"Master Sergeant Gellar," Alex said. "Did we win?"

"The exercise is incomplete. Return to base."

"Incomplete? What gives?" Ash asked. "Ace was still in the fight."

"It wasn't a combat exercise, Private Timmons, which is precisely why you failed."

"Dang, that's harsh," Sly said.

"At least I wasn't the first one hit," Ash said.

"Nyx, do you know what's going on?" Alex asked.

*Negative. No word up here.*

"Maybe we're being recalled for failing," Alex said.

He hadn't been hit, and in all likelihood would have survived the engagement, real or simulated. They had also identified the targets they were sent to find, but operating an FA Titan came with the heavy responsibility of ensuring the battle suit, which cost over a hundred million credits to manufacture, wasn't needlessly lost. A lump of fear formed in Alex's stomach. Perhaps ordering his team to dive in an effort to avoid the missiles was a mistake. The loss of three Titans on a reconnaissance mission was probably considered a total failure. It made Alex question whether he was really good enough to be entrusted with the most advanced battle suit in the CDF fleet.

He was spiraling down toward the base as he worked to remove the fear of failing from his mind. The mission results were a neutral circumstance; it was his thoughts about the mission that were making him afraid. Echo Company had a wide landing platform, and once he was down to five hundred meters, he let the Titan Trainer's repulsers do the work. The unit descended slowly. Alex thought it was like being on an elevator, except he could see through the walls.

*Good luck, Alex. I'll talk you soon.*

"Roger that, Nyx. Looking forward to it."

The battle suit landed easily, and the chest piece on the humanoid device popped forward with a hiss. Alex took a deep breath of the cool air. It was one of his favorite things about Helena Prime. After living most of his life on a level-three planet that required a re-breather every time he set foot outside, breathing the open air on the CDF training planet was a gift in itself.

Ash was already on the ground, and Sly landed just as Alex was climbing out of his training unit. Master Sergeant Gellar walked out of the hangar and waved them in.

"On the double, you three," she barked. "The CO's waiting."

They jogged across the tarmac together.

"We do something wrong?" Sly asked.

"If so, we blame Ace," Ash said. "He's got goodwill credit to burn."

"Very funny," Alex said.

"It's about time," Gellar snapped.

She was holding the door open, and Alex followed Ash inside. It took a second for his eyes to adjust, but when they did, he saw the rest of Echo Company lined up nearby. He hurried over and joined them. Chief Landry was nowhere in sight, but as soon as Sly came up beside Alex, the CO appeared from a room on the far side of the hangar.

"Atten-shun!" Master Sergeant Gellar barked in a loud voice. "Commander on deck."

"As you were," he said as he came striding over toward the group. "I have news."

Alex, like the rest of the squad, waited for him to share the news. There was a grin on the chief's face, so Alex assumed the news was good and not bad. He felt himself relax just slightly. At least they weren't in trouble. Whatever news the chief had, at least it wouldn't include a ticket back to the mining world of NP8261 where Alex had grown up.

"Ahzco has won a bid for mineral rights on a brand-new planet, and the brass is calling for a full engagement."

Landry paused to let the weight of that news sink in. Alex understood from his studies as an operator with the CDF that a full engagement meant personnel on the ground and in orbit. It normally combined multiple squads with different specialties.

"Fortunately for us," Chief Landry continued, "the CDF is stretched thin, and they're calling up the training units. That means us. We go wheels up in two hours at the spaceport. So grab your gear, people. We're being deployed on an actual mission in deep space."

Alex felt the knot of fear that had been in his stomach return. A combat mission? They weren't really ready for that. Alex wasn't a coward, but he didn't like the thought of Echo Company in a battle that they weren't fully trained for. People whom he was beginning to think of as friends might die. His blood ran cold through his veins at the very thought of it.

"You heard the man—the clock is ticking," Master Sergeant Gellar shouted at them. "Get your gear packed and be back here in fifty-nine minutes, or I'll come looking for you. And let me tell you, none of you want that."

"Yes, Master Sergeant!" the entire company shouted in reply.

Alex felt numb. He wanted to ask Nyx if being deployed so soon was normal. She had become more than just a voice in his head. They were friends—in fact, she was his closest friend. But there was no time to send a message, and apart from his battle suit, he couldn't communicate with her. All he could do was obey his CO and hope for the best.

# Chapter 3

Alex didn't have a lot of gear. Three sets of training fatigues and three sets of compression wear were rolled neatly and tucked into his rucksack. He also had socks, underwear, and toiletries in the bag, along with one set of civilian clothes and his heavy leather coat. The bag was heavy, but the padded strap made carrying it easy enough. His Flex PIL was in the thigh pocket of the fatigues he wore, and his lace-up boots thumped on the concrete as he hurried from his barracks back toward Echo Company's hangar.

"Yo, Ace," Newt called. He was the second tallest member of the squad, with piercing blue eyes that stood out from the dusky hue of his skin.

"What's up, Newt?" Alex called back as Kyle Newton jogged to catch up. He had an identical rucksack slung over one shoulder.

"You think we'll get promoted?" Newt asked.

"Why?"

"Because we're being deployed. They're supposed to promote us to corporal once we're deployed."

"I think we have to complete training first," Alex said.

"But surely we've done that if they're sending us on a mission, right?"

"I guess so," Alex said, but in truth he wasn't really sure.

It didn't make sense to him that they would send Echo Company on a mission when he and his team hadn't even trained with weapons on the FA Titans. And Alex didn't like the idea of going back to a ground-based battle suit. There was nothing wrong with the other MBS's, but he had fallen in love with flying. Everything else now seemed lesser to him somehow.

"Oh man, a bump in pay, a second stripe, and some excitement," Newt said. "This gig gets better all the time."

Alex couldn't disagree. He had no idea how much more money or prestige being a corporal would earn them, but it did sound nice. The only real drawback was not being able to go and visit his parents. Vice President Loman had assured him that once Alex finished training, he would have time and liberty for a visit to his parents' new home on Skandia Seven. It seemed that idea was now off the table. If he was going to see his family again, he would have to survive long enough.

"Do you know where we're going?" Alex asked.

"No, not really," Newt said.

Alex was learning more about his squad mates with each passing day. Newt was from a level-one world and had been well-educated at an all-boys school. His father was some type of government worker, and Alex couldn't remember the name of the world his friend had grown up on. He silently scolded himself for not paying more attention in galactic geography.

"The chief said we won the mineral rights, which must mean it isn't a privately owned world," Newt said. "The Free Trade Association is working its way through the galactic arm, opening up new worlds that are discovered to be habitable. I'm guessing it's one of those."

"That's a long way from here," Alex said.

"No doubt. We'll have plenty of time to train on simulators, I would guess."

It wasn't as satisfying as being in a real Titan mechanized battle suit, but a simulator was better than nothing. And they might even end up on a ship with their controllers. The one silver lining to being deployed was the chance to spend more time with Nyx.

"I guess we'll find out soon enough," Alex said.

"What are you two yapping about?"

Alex and Newt both turned around at the same time. Oggy was just behind them, with Nuk and Tig on either side. They were united in their disdain for Alex, who they considered an interloper. Alex knew their feelings sprang from jealously, but it was hard not to resent them for the way they continued to treat him.

"Just talking about the deployment," Newt said, "and the possibility of promotion."

"What would *you* know about it?" Tig said.

"Let's go," Alex recommended.

"You know, one of these days, Ace," Oggy said, his voice dripping with hostility, "we're going to find out who really is the best."

"It's not a contest, Oggy," Alex said.

"That's what losers always say," Nuk chimed in.

"I say you got lucky on that training exercise," Oggy continued, referring to an escape and evade field exercise that had pitted the entire squad against Alex. "If I had been suited up, you wouldn't have made it halfway to the finish line."

"You won that exercise, Oggy," Alex pointed out.

"Yeah, you shot him in the back, remember?" Newt said.

"It wasn't a fair test, but one's coming," Oggy said. "Mark my words."

They were back at the hangar, and while Oggy showed no signs of easing his hostility toward Alex, he was smart enough to keep his mouth shut around Master Sergeant Gellar and Chief Landry. They were both waiting, just inside.

"Stow your gear and get on the transit," Gellar said. "We'll head to the spaceport as soon as everyone gets back."

There were a few other trainees already on the transit, which was a ground-based people-mover. Alex guessed it would hold fifteen passengers plus a driver. The driver's seat was empty along with the passenger seat beside it. Alex threw his rucksack into the back with the others and then sat in the middle. The transport had no doors or walls—just a floor, seats, and a roof with a few supports in the middle. Newt sat beside him, while Oggy and his friends sat in the back. Once the entire squad had arrived, Master Sergeant Gellar took the controls and drove them out of the hangar. The sun was going down, and the buildings around them took on an orange hue. As they waited for Chief Landry, Alex couldn't help but wonder if he would ever make it back to the CDF training world. He knew there were other worlds in the galaxy that would make Helena Prime seem primitive, but Alex thought it was a wonderful place.

The temperature was dropping, as it did every night on Helena Prime. Once the sun went down, the planet got cold. Most of the water was underground, and only certain types of imported flora could grow on the world. Alex thought the CDF had made Helena Prime into a paradise of sorts: a few towns, surrounded by vast deserts, each one a small oasis on an otherwise forbidding planet. He was roused from his internal musing by Ash. She was bold and often unashamedly loud, but there was a cheerfulness to her that Alex admired. She elbowed him in the ribs.

"I'll bet you're glad to be getting off this rock," she said with a chuckle. "I know I am."

Alex took a deep breath of the cool evening air. "Actually, I like it here."

"Ace is from some backwater world," Newt said. "It doesn't even have a name."

"Really? A no-name planet?" Ash asked. "That must have sucked."

"It wasn't a pleasant place," Alex admitted. "We called it the Rock. It makes Helena Prime seem like paradise."

"We've got to show this country bumpkin a good time, Newt," Ash said. "Have you ever even been to a rager?"

"I've seen them in holo-films," Alex said.

Ash laughed so hard that Alex and Newt couldn't help but join in. It helped ease the tension Alex felt about the mission. When Chief Landry came out of the hangar and got into the transport beside Master Sergeant Gellar, Alex felt a sudden desire to hang onto something from the base. Seeing the dark hangar made him sad for some reason.

"Cheer up, Ace," Ash teased. "Life is about to get a lot better really fast."

"Yeah," Sly said, leaning forward from the seat behind them. "Let's just hope it doesn't get a lot shorter, too."

# Chapter 4

The ride to the spaceport seemed short. Echo Company was joined by Delta, Charlie, and Bravo companies as they waited to board the shuttle that would take them up to the TROY space station.

Each group stayed together, eyeing the other squads with skepticism. Alex hadn't realized just how competitive the CDF was, and he couldn't help but wonder how far along in their training the other companies were.

"Maybe they weren't training anymore," Sly said. "Maybe they were just waiting to be called up."

"They don't look any more ready than we do," Ashton said.

Alex could see the looks on the faces of the other squads. There was suspicion, anxiety, and lots of uncertainty.

"I don't think any of them have been on a real mission yet," Alex said. "This is a first for all of us."

The operators were herded onto the shuttle. Alex sat between Newt and Ash, with Sly just across the short aisle. The officers were in another cabin, and Master Sergeant Gellar joined the other NCO's to make sure everyone was well-behaved. The flight up was easy, if not peaceful. Alex felt too unsettled, too ill-prepared to have confidence. But the operators made small talk and cracked jokes for the hour-long flight up to TROY. Once the shuttle docked, the master sergeants began barking orders.

"Everyone line up," Gellar shouted. "We are moving directly to the CDF carrier *Republic*. You will follow me, keep up, and keep your mouths shut. Am I making myself clear?"

Alex thought Master Sergeant Gellar was a scary woman when she wanted to be. She wasn't tall, but he had seen the muscles flexing beneath her compression shirt when they trained. Her hair was dark—almost black—and shaved on the sides. She kept the top portion longer but bound up in a tight braid. Alex thought she might have a pleasant face if she didn't frown so much and her eyes didn't seem so cold. The master sergeant could be friendly at times, but when she gave orders there was no doubt about following them.

Echo Company retrieved their rucksacks and followed Gellar from the shuttle. Alex recognized the space station. He had spent time there following the incident with Vice President Loman Haley. There were times, especially at night, when the fear he felt in that encounter gripped him. The VP had him brought in for questioning, but it was Chief McKinna and Colonel Bixby that had betrayed Loman Haley. Alex had been forced to watch while they tortured the VP—and if not for Alex's intervention, they would have killed him. Afterward, Alex had spent a few days resting in the medical bay before spending one brilliant afternoon with Nyx. The pleasantness of that day made him smile.

"What are you grinning about?" Oggy sneered. "You act like you've never been off-world before."

"He's been here before," Sly said. "He saved Vice President Haley here, remember? You're such a bonehead."

"Can that chatter," Master Sergeant Gellar growled from the front of the line.

Alex was glad he hadn't replied. The last thing he wanted was for Gellar to make an example of him in front of the other squads.

"Better sleep with one eye open, Sly," Oggy hissed between clenched teeth.

"Ignore him," Alex whispered.

They turned a corner and went down a long docking arm. At the end was an airlock guarded by two operators in Patrol battle suits. Master Sergeant Gellar scanned her ID, then took the squad inside. Alex wondered where Chief Landry was, but he knew better than to ask.

The inside of the ship was different than any spacecraft Alex had been on before. In some ways it reminded him of his home on NP8261. The deck was made of dull metal grates, the walls and ceilings were made of glow panels, and the corridor they were in was narrow and only a little taller than Alex. There were pipes in the corners where the walls met the ceiling, and as they progressed down the hallway, they passed dark metal doors with numbers painted on them in glowing white.

Eventually they came to a room with a large "E" printed on the door. It slid open when Master Sergeant Gellar flashed her ID at the control panel. She led the group inside.

"This is our berth," Master Sergeant Gellar said. "Bunks are already assigned. No fighting, no trading. Store your compression fatigues and toiletries in the locker at the foot of your bunk. The rest of your gear will be stowed in a locked compartment. Let's settle in. Company meeting in ten minutes."

Alex joined the others looking for their bunks. The berth was a long, narrow room with bathroom facilities at the far end. On the starboard side of the room were four rows of recessed bunks stacked three high. They were small compartments built into the wall with lockers in between. On the port side of the room were two private berths. In between, there were three tables, each with four chairs. Everything was bolted to the floor. The berth was spartan but clean. Ash, Newt, and Sly were all in row, but Alex couldn't find a bunk assigned to him.

He turned and found Master Sergeant Gellar coming out of one of the private rooms on the port side of their berth.

"I can't find my bunk, Master Sergeant," Alex said quietly.

"Guess you'll have to go back down and wait for another assignment, Ace," Oggy said with a cackle of laughter from Nuk and Tig.

Gellar didn't smile, nor did she frown. She just pointed toward the other private room. Alex glanced over and saw his name on the plate next to the door.

"It locks," Gellar said. "I'd use that, if I were you."

"Holy crap, Ace," Ash said, slapping him on the back. "You totally scored."

"It pays to be Alpha team leader," Sly said, looking over his shoulder at Oggy. "I guess you get to stay, after all."

Alex, followed closely by his three fellow Titan operators, stepped into the private room. It was small, but there was a standard bunk, a full-sized locker, a display screen, and a small desk with a chair on either side.

"Dang, man, you are so lucky," Newt said.

"This is awesome," Ash added.

Alex set his rucksack on the bed, then turned to the others.

"Let's get our stuff stowed," he said. "Master Sergeant Gellar wants us ready in a few minutes."

"Give us a second to ponder the greatness," Newt said.

"You know we're going to be in here all the time," Ash said. "This is de facto Titans' room."

"I'm fine with that," Alex said. "I'd trade with any one of you if I could."

"You should have seen the look on Oggy's face," Sly said. "Man, was he pissed when he saw that you got your own room."

"It's not going to make our lives any easier," Alex said. "You all know at some point he's going to take his frustration out on us."

"I'm not afraid of him," Ash said. Alex didn't think Ashton was afraid of anything. "He comes at me, I'll cave his face in."

"No, we can't do that," Alex said. "We're a team, remember? Echo company works together. We can't be fighting."

"Then he needs to learn to keep his trap shut," Ash replied.

"Let's watch out for them," Alex said. "And in the meantime, make yourself at home."

# Chapter 5

"Until further notice, there are only four areas of the ship you are allowed to be in," Master Sergeant Gellar announced.

Echo Company, including Alex, was lined up in front of the recessed bunks in their quarters. Each member stood at attention as they listened to the briefing from Gellar.

"Those areas are the chow hall, the recreation room, the simulator bay, and here in this berth," Gellar continued. "The hall outside leads to all four spaces. Do not go beyond the chow hall. Do not go to any other levels on the ship. Do not go into another squad's berth. Am I making myself absolutely clear?"

"Yes, Master Sergeant," the squad said in unison.

"Outstanding. We still have a lot of work to do, people. Don't mistake this deployment as an endorsement of your abilities. I've seen monkeys operate battle suits better than most of you. Tomorrow, we will begin a very tightly regimented schedule of training. Check your Flex PIL's for specifics. And remember, you are on a spaceship. If you start to feel like the walls are closing in, you come straight to me. There's no fresh air, and artificial gravity is low. Proper exercise and nutrition are essential for optimal health. There is the possibility of combat in the near future, people. Do you hear what I'm saying? Not field exercises, not simulations—actual combat that can and often does end in death for those who are not prepared—so get your minds right. This is not a vacation, and it's certainly not a pleasure cruise. We will be working hard. You have one hour before chow, and after that I suggest you get some rack time. Tomorrow will be a rude awakening for many of you. Echo Company, dismissed!"

Alex and the rest of the squad relaxed. He had already stowed his belongings and set the lock on the door to his little room. He and his Titan team set out to find the simulator bay. When they stepped out of their berth, the hallway was already buzzing with talk and laughter.

"Man, it feels like we're back in school," Newt said.

"Can you believe we're stuck down here?" Ash said. "Are we not good enough to have access to the entire ship?"

"I don't think we're going to have time to explore the ship," Alex said as they stepped into the first room they came to. It was long and narrow. There were MBS-specific simulators under large signs. Alex guessed there were over a hundred in the long room.

"Dang," Sly said. "That's one big game room."

"We won't have to take turns," Ash said.

They moved across the hallway to the recreation room. It was much larger than any of the other spaces. One end was filled with tables and chairs. Several wall panels had video capabilities. There were already people sitting around talking or watching videos with blocky headphones covering their ears. The sitting area had a low ceiling like the rest of the spaces on the ship, but beyond it was an exercise space with bright therapy lights. There were several grappling mats and an open space for exercise. Alex saw medicine balls and yoga mats arranged neatly against the far wall. Beyond the exercise space was a circuit-training area with machines that could work the entire body. Above the exercise areas, the ceiling was much higher. Alex guessed it was three or four levels, at least. The area wasn't just spacious—it was another part of the recreation room.

"Oh man, I gotta try that," Ash said.

Above the exercise area was a zero-gravity bubble. Alex had seen them on holo-films, but never in real life. There were already several people floating and spinning in midair. Alex thought he could see launch areas on the other levels.

"How do we get up there?" Sly asked.

"Stairs," Newt pointed out.

Across the sitting area, a narrow set of stairs led up to the space above.

"There must be a launch area up there," Ash said.

The group hurried across the sitting area and bounded up the stairs, single-file. Above the lounge was in fact a space for launching out into the zero-gravity bubble. Rules were posted on a wall, and small cubbies could be used for storing personal possessions. Alex saw that Personal Information Links were not allowed in the bubble.

"Why do you think that is?" Newt asked.

"So you won't collide with something or someone while you're looking at your PIL," Sly said.

"Or so you don't crack it if you crash," Ash said.

"No hard jewelry or unattached possessions," Alex read.

"No food or drinks, either," Sly pointed out. "That could get messy."

"I have to try it," Ash said as she pulled her PIL from her pocket.

"We're supposed to go to the chow hall," Alex reminded them.

"Just a few minutes," Ash said. "I promise."

"Can't hurt," Sly said, putting his own PIL into the cubby with Ashton's.

"Come on, Ace," Newt added. "It looks like fun."

"Fine," Alex said.

The truth was, he wanted to try the zero-gravity bubble as much as the others. He wanted to feel like he was flying again. More than anything, Alex longed for the sense of freedom he had discovered in the Fast-Attack Titan battle suit.

He stowed his Flex PIL with the others, and they stood at the edge of the launch platform.

"What do we do?" Newt asked.

"Jump, I suppose," Sly said.

"On three," Ash said. "One, two, three!"

They all jumped together. Alex felt the lack of gravity instantly. His mind expected his body to fall and crash onto the mats below. Fear was like a bad taste in his mouth, but he ignored it. As soon as his body passed the edge of the platform, the pull of gravity had disappeared. He kept going up and up.

"This is crazy!" Ash declared.

She reached out and grabbed Alex's arm. At first he thought she was scared, which was surprising. Ash was somewhat of a daredevil; she loved anything fast, especially flying in the Titan battle suits. But she hadn't grabbed his arm in fear—instead, she grabbed him in order to quickly push herself off and send herself flipping through the air in a new direction.

The push also sent Alex on a new course. His legs were rising up until he was horizontal, staring down at the grappling mats below. His legs continued rising up until his head was pointing down toward the ground, but it didn't feel any different. His world appeared to have flipped, almost as if the ship were spinning around him.

Unlike Ash, he enjoyed going slowly. His muscles relaxed, and he could feel the tension of the day melting away. There was so much freedom in the bubble that part of him never wanted to leave. He thought that living in zero-gravity, despite the well-documented health risks, had its advantages.

The others bounced off the walls and flew like comic book superheroes while Alex drifted slowly. Eventually they all returned to the launch deck. When Alex broke free from the bubble, he dropped to the deck as if his body weight was too much to bear.

"Oh, that sucks," Ash said.

"I wasn't this heavy before," Newt grumbled.

"Even breathing is hard," Sly said.

"It's all in your head," Alex said as he stood up, but it seemed like more than just a mental illusion. His legs trembled, and the ship's gravity felt oppressive.

"Too much of a good thing, maybe," Ash said as they stumbled over to the cubby and retrieved their PILs.

"I'm starving," Sly said. "What do you think the chow is like on this ship?"

"Let's find out," Alex said.

He cast one last look back over his shoulder. His body felt stiff, clumsy, and much too heavy in regular gravity. The people in the bubble all looked happy, graceful, and serene. He knew one thing for sure: he would be back to the bubble as often as possible.

# Chapter 6

The door opened, and Loman Haley turned from where he stood looking out the massive window of his office. Zan Fordham was a manager in the RDT division. Security had its share of climbers, although most were in the admin track. Haley had seen Zan Fordham's performance reports. He was the type of person who fudged the numbers when it came to what his people actually produced. None of his colleagues liked him, but he had some connections in the company and on the board of directors. None were as influential as Lynn Faulk, who had obviously been grooming him to be her lackey and Loman's replacement.

"Mr. Haley, it's a pleasure to finely meet you, sir," Fordham said.

Zan was overweight but fastidious about his appearance, and single. No surprise there, Loman thought. His designer clothes didn't hide his self-indulgent nature and overbearing personality. The pompous manager was looking around as if he were taking stock of Loman's office and deciding what to change once he took over.

"Mr. Fordham, welcome to Arcadia," Loman said.

The prospect of being kind to Zan, whom Loman saw as an interloper, was not pleasant, but he understood what was at stake. He was about to embark upon a battle of wits and wills for his job, but there was more hanging in the balance than Loman's livelihood. If it were just about money, he would have left Ahzco long ago. Loman had more than enough stashed away in his credit accounts and stock options. His real concern was for the employees who counted on the CDF to keep them safe. If Ahzco went out of business because other corporations stole their proprietary assets, hundreds of thousands of people would lose their jobs and be left destitute. Ahzco had assumed responsibility for the employees on the worlds it held as private property, and Loman couldn't let them down. If someone was waiting in the wings to take over, someone truly capable and with integrity, Loman wouldn't stand in their way—but that person had yet to appear, so he had no choice but to stand his ground.

"It's a pleasure to be here," Zan said.

"I trust the company has set you up in acceptable quarters until you can find a place of your own?"

"Oh, yes. I'm in a suite at the Excelsior. It's quite nice."

Of course it was. At over a thousand credits a day, it should be. Loman was not opposed to people reaping the rewards for their hard work and ingenuity, but he was sure that Zan's only accomplishment was knowing the right people.

"All right then, I've had my computer compiling the records for our division," Loman said. "I know a man of your stature will want to get up to speed right away."

"Of course, of course," Fordham said.

"It's all proprietary, so it can't leave the offices," Loman continued. "I've had Raz prepare you a space. It isn't much, but it's private. Remember, no one can see the files."

"I do understand confidentiality, sir," Zan said, with more than a little condescension in his voice. "I worked in research and development, after all."

"Oh, I haven't forgotten," Loman said. "You were a manager, I believe. Well, don't let me keep you. There's a lot of information to familiarize yourself with. Once you've gone over it all, we can begin discussions on what your role will be."

"I was under the impression that we would be dividing your current duties," Zan said. "Co-managing the security division."

Loman walked toward Zan, his temper roiling just below the surface. He wanted to have the greedy overseer thrown from the building, perhaps from the top floor, but instead he smiled and extended a hand. Zan took it in a limp, clammy grip.

"I'm a big believer in people, Zan," Loman said. "You don't mind if I use your first name, do you? We all have talents, and we're most fulfilled when we get to use our talents to make the company a better place to work."

"And improve the bottom line," Zan Fordham said with a chuckle.

"Of course, that too," Loman said. "Security is all about people. It's our job to make sure that every employee working for Ahzco is safe. It's a job I take very seriously."

Loman turned Zan toward the office door.

"I wouldn't entrust the safety of our people to just anyone. So while you have the chairwoman's confidence, you'll need to prove yourself to me before you're anything more than a drain on my time and resources. Go over the files. Impress me with your work ethic. Show me you have the integrity and drive to be an advocate for the employees of this company, and I'll give you all the responsibilities you want."

Loman gave the newcomer a little push toward the door. Zan stumbled toward it, and the door opened. Raz was looming just beyond, a hulking reminder of Loman's authority. Zan looked up at the big man, then turned back. His skin seemed pale, and it appeared that sweat had sprung out on the chubby man's upper lip.

"Ms. Faulk won't like this," he said.

"She doesn't have to," Loman said. "Raz, show him to his office."

Raz nodded, and the office door closed. Loman felt his entire body sag under the weight of his own responsibility. Was he stiff-arming Zan because of his passion for keeping the employees of Ahzco safe? Or was he really just protecting his own ego? It was becoming harder and harder to say for certain. The pain from the wound in his side was a constant irritation. He had pain meds that would make him blissfully unaware of the pain, but it also created a mental fog, and he couldn't afford to get caught off guard. There was blood in the water, and the predators were circling. Zan Fordham seemed like a dunce, but the last thing Loman could afford to do was underestimate the man. His stunt with the division files would only keep him busy for a few days. After that, he would have to be dealt with in a more decisive manner. That didn't give Loman a lot of time, and he was certain that Lynn Faulk had her own plans to send him packing. It was stressful, and Loman felt it through his entire body. His shoulders felt tight, his neck stiff, his back ached, his chest was tight, and his legs felt heavy—but he couldn't fail. He needed to find a way to keep Chairwoman Faulk's restructuring plan from giving her complete control of the company.

He dropped into his chair. His mouth was dry, and his hands felt shaky. He wanted a drink—perhaps *needed* a drink—but he couldn't take the chance. Alcohol in company headquarters was forbidden. It was his rule, and he was in charge of enforcing the rules. If he broke one and Zan Fordham found out, he would be finished. Instead of a drink, he picked up a stress ball, squeezed it tight in his fist, and did his best to ignore the pain in his side.

"Give me a status update for the *Republic*," Loman ordered his computer.

A chime sounded and the robotic voice replied, "the CDF carrier *Republic* is in transit to leave the Helena system."

"What's their travel time to Carthage system?"

"Eight days and seventeen hours into the system. They are following the free trade route but will not need to stop in transit."

A week, Loman thought. Just enough time for the struggle with Faulk and her minion Zan Fordham to really get underway.

"Is Echo Company on board?"

"That is correct. Echo Company is the junior squad and will be assigned reserve duties."

Reserves—Alex Evans won't be too happy about that, Loman thought. But it was probably all for the best. There was a chance that the prospectors on Carthage Prime wouldn't come under attack. He could always hope for that, but the odds weren't in Loman's favor. If there was fighting, no one wanted to be in the reserves, forced to watch others face the dangers head-on.

"Keep up with their progress," Loman ordered the AI. "I want to know if they encounter anything that might keep them from reaching the system."

The computer replied with a single chime. Loman wished all his employees could be so agreeable. Lately it seemed like they all were all trying to kill him.

# Chapter 7

Dinner on the *Republic* was a strange culinary experience. The food was issued from automated dispensers. They had a choice of three options: goulash, Salisbury steak, and vegetarian enchiladas. Alex chose steak and was given a tray with a protein patty, runny instant potatoes, a vegetable medley, and a stale dinner roll. The protein and potatoes were covered with a spicy, dark gravy.

"This is disgusting," Newt said as he flicked at his food with a fork.

"The goulash isn't bad," Sly said.

"The enchiladas don't have much taste to them," Ash said. "It's just sort of warm and pasty."

"Fuel for the body," Alex said.

He didn't enjoy the taste of his food. It was nothing like the fresh meals they were served on Helena Prime, but he was accustomed to bad food, air that would kill you, and little to no sunlight.

"Easy for you to say," Sly said. "I can't eat this."

"You get hungry enough, you'll eat anything," Alex said

"You know, when it's just us around, you don't have to defend the CDF at every turn," Sly said. "You can admit the food is bad."

"I never said it tasted good," Alex said, swallowing down the chunk of protein he had been chewing. It was mushy and more like paste than meat. The gravy had spices that were almost shocking to the taste buds. "I just said you should eat it."

"At least you don't have to worry about getting fat," Ash said.

"Funny, real funny," Sly said. "I'm beginning to think this was an epic mistake. I could have gone to university on the Oxford station. I hear the food there is incredible."

"And I'm guessing no one would ever shoot at you, either," Ash said. "You did make a mistake."

"Come on, this is a tiny inconvenience," Alex said. "So the food's bad. Big deal. You get to fly a Titan, man. What else in the universe compares with that?"

"He's right. Eyes on the prize, Sly," Newt added.

"Fine, whatever," Sly grumbled. "I just have standards, you know? I'm putting my neck on the line, and the least the CDF can do is give us a decent meal."

They didn't waste time eating. As soon as his hunger was sated, Alex tossed the remainder of the highly processed meal into the garbage bin.

"What do you bet they're recycling the food we don't eat?" Sly said. "That Salisbury steak tasted like it was made up of other stuff."

"Then you should eat it all," Ash said. "That way, you're not contributing to the poor food quality."

"You didn't eat all of yours," he argued.

"A lady always leaves some food on her plate," Ashton said. "That's what my mother always said."

"Did they say that ladies drive like maniacs with their hair on fire?" Newt asked.

"Very funny, but you all wish you had my skills," Ash replied.

"Speaking of," Alex said as he looked at his Flex PIL, "have you guys seen the schedule Master Sergeant Gellar posted?"

"No, and I don't like the way you're talking about it," Sly said.

They all looked at their Personal Information Links. The schedule was the first thing that popped up when they powered their devices on.

"Physical training at 0600?" Sly said. "That's insane."

"Simulators from 0830 until lunch," Ash said.

"What's Strategy and Tactics?" Newt asked.

"I guess we'll find out tomorrow," Alex said.

"Hand-to-hand combat sounds fun," Ash said. "So does zero-gravity training."

"What do we need that for?" Newt wondered.

"In case the ship comes under fire, you dolt," Sly said. "One hit and we could lose artificial gravity. You have to be able to make your way to an escape pod in zero-G."

"Wow, Master Sergeant Gellar wasn't kidding," Alex said. "Three sim exercises a day?"

"I guess we'll learn how to use the weapons systems," Ash said. "Can't wait."

After dinner they headed to their quarters. The four Titan operators sat in Alex's room, talking and joking, but knowing they had an early start in the morning, they decided to call it a day after about an hour.

Alex lay on his bed, staring up at the low ceiling and wondering why it seemed like he was consistently receiving special treatment. It wasn't that he was ungrateful, and he understood that he had saved the head of the entire CDF division of a mega-company from being murdered, but it still seemed odd to him. Nothing in his life had prepared him for the good fortune he had enjoyed since the attack on NP8261. The entire course of his life and the lives of his family had been altered when Alex had climbed into that MP Defender battle suit.

At some point he drifted off to sleep, but his Flex PIL, which was wrapped around his forearm like a long cuff, woke him at a quarter till six. After a quick trip to the bathroom, he was standing at attention beside his friends when Master Sergeant Gellar stepped from her private quarters.

"You're all up," she said. "Wonders will never cease. I hope you all slept well because you're in for a treat. A battle suit is only as good as the operator inside. As long as we're on this ship, we will strive to reach and maintain optimal physical fitness. Follow me."

The hallway outside their berth was quiet and empty. The recreation room was also empty. It felt like Echo Company were the only people on the ship. Master Sergeant Gellar led the squad of thirteen operators across the grappling mats to the exercise equipment. There were enough stations for each person, including Gellar. She used a master control panel to lock in the routine.

"This is the circuit training center," she announced. "Once we begin, each of your machines will lead you through a series of exercises. You will work the machine for forty-five seconds, followed by a thirty-second rest period. Today, you'll do two sets of all ten exercises. A set is considered at least eight repetitions of each exercise. If you don't complete a set in the forty-five second time limit, that exercise will start over. Any questions?"

Alex had questions, but he remained silent. No one wanted to appear weak.

"All right, everyone at their stations," Master Sergeant Gellar shouted. "Begin!"

The first few exercises Alex completed without problems. They weren't easy. The machine began with low resistance that increased until it sensed that the user was struggling, at which point it began to decrease the difficulty. After ten minutes, Alex was sweating and his muscles were trembling.

"This is killing me," Newt said.

"Just wait until tomorrow," Ash said. "We're going to be so sore we won't be able to move."

On his fifth exercise, Alex failed to get all eight repetitions in the time allotted. The machine beeped at him, and he saw that it was resetting. After that, he went all out, and managed to finish with only one other failure. The total workout lasted only half an hour, but when it ended Alex could barely stand.

"What kind of cruel punishment is this?" Newt said when he saw that Alex was finished. "Are you done?"

"Yeah," Alex said, bending over and propping himself on his knees.

Sly walked by, looking like the circuit workout was a breeze.

"You guys aren't done yet?" Sly asked.

"Shut him up," Ash said, just as her machine chimed to indicate she had finished the workout.

"I'm hitting the showers," Sly said.

"Go ahead, I'll wait on Newt," Alex said, trying to cover up the fact that he could barely stand.

"Didn't you guys play ball in high school?" Sly asked. "We worked out harder than this every day."

"That's what's wrong with you," Ash said. "You're a jock."

"Hey, I was a good student, too," Sly said.

"We'll meet you in the chow hall," Alex said.

Ash and Sly headed out. Alex gave Newt some encouragement, and he soon finished. When they left, there were only a few members of the squad still working on the machines. They looked miserable. Master Sergeant Gellar was still working, too. She was pushing and pulling as if the resistance was of no concern. Alex could see a look of total concentration on her face, and he made up his mind to give the physical training more effort the next day.

Showered, changed, and ravenous, they made their way to the chow hall. Breakfast was a pile of scrambled eggs reconstituted from powder, sausage links made of protein powder, dehydrated fruit, and juice from a mix. They all ate without complaining and actually went back for second helpings. Once they were refueled, they headed for the simulator bay. Master Sergeant Gellar wasn't there, but another master sergeant assigned them to simulators in the FA Titan section. Most of their squad mates were getting settled into the other sim stations. There were plenty of other operators running the machines, but no one else was in the Titan section.

"Looks like it's just us," Ash said.

"Maybe the others have a different training schedule," Alex said.

The four Echo Company fliers climbed into the machines and let their INC sync with the system. The low hum of the unit's electromagnetic waves was like music in Alex's mind as his INC chip connected to the simulator's computer. The device closed up around him.

*Morning, Alex.*

"Hey Nyx, good morning. Are you on board the *Republic*?"

*I am. We're being kept on a short leash, though. No fraternizing with operators.*

"Yeah, we're confined to a small area too. Any idea what's going on?"

*Just the general call to action. Running security on a new planet.*

"Well, if you hear anything different, let me know. Master Sergeant Gellar has us on a busy schedule. We've got no downtime."

*Sounds brutal.*

"So far it has been, but at least we're being deployed. That's good news, right? Maybe after we get adjusted to life on the ship, they'll let us mingle with the rest of the crew."

*I hope so. You ready to fly?*

"Always. What are we doing today?"

*Looks like a weapons sim. I'll run the systems and navigate. You keep us in the air and shoot the bad guys.*

"Sounds like fun. Let's do it."

# Chapter 8

The FA Titan was a heavily armed, multi-environment, mechanized battle suit. It had quickly become the workhorse of the CDF's combat operations. There were four classes of MBS's: military & police, all-terrain, asset recovery, and fast-attack. The Minotaur was a fast-moving, ground-based battle suit. The Titan was for airborne attacks and was armed appropriately with shortwave laser cannons, air-to-air missiles, air-to-ground missiles, defensive measures, and a multi-purpose projectile repeater that could fire a wide range of bullets from dart-shaped flechettes to armor-piercing, depleted uranium rounds.

The Titan was terrifying because of its speed and maneuverability. Ground units had trouble targeting the Titan, which could fly in atmosphere, hard vacuum, and even underwater. Alex had not been trained on the latter, but he knew the suits were capable. Only the most talented operators were allowed to fly the FA Titan, and Alex took pride in that fact. But the Titan also required nearly twice as much training. While every other member of Echo Company had several blocks of free time in their schedule, Alex and his team of Titan operators had no time off. Their days were packed from the time they woke up at 0600 ship time until they dropped into bed, exhausted, exactly sixteen hours later. Other than mealtimes, they were in a constant state of activity, including two sessions of simulator training that lasted four hours each.

It was grueling, and by the fifth day Alex was feeling the strain. His mind was filled with information, and while the simulators gave him some degree of experience with the ideas and theories he was presented each day, especially in the Strategy and Tactics class they were assigned to take, it wasn't the same as actually flying a battle suit in a combat situation. The computer's unyielding adherence to its preprogrammed parameters didn't allow for improvisation on the operator's part. The simulation had one right response to every obstacle presented. In that way, it felt more like memorizing answers to a test rather than learning the information that Alex was being tested on.

The morning PT sessions were getting harder, too. Master Sergeant Gellar had increased the sets for each exercise. It was now taking the operators forty-five to sixty minutes each morning to complete their sessions, and rumors had begun to circulate that Gellar planned on adding time on the cardio machines, as well.

Alex didn't mind the PT or the classes or even having no time off, but he was beginning to wonder how much he could take. In comparison, his basic training and operator training on Helena Prime seemed like breeze. He felt as though Master Sergeant Gellar and Chief Landry were trying to squeeze in weeks worth of training in only a few days.

"I checked," Ash said. "Every chance I get between other training sessions I go into the simulator bay. There's never anyone else on the Titans."

"So we're the only ones?" Newt asked.

"The only ones so far," Alex said. "And who knows, there could be a dozen veteran companies on a different part of the ship."

"Yeah, but it's kind of cool," Sly said. They were eating dinner, and no one was complaining about the food anymore. It was just as tasteless as their first meal on the ship, but their rigorous schedule made them appreciate the downtime, and their need for calories was way up.

"We're the elite, you know," Sly went on. "The best of the best."

"Yeah, but if they don't let up soon, we'll all be too exhausted to fight," Ash said.

"We haven't even reached the Carthage system," Alex pointed out. "I don't see them giving us a break until we do."

"Nothing lasts forever," Newt said. "My mother always said a person can endure anything if they know it will end at some point."

"What did you mother do?" Sly asked.

"She was a clerical worker," Newt said, "but that's beside the point."

"At least we're too busy to worry about Oggy," Alex said as his nemesis entered the chow hall.

"You think we'll be doing squad exercises or simulations soon?" Ash asked. "I talked to Lav, and they're segregated, too. Everyone's working in groups depending on their MBS."

"That would be my guess, but who can say for sure?" Alex said. "It just seems like they're expecting real trouble."

"New planet," Sly said. "It must have something they want pretty bad. Five squads are a lot of firepower."

"Or maybe it's all part of the training," Alex said. "A staged combat op just to see how the new operators respond sounds like something they would do."

"Maybe," Ash said. "But it seems a little extreme for a training exercise."

"It's not like we can treat it differently," Newt said. "We have to assume it's real, no matter what we believe."

After dinner they returned to the simulation bay for the second training exercise of the day. Alex dropped into his simulator and powered it on. The machine closed in around him like a snug cocoon. He was beginning to enjoy the feeling of being enclosed. In many ways, it was the only privacy he had during his waking hours. Even the showers were communal. There were separate facilities for men and women, but no privacy.

*Welcome back, Alex. How are you feeling?*

"Tired," he replied truthfully. "You?"

*Would you be upset to know I sneak in a nap in the afternoons?*

"Jealous, maybe, but not upset," Alex said.

*Our training is different. I've been working as a controller for almost a year already. And most of that was spent on board a training ship. We have a little more freedom than the rest of you.*

"Is it always that way for operators?"

*Negative. Veterans have freedom to access all the enlisted spaces on the ship. The officers have their own spaces, but for the most part it's like being in a small, self-contained community. There are a couple of enlisted bars on the ship with a two-drink limit, a holo-film theater, and even a library.*

"Sounds like fun," Alex said. "Maybe you can give me a tour soon."

*Count on it. You ready to fly?*

"Roger that," Alex said.

The simulator came to life. They had run weapons exercises in atmosphere at the beginning of the week, and they were learning to fly in hard vacuum with zero-gravity. Their training in the zero-G bubble was helping, but like anything new it was taking some time to gain proficiency.

*First up is a ship-to-ship transfer.*

"Where's the other ship?" Alex asked. "I can't see it."

*It's on the other side of the planet. You'll have to lead your team around in orbit, then make a safe landing.*

Alex switched to his team channel on the simulator's com-link. "You guys ready?"

"Always," Ash said.

"Roger that," Sly replied.

"Yes, team leader," Newt said.

"All right, let's launch," Alex said. "Thrusts once we're clear of the ship."

He didn't have to tell them how long to let their thrusters propel them through space. Each operator was paired with a controller. Alex had Nyx, and she gave him exact instructions. She was part navigator, part co-pilot. Her main job was to feed him the information he needed so that he could focus completely on what was happening around him. In the case of a battle, Alex would need to be able to react to enemies and couldn't be distracted by instrument readings or radar feeds. In an emergency, Nyx could even fly the battle suit, but her perspective was different from his. Alex could feel the battle suit around him like a thick second skin. When gravity was a factor, he could feel the way the Titan was flying. Of course, the simulator couldn't replicate that very well, but in an actual mission, his piloting skills would be invaluable.

They did a measured thrust for half a minute, building up enough speed to circle around to the far side of the planet in just under two hours. It would be a long, boring flight, unless the simulation had some surprises in store. Their counter-burn to slow down would take much longer since their pace would be increased by the planet's gravity. Alex didn't worry about the details. The controllers would see about all that. His focus was on keeping his team together and avoiding trouble until the other ship came into view. When that happened, they could slow down, and Alex would land the simulated battle suit on the designated section of the target ship. He could imagine the need to board another ship in a space battle, but he didn't really relish the thought of it. Fighting on board a spaceship would be difficult, even deadly. The armor on the Titan battle suit would give them some measure of safety, but the close confines would make maneuvering challenging. Still, if the need arose, he would be ready. The Titan operators were considered the elite division in the CDF, and he was willing to do whatever it took to make sure he was the best he could be.

# Chapter 9

Loman stared at the holograph of Ciara Prince. He could tell by her posture and the look on her face that she wasn't happy. He didn't blame her; it was never pleasant to tell the boss bad news.

"So we know nothing," Loman said.

"Whoever was behind the attack seems to have dropped out of the picture," Ciara said. "They might be laying low, or they might be out of the game. There's been no talk and certainly no activity that we can find. My entire team has come up empty."

Loman wanted to criticize her team, but he knew they were the best investigators in the company. He couldn't afford to believe that she was right, but on the other hand, he couldn't really argue the point, either. If there was no news, he couldn't fault her for that.

"Well, don't give up," he said. "It's possible the attacks were an effort to keep us from bidding on the Carthage mineral rights."

"That would mean that whoever was behind the attacks on our colony ship and the Perrin system would have to have inside information."

"No surprise there," Loman said. "We had it, just not as soon as someone else."

"Well, that gives me another avenue to explore. Maybe if I find a leak in the Free Trade Association, it will lead to whoever was behind the attacks on the company."

Loman nodded. He was impressed at her drive and ingenuity. The door swished open, and he frowned. His new partner, as ordered by the board of directors, had formed the habit of entering his office without notice.

"Check it out and get back to me," Loman said. "I've got to run."

She nodded, and the hologram faded away.

"Who was that?" Zan Fordham asked.

"One of our security administrators giving a report," Loman said.

"Concerning?"

"An investigation. How's the research going?"

"I'm done," Zan said irritably. "And don't think that I don't know what you're doing."

"What I'm doing?" Loman asked, feigning ignorance.

"You're trying to brush me off and bury me with busy work."

"That's not true," Loman said. "If we're going to co-lead the security division, we both have to be up to speed on what's going on."

"Somehow I doubt you know all that information," Zan challenged.

"Oh, I might surprise you."

"Really? Then you won't mind a little test."

"Zan, I appreciate your enthusiasm for the task you've been given, but we really don't have time to play games."

"Actually, I insist," Zan said with a wicked grin. "I do have a report to make to Chairwoman Faulk, after all."

Loman grimaced, but he'd been expecting such a move. Few people in the company knew that Loman had an INC chip and could connect with his AI computer. He didn't do it often—the Implanted Neural Controller was meant to help operators pilot battle suits—but there were other uses to the advanced technology. He nodded to Zan while mentally syncing with his computer.

"You know the number of employees on the gas refinery in orbit around Atlantis Eleven?"

Loman cleared his throat. He could see the look of delight in the manager's beady eyes. He mentally asked the question to his computer.

*Four hundred and ninety-eight, with two companies of CDF operators on board in case of emergency.*

"Four hundred and ninety-eight," Loman said. "Including two companies of CDF operators. Now, can we please get to work?"

The look on Zan's face was undiluted fury. His cheeks flushed, and a vein began to bulge in his forehead.

"How could you possibly know that?" Zan demanded.

"Because it's my job to know. I keep tabs on all security personnel. I was reviewing the risk on Atlantis Eleven not long ago."

"Fine, then what about the garrison on Solomon in the Zionist system?"

*There are twenty-two operators stationed on the planet Solomon. All specialize in AT Defender battle suits.*

"Twenty-two," Loman said. "All running AT Defenders. This is getting old."

"You're tricking me," Zan said.

"You're paranoid."

"Am I? It's not my job on the line."

"Who said anything about someone's job being in jeopardy? Do you know something I don't?"

Fordham looked down, and Loman wasn't sure if the manager was angrier at Loman or himself. Of course, everyone in senior management knew they were fighting for their jobs. Chairwoman Faulk wanted her cronies running each division, giving her complete control of the largest corporation in the galaxy. Loman had a sneaking suspicion that once she got what she wanted, her puppets leading the company would run it straight into the ground. She would become the most powerful woman in the galaxy, but only if she could successfully push him out—and he was determined not to let that happen.

"If you're through testing me, let's talk about what you'll be doing," Loman said.

"My assignment is to prepare to run the entire division. We're co-directors now."

Loman had to give himself a moment to calm down. He wanted to scream at Fordham that he was nothing but a weasel, selling his integrity to Lynn Faulk in exchange for position and money. But direct confrontation would not get Loman the results he desired, no matter how satisfying putting Zan in his place might feel in the moment.

"All right, well, how do you see that working out?" Loman asked.

"I need a real office, for one thing," Zan snapped. "At least as big as this one."

"Take it," Loman said, trying not to sound bitter. "I'll move my things out today."

Zan started to say something. He even opened his mouth, ready to fight for his right to an office, but Loman's concession took him by surprise. He closed his mouth and stared at Loman for a few seconds.

"Really?"

"Absolutely," Loman said. "I'm a believer in getting things done. There is a lot of work in this division. I'm happy for the help."

"Don't think you can bury me in more paperwork."

"I won't. The most pressing concern is finding Colonel Bixby's replacement. Why don't we dive into that tomorrow morning, as soon as you're settled?"

"Where are you moving to?" Zan asked.

"The office you were using, I suppose," Loman said. "I don't need all this space. Why don't you go pick out a few items to make this office your own. We have an account at Bailey's. I'll have Raz help me move my personal things out."

"Okay," Zan said, still a little confused by Loman suddenly playing nice.

"Take the afternoon," Loman said. "We'll meet in the morning and get started."

"First thing?"

"As soon as you're here," Loman replied.

"I'll be here right at nine. I'm a very punctual person."

Loman started to laugh but held himself in check. Being VP of security for a mega-corporation was more than a full-time job. The work never ended. Loman was usually in the office by 0700, and it wasn't unusual to stay until everyone else had gone home. Even when he was away from the office, he was always on call. Loman took his job seriously, and he expected those who worked closest with him to do the same, but he would gladly make an exception for Zan.

"That sounds perfect," Loman said.

The manager left with a smile on his round face and a spring in his step. Loman sent a mental command to his computer to begin compartmentalizing and locking off certain files and folders of information. He pressed a button on his phone to activate the intercom.

"Raz, call building maintenance. I need my office cleared out ASAP."

"Yes, Mr. Haley. Should I send the furniture someplace specific?"

"Storage for now," Loman said. "And set up a computer node in the room Loman's been working on. I'll be using that space for the foreseeable future."

"Yes, sir."

Loman looked out the window. He would miss the view, but the sacrifice was worth it. He just needed more time to deal with the growing list of enemies who were looking to take him down. Giving Zan Fordham a corner office with a view would satisfy his ambition and make him feel superior to Loman. The greedy little manager might be Chairwoman Faulk's puppet, but that didn't mean Loman couldn't pull his strings.

# Chapter 10

It took the *Republic* eight days to reach the Carthage system. Nyx had been training each day with Alex and his team of Titan operators. They were becoming a dependable, cohesive unit, which gave Nyx a certain amount of pride. She spent some time with the other three controllers working with Ash, Newt, and Sly, but unlike their counterparts, the controllers hadn't really formed a bond.

Nyx guessed it was most likely a result of the type of person recruited to be a controller. She had picked up on the fact that most of her peers were very much like her: introverted, analytical, rule-following computer enthusiasts. Socializing just wasn't in their nature, and of course it didn't help that most of their training had taken place alone in front of a computer console. They didn't persevere through daunting challenges together or work in groups. They didn't even have to share quarters. Controllers spent most of their time on CDF carrier ships or orbital space stations. They were assigned to small, narrow rooms in their own wing of the ship, not far from the entertainment section, but isolated enough that they felt safe.

Nyx had grown up on a scientific space station and had gone through a phase in which she'd felt the need to explore. But her first trip to a planet had made her quickly realize that she felt too exposed in large, open spaces. Since then, she worked to keep her world small and controllable. She didn't mind visiting other places for short periods of time, but it was much better to keep things contained. When she'd been sent to the *Republic*, an officer had assigned her a room and a computer console in the control center. She'd quickly made those two spaces her own and hadn't yet taken much time to explore the common areas of the ship. There was no rush and no real desire to mingle, despite the fact that she sometimes felt lonely.

Her operator ran simulations twice a day, and outside of those simulations she was free to do as she pleased. It made Nyx happy to spend most of her time at her computer console, even when she wasn't running sims with Alex. So she was at her station when the ship passed through the space tunnel and appeared in the Carthage system. She was tapped into the ship's command network, remotely viewing the reports and orders being given by the senior officers. She saw a video feed of the system. It looked normal to her. Carthage Prime was the focus and still thousands of kilometers away from the ship's position. It was a bright white oval, almost egg-shaped, with one end pointing toward the system's yellow star. That end was green and blue, but the rest of the planet was clearly swathed in a thick layer of ice and snow.

A bulky freighter was orbiting the planet, and Nyx could see that supplies were being ferried down. She couldn't hear the communications back and forth, but from the commands given, she guessed that the freighter had supplies for a colony or at least an exploratory team that would descend to the southern hemisphere of the planet. She had no idea why they were there or what they hoped to accomplish. Her orders were simple: to assist Alex in whatever capacity was needed for the security of the company's employees and assets in the Carthage system.

Nyx didn't mind not knowing more. She was curious enough, but she also relished the simplicity of her responsibilities.

The order she was waiting for came through less than an hour after reaching the system. Squads were being given the order to prepare to make their way down to the surface of the planet. Her console didn't have specifics—only that Bravo, Charlie, Delta and Echo Companies were to prepare for departure immediately upon reaching orbit. A timer began counting down on her screen. There were just under twenty-three hours before they would reach orbit. She felt a thrill race through her body. She didn't want to fight, but she wanted to be challenged. The last thing on her mind was the possibility that Alex or someone else might get hurt. Instead, she was focused solely on running a serious operation, one that would test her wits with other professionals. As odd as it might sound, she was excited by the prospect.

Her Flex PIL, which she kept wrapped around her forearm, vibrated. It was a reminder to eat before the morning training session began, and she got up slowly from her console, wondering if there would be any more trainings now that they were on the cusp of an actual mission.

She had no problems with training; it was an essential function to maintain mission readiness, but she couldn't deny the feeling that it was somehow beneath her. Nyx West was ready for more than just a computer-generated scenario. She was about to get up when a message popped up on her screen. It was her specific orders, direct from her commanding officer Lieutenant Sanders.

*Attention Corporal West, N*

*Mission specifics require you to continue simulator training with Titan operators on board the CDF Republic. Privates Evans, Timmons, Lasiter, and Newton are ordered to remain on board until further notice.*

Nyx felt an overwhelming sense of dread. If Alex wasn't being called up, did that mean something was wrong? And how would he take the news? She didn't know, and she certainly didn't want to be the one to tell him. She turned from her console and saw Lieutenant Alyssa Sanders approaching. By the time Nyx's CO reached her, the controllers for the other Titan operators had gathered close. Sanders held up her hand to silence the group.

"It's not my decision," Sanders said.

"Is something wrong?" Nyx asked. "Is that why we're being held back?"

"No, there's nothing wrong," Sanders said. "I'm giving you the orders I was given. Nothing changes. You keep training."

"The operators won't be happy," one of the other controllers pointed out.

"If so, they can take it to their CO. For now, we have our orders and we carry them out regardless of how we feel personally. Is that understood?"

The controller division was often more like a corporate position than a military one. The entire division exuded calm efficiency. No orders were shouted and no weapons were used—unless computers were classified as weapons—and orders didn't seem heavy or absolute.

"Yes, Lieutenant," the four controllers said quietly.

"Very good. Do your best to keep your operators calm. There's bound to be plenty of ruckus as the squads are shipped out. Let's not get caught up in the furor."

She walked away, and Nyx felt as if her own hopes and dreams had been dashed. Obviously there would be other missions, but after so much training and anticipation, to be held back seemed cruel.

Nyx glanced at her Flex PIL and saw that she had twenty minutes until she needed to be back at her console and ready for Alex to arrive. The thought of his disappointment was almost too much to bear, but she reminded herself that it wasn't her fault. She walked quickly to the nearest vending machine. She could have gone to the chow hall, but it would be busy, and the food would need to be eaten there. Instead, she got herself a package of salty cheese crisps, sweet shortbread cookies, and a bottle of water. It would be enough to see her through the four-hour training session, and she could get a proper meal at lunchtime.

When she got back to her console, she gave the planet on her screens one last look before switching over to simulators. There was no way to know which simulator in the row of Titan training stations Alex would utilize. She would have to wait for her operator to sync to one of the simulators, and then she could join him. As she slowly ate her snacks, alternating one bite of sweet cookie with one bite of salty cracker, she wondered if he would know when she talked to him. The thought of their mutual disappointment made her want to see him more than ever. Just knowing they were on the same ship but separated from one other was grueling. Everything she wanted was postponed and put off for a later time. She couldn't help but wonder, as she waited, if their time would ever come.

# Chapter 11

"You want to run that by me again?" Ash demanded.

They were gathered in Alex's room while the rest of the squad got the good news that they were leaving the ship. The room was soundproof, probably so that the officers could get plenty of rest even if their squads were being loud in the common area just outside. Alex couldn't hear Master Sergeant Gellar's orders to the rest of Echo Company, and thankfully, no one could hear Ash's string of curses when Alex gave the other Titan operators the bad news.

Alex had just come from Master Sergeant Gellar's room, where Chief Landry had been waiting. He'd felt strange being in the master sergeant's private space, but it was exactly like his own and just as spartan. Gellar hadn't bothered to make herself at home. It was a place to sleep and change clothes, nothing else.

The news that his team wasn't deploying with the others felt like a knife in his guts. Master Sergeant Gellar was taking Echo Company down with the other squads, but Alex and his Titan operators were ordered to remain on the ship and continue training.

"This isn't fair," Newt said.

"Chief Landry is staying with us," Alex said, trying to keep his friends calm.

"Oh, joy," Sly said. "The chief is going to babysit."

"Did they at least give you a reason?" Ash demanded.

"No," Alex said. "The orders are from higher up, and all I know is what they told me."

"Is it because we're not ready?" Newt asked.

"Screw that, I'm ready," Sly snapped.

"We're more prepared than the rest of Echo Company," Ash said. "This blows."

"We must have done something wrong," Newt continued. "They wouldn't single us out otherwise."

"Titan training is longer than the other MBS's," Alex said. "Maybe that's all it is."

The door to the room opened without warning, and Chief Landry stepped inside. The four privates all snapped to attention.

"At ease," he said in a calm voice.

Alex looked past the handsome officer and saw Oggy laughing at him and pointing from the common room.

"Sir, this isn't right," Ash said.

"Yeah, we should be going too," Sly agreed.

"Perhaps, but orders are orders," Landry said. "We've all got our orders, and whether we like them or not, we will obey. Is that clear?"

"Yes, Chief," they all said in unison.

"Good, because you've got a training sim to get to. Remember, you're still Echo Company, and I expect you to represent us well. Don't let anyone goad you into doing something that you'll regret."

Alex immediately thought of Oggy and his friends, but he pushed the thought from his mind as Chief Landry left. He glanced at his PIL. They had two minutes to reach the simulator bay.

"He's right. Let's go," Alex said.

"Stupid orders," Sly replied, but he was following Alex out of the small room.

"I'm sick of the simulators," Ash said. "I want to fly, not play games all day."

"Our time is coming," Alex said, but there wasn't much enthusiasm in his voice.

The corridor was busy, and Alex could hear the excitement in the voices of the other operators. It made his own disappointment sting even more. All he had wanted was to find a place where he fit in, and once he thought he'd found it, he felt like an outsider again. His only comfort was that he wasn't alone, and yet he felt horrible for even thinking that. His team deserved to be involved in the mission. They were the best operators in Echo Company. Alex knew it was true, so he couldn't comprehend why they were being left behind.

The corridor was full of people, but the simulator bay was completely empty. They walked down the narrow aisle between the machines, feeling more bitter with every step.

"There has to be a reason," Newt said.

"Whatever it is," Ash said, "I hate it."

"At least we won't have to see Oggy's ugly mug much longer," Sly said. "This place will be much more comfortable without everyone crowding us all the time."

Alex climbed into his simulator without saying anything. He wanted to get through the exercise and be done. Maybe he could take out his aggression on the wrestling mat during hand-to-hand combat training. He hit the button to activate the simulator and waited while the device closed up around him. It smelled like sweat inside, and for a moment it was completely dark. He waited to sync his INC to the simulator, relishing the darkness. For a moment he imagined he had simply disappeared and his problems couldn't find him. But he knew he couldn't hide —in fact, he didn't want to. He wanted to overcome them. He let the INC connect with the simulator with a satisfying snap. The EM waves began a low, soothing song that played in the background of his mind as the simulator came to life around him. He flexed his arms and legs while the program loaded.

*How are you, Alex?*

"You heard?"

*Yes.*

"It sucks. No one can tell us why we aren't going down with the others."

*I questioned my CO and got no answers. I'm sorry.*

"Me too," Alex said. "I know this isn't what you were hoping for. What's the exercise today?"

*Planetary insertion from hard vacuum.*

"Sounds exciting," Alex lied.

The simulation was boring. Alex and the rest of his team flew from a ship in orbit, across space, and into the atmosphere of a simulated planet. There were no enemies, no combat—just the boring lessons of transitioning from space to atmosphere. Alex learned a few things, but most of the work was on the controller side of things. They had to plot the correct trajectory, make the changes to the battle suit once they entered atmosphere, and help the operator reach the designated zone to complete each run.

When they finished, Alex was more discouraged than ever. They went to lunch and ate cold sandwiches and pasta salad. They were halfway finished with the meal when Oggy, Nuk, and Tig sat down beside them at the long, rectangular table.

"Well, well, how the mighty have fallen," Oggy said with a smirk.

"Can it, Og, we're not in the mood," Ash snarled.

"There's no law against speaking your mind," Tig said.

"Don't get so wound up, Ash," Nuk said. "You wouldn't want people to see you cry."

"All this time people were thinking you were the chosen one, Ace," Oggy said. "But you're actually not even good enough to deploy with the rest of the squad."

The three Minotaur operators burst out laughing, and Alex could feel his anger rising. He wanted to leap across the table and smash Oggy's face, but fighting outside of the combat training sessions was strictly forbidden. No matter what Oggy said, Alex had to keep his cool if he wanted to keep flying.

"You'll be crying for our help if you aren't careful," Newt said.

"That'll be the day," Oggy growled.

"Yeah, man, combat's no joke," Sly said. "Better watch your six out there, some people are known for shooting in the back."

A hush fell over the table. It was all too clear that everyone was itching for a fight, but Alex couldn't let that happen. Oggy hated them because of Alex and because they had earned the right to be Titan operators. If they threw it all away over a fistfight, he would never forgive himself. He dropped the bland sandwich on his tray and stood up. Oggy tensed, ready to react to an attack, but Alex calmly stepped away from the table.

"Run back to your simulators, Ace," Oggy called out. "That's the only action you're going to see."

Alex didn't turn back. His hand gripped the plastic food tray so hard they shook, but he kept walking. When he reached the trash receptacle, he dumped his half-eaten lunch and fed the tray into the automated washing bin.

"That guy is such a jerk," Newt said.

"Someone needs to teach him a lesson," Sly said.

"I wouldn't mind volunteering," Ash said.

Alex stared across the chow hall to where Oggy and his friends were laughing. "He's going to regret being so flippant. I don't know when, but he'll lead people into trouble and then he'll have to face the consequences."

"My mom said some people have to learn the hard way," Newt added.

"They do indeed, Newt," Alex said.

# Chapter 12

The drop ships were launching from bays on either side of the massive carrier ship. Nyx was watching from her controller station. Most of her peers had turned up to see the mass exodus. Cameras were capturing the ships as they maneuvered past the carrier and toward the glistening planet below. Nyx was trying to hold back the bitterness that was threatening to overwhelm her. Alex's disappointment at being left behind was palpable, and she wanted more than anything to make him feel better. Unfortunately, she was powerless—just another spectator as the large security force made their spectacular entry to a new world.

The first sign of trouble came from one of the drop ships near the *Republic's* bow. Light suddenly flared from the engine, and the drop ship began to drift sideways.

"D-S-2-9er-7, what is your status?" came the calm inquiry from the carrier's officers.

"Mayday, mayday, mayday, a frightened voice replied. Our starboard engine has suffered a catastrophic failure. We have...a breech..."

The report ended in an ominous silence. Nyx was standing at her station. She could see over the short dividers to where the other controllers were watching the descent from their own station.

"D-S-2-9er-7, can you maneuver? Bring your vessel to coordinates one, one, four, and wait for rescue."

The only response was a section of the drop ship's hull exploding out from the vessel, with a gush of visible gas. It was obvious from the way the ship was drifting toward the planet that it had no control left, and the breech in the hull was visible even from a distance.

Nyx's console beeped, and her Flex PIL vibrated. She dropped into her seat and clicked on the message.

*Emergency Action Message: Prepare for recovery maneuvers. Operators are being mobilized. Stand by for orders.*

There was an icon that would link her to a mechanized battle suit, but to her surprise it wasn't an FA Titan, but rather an AR Valkyrie. Alex didn't have experience in a Valkyrie, and Nyx hadn't run sims in the asset recovery vehicle in a long time. She knew that the Valkyries were large, powerful battle suits, designed to recover other MBS's that were disabled on the battlefield. They were slow with heavy armor and almost no weapons. Instead, they had electromagnetic lines on either side that could connect to a machine, anything made of metal, and tow it back across enemy lines. The propulsion was similar to the Titan, but the mass of the suit was greater. The Titan was sleek, while the Valkyrie was bulky with more powerful engines. Fortunately, they wouldn't need the engines in zero-gravity; thrusters would be enough to maneuver with, but if they weren't careful, they could crash into one another and double the number of casualties.

Her computer beeped again, and she opened her orders.

*Emergency Action Message: Crew of DS297 is lost. Operators may be alive in their mechanized battle suits. Echo Company will cross from the Republic to DS297, locate and retrieve the MBS's in the drop ship's cargo compartment, and retrieve all CDF assets.*

It was a rescue mission...if there was anyone left alive on board, Nyx thought. Otherwise it was merely a salvage mission. She hoped that the operators were in their battle suits, but even so, the ground units weren't made for prolonged hard vacuum. Their oxygen levels wouldn't last long, and if the operators ran out of air to breathe, their heavily armored battle suits would be nothing more than coffins.

She ran a quick systems check on the Valkyrie. It was all she could do other than hope for the best and wait for Alex to arrive. Alarms began to sound through the ship, and a sense of fear filled Nyx as she waited. It appeared they would see action, of a sort, after all. It might not be combat, but it was just as deadly, and the stakes were beginning to weigh on her. Lives were on the line. No more simulations. If they failed, people would die—maybe even Alex. That outcome scared Nyx, but it also steeled her resolve. They would be on a dangerous mission in unfamiliar gear, and that meant her job was even more important. She was determined not to let her partner down.

# Chapter 13

Alex was thankful the corridors were empty. He and his team were being rushed through the ship that felt deserted after the four squads had left for deployment on Carthage Prime. From the looks of things, there were even more squads on the enormous carrier, but all had been shut down. Chief Landry was leading the way, weaving through the corridors and making Alex feel lost.

The alarm blaring throughout the ship was enough to make Alex feel on the verge of panic. He forced his mind to focus on following Chief Landry. That was all he had to do—just keep up. They had no idea what was happening or where Landry was taking them. Something was wrong—that much was obvious—but he had no idea if it was an attack or simply just a drill.

They turned from the narrow corridor they had been racing down into a large room that reminded Alex of the security hangar on NP8261. There were battle suits hanging in harnesses and technicians working around four bulky AR Valkyries.

"Okay, listen to me," Chief Landry said as he turned to face Alex's team. He had to shout to be heard over the alarm. "One of the drop ships had a malfunction. The engine blew, the hull is compromised, and it's drifting into a decaying orbit."

"What about the operators on board?" Ash asked.

"They should still be alive," Landry said. "Their battle suits can survive hard vacuum, but we need to get them off the ship and back onto the carrier."

"We?" Sly asked.

"That's right. The four of you are going after them in these Valkyries."

"We haven't trained on Valkyries," Newt said.

"There's no time to worry about that now," the chief said. "You'll be in zero-G using thrusters, so it won't be that different from the Titans you've been training in. Listen to your controllers—they'll help. You get to the drop ship, pull the survivors out, and come straight back here. I'll be on the command channel walking you through the entire process."

"We can do it," Alex said, although he felt terrified.

"That's the right attitude, Evans. Work this as a team and stay cool," Landry ordered. "You'll be just fine."

He left them standing in the hangar, and Alex stepped toward the technicians.

"We're your operators," Alex said.

The technician, a burly man with a bushy beard streaked with gray whiskers, nodded. "The Valkyries are ready for you."

A short ladder was set up, and Alex climbed into the Valkyrie. It was like putting on a coat that was several sizes too large. He hit the button to power up the suit, and it began to close around him. Syncing his INC was simple enough, and as soon as he did, Nyx's voice filled his mind.

*Alex, I'm here. Don't worry.*

"King of hard not to," Alex said. "How far out is the drop ship?"

*About eighty klicks.*

"What do I need to know about the Valkyrie?"

*That it's built for this type of mission is the first thing. Secondly, it uses electromagnets to secure whatever assets*

*you're trying to recover. You'll use one to secure your MBS
to the drop ship and the other to pull out the survivors.*

"Sounds simple enough," Alex said.

In truth, it didn't sound simple, and he was anything
but calm. He used the mental exercises Master Sergeant
Grossman had taught him, setting his fears aside and
focusing on what he knew to be true. His team wasn't
trained in the Valkyries, but they were all trained fliers. It
wasn't a combat mission—just a rescue—and whoever was
in command of the CDF operation had enough faith in
them to send them out. That had to mean he, or she, had
enough confidence that they would make it back, as well.

"All right, team, let's check comms," Alex said.

"I'm ready," Ash said.

"Locked and loaded," Sly added.

"All systems are ready, team leader," Newt said.

"Good," Alex said. "Here's how we're doing this.
Ash and I will make contact with the drop ship. From
there, we'll assess and begin the recovery. If you have an
idea, share it. We only get one shot to save those operators,
and I don't want to blow it."

*Good pep talk*, Nyx said. Her voice was in his
mind; sometimes he couldn't even tell the difference
between his own thoughts and hers.

The harnesses holding up the Valkyries began to
move. Alex resisted the urge to move around. Instead, he
relaxed his hands on the controls and worked to keep his
mind calm. The Valkyrie was essentially a big engine. He
could feel the power vibrating through the seat he was on.
His legs were to either side, as if he were sitting astride the
motor. He could feel the power through his INC as well—a

deep, thrumming sense of great energy just waiting to be harnessed and applied.

The suits were moved through an opening in the wall from the hangar to what appeared to be a launch area. They were set down on the deck, and then the harnesses disengaged.

*You're in position for launch*, Nyx said. *Stand by.*

"How does this work?" Alex asked.

*The launch area will seal off, then the outer bay doors will open like a big air lock. There's a magnet barrier that protects the launch bay from hard vacuum. Once the ship lowers that shielding, you will be pushed out by the launching arms behind you.*

"All right, sounds simple enough," Alex said.

"Valkyrie team," Chief Landry's voice sounded strange through the battle suit's internal speakers, "you should have the coordinates to the drop ship. The other vessels are all well clear. You should have easy access to the target."

"Copy that," Alex said.

The outer doors began to slide apart, revealing space and the brilliant white planet beyond. It was Alex's first look at Carthage Prime.

"Looks cold," Ash said.

"Like a giant ice ball," Sly said. "Maybe staying here wasn't such a bad choice, after all."

"Let's stay focused," Alex said. "Lives are on the line."

"Roger that," Ash said.

"Copy," Newt replied.

*They're lowering the magnetic shield*, Nyx said.

"Valkyrie team, prepare for launch," Chief Landry said. "Make us proud."

Alex's mouth felt dry, and his body felt trembly and weak. He was going into space, and if things didn't work out, he might not ever return. He felt sweat on his forehead and wished that he could reach his face to wipe it away, but the suit was closed tight around him. There was a sudden lurch, the carrier ship disappeared behind him, and Alex was free in outer space. Drifting in zero-gravity had never seemed frightening before, but now Alex felt small, and the Valkyrie battle suit seemed insubstantial around him.

*You okay, Alex?*

Nyx's voice, even though it sounded to Alex like his own, shook him out of the fog of fear.

"Yeah, I'm good," Alex said.

He imagined the Valkyrie, with its extendable rescue arms folded up tight on either side, thrusting slightly on the starboard bow. Compressed air shot from a tiny nozzle and began to turn the boxy battle suit. That tiny bit of control over his movements gave Alex a surge of confidence.

"All right, team," Alex said. "Time to show what we can do."

"Hell yeah," Sly said.

"No problem," Ash said.

"Lead the way, Ace," Newt said.

Alex had his Valkyrie turned and moving steadily toward the drop ship. It was the only other vessel besides the hulking carrier in sight. Alex couldn't help but look at the massive ship as he flew past her. The sunlight reflecting from the icy world to his right illuminated the CDF carrier

*Republic* so that Alex could see the dull grey metal, the painted lettering on her sides, and the large doors to the launching bays. Lights were positioned on the exterior of the ship, and there were even windows on certain areas.

*Forty kilometers,* Nyx said. *You'll need to begin slowing down soon.*

"Roger that," Alex said as he began to feather the bow thrusters.

"Oh, man, there's a huge part of the hull missing," Newt said as they approached the drop ship.

"Are we sure anyone survived?" Sly asked.

Chief Landry's voice sounded distant over the Valkyrie's internal communications system. "We have confirmation that Charlie Company is alive. They're locked down in the drop ship's cargo bay."

"Will we be able to remove the docking clamps?" Ash asked.

"We can do that remotely," Chief Landry said. "But once we do, they'll all be floating free inside."

"How many are in there, Chief?"

"Nine Destroyers and three Interceptors," Landry replied, his voice laced with a thin stream of static.

*Alex, bring your MBS to stop beside the drop ship,* Nyx said. *I'll walk you through the process from there.*

"Got it, Nyx," Alex said, before switching to the company channel. "Ash, Sly, Newt, hang back a little. Let me get in position before you move in."

"Roger that, team leader," Ash said.

*You're one kilometer out, Alex. Try to reach a full stop about fifteen meters from the drop ship.*

"Without crashing?" Alex said in a weak attempt at humor.

*That would be best,* Nyx replied.

# Chapter 14

Alex was drifting toward the drop ship, which was much larger up close than it appeared from a distance. It was spinning like a football as it drifted sideways toward Carthage Prime.

"I'm in position," Alex said.

*Right, good job. Now, I've activated the recovery line on your left side. You want to aim it just like a weapon, then extend it.*

"Extend the recovery arm?"

*No, not the arm. It's too fragile for this maneuver. Extend the line. There's a magnet on the end, which I'll power on when it gets close to the drop ship's hull.*

"Okay," Alex said. "Just point and shoot."

*This will be your anchor point,* Nyx explained. *You need to connect it the drop ship's hull near the rent in the hull. Can you do that?*

"Sure," Alex said, trying his best to stay positive.

The mission was scary in some respects. Being in a battle suit and hovering in space was frightening in many respects. But Alex was able to put that fear aside and focus on the task at hand. His main concern was messing up. It didn't take a physicist to see that connecting to a spinning ship was going to be dangerous.

*Now, once we connect to the drop ship, I'll reel you in while you focus on staying in line with the recovery cable. If you don't, the motion of the ship will get it tangled and you could damage the Valkyrie suit.*

"That sounds bad," Alex said.

*It's not good.*

"Steady, Alex," Ash said. "You've got this."

"You better hope so, Ash. You're next," Alex replied.

He let the ship spin all the way around twice. The drop ships were simple vessels: a rectangular cargo hold built on top of two engines with a triangular cab for the pilots up front. The large windows were reflective, and Alex was grateful that he couldn't see inside. He didn't know for certain what exposure to hard vacuum would do to a human body, and he wasn't in a hurry to find out.

The hole in the ship's hull looked like something inside had exploded. The damaged engine was obviously the culprit. One of the two was blackened with the metal mounts twisted or ripped off. The hole included half of the faulty engine and a large portion of the port side wall of the cargo bay.

Alex let the magnet sneak closer and closer to the target. When it was just a meter away from the drop ship, Nyx took over.

*Powering on the electromagnet now.*

Alex hit his thrusters. He had to maneuver in an arc to keep pace with the drop ship's spin. He was far from perfect, but he managed to stay close enough that the line didn't tangle, and Nyx pulled him onto the hull.

"Contact," he said. "Hold is secure."

*Can you see into the ship?*

Alex had to let out a little slack on the recovery line, but he was then able to lean his starboard side toward the hole in the ship's hull.

"Yeah," Alex said.

The interior was dark, and there was debris floating around. He could just make out the nearest MBS.

"Good work, Evans," Chief Landry said. "Hold that position."

*We've got a good visual,* Nyx said. *Ashton's controller should be able to guide her into place now.*

"Good luck, Ash," Alex said.

"Ha, I'll make this look easy," Ash said.

She wasn't kidding. Alex could only see her when the drop ship rotated toward her, but she eased in, smoothly and gracefully, extended her recovery line, and made contact with the ship on the far side of the hull breech from Alex.

"Contact," Ash said.

"What about us?" Sly asked.

"Once the *Republic* releases the docking clamps, we'll pull them out," Alex said.

"And throw them to you," Ash said, with a mischievous chuckle.

"What?" Newt asked.

"We'll pull them out and push them toward you," Alex said. "You'll catch them with your recovery lines and secure them to your battle suit. We all have to carry three."

"*Republic* Valkyrie team is in place," Ash said. "You can release the docking clamps."

"Roger that, Valkyrie team," a voice said.

Alex didn't recognize the voice but assumed it came from one of the officers on the carrier ship. The docking clamp released with a loud *thunk* that vibrated through the ship. Alex saw the mechanized battle suits slowly rise up from the deck of the drop ship.

*No time to waste. The longer they're in there, the more likely they'll bump into something that might damage them or make the drop ship unstable.*

"Roger that," Alex said, raising his right arm and extending the recovery line. "Extending the cable into the ship. Ash, we better do this one at a time so we don't cause an accident."

"I agree," Ash said. "I'm standing by."

There was no sound in space, and Alex couldn't feel the magnet recovery line, but something in his mind sensed the electromagnet connecting to one of the battle suits.

*I've got contact. Reel it back in, Alex.*

He did as instructed, and the first battle suit was brought out of the drop ship. Making contact with the hull was impossible to avoid, but Alex felt confident that the Destroyer armor was strong enough to take it. He extracted the MBS slowly, and once it was completely outside the drop ship, he pushed it out toward Newt.

"Releasing the first MBS," Alex said. "It's heading your way, Newt."

"I see it," Newt replied.

"It's like playing catch in the park," Sly added.

Ash was busy pulling out the next MBS from the drop ship, so Alex watched Newt extend a retrieval line. The magnetic end snapped onto the drifting MBS, and Newt began using his thrusters to arrest the movement of the rescued operator.

"One down," Alex said.

"Here's the second," Ash said as she nudged an AT Interceptor toward Sly.

The first six rescues were easy. Newt and Sly caught them, secured them to the recovery lines that were part of the Valkyrie, then began the journey back to the *Republic*. Ash separated from the drop ship and caught the next three, then waited for Alex. He pulled the last three MBS's from the drop ship and sent them drifting in the direction of the *Republic*.

"You sure you can catch them?" Ash asked.

"Shouldn't be a problem," Alex said.

*We've got this,* Nyx assured him.

The drop ship was left behind, venting debris and slowly being pulled down toward Carthage Prime. It was a little sad to see the ship abandoned, but Alex knew it was a total loss. He gave his thrusters a nudge and started after the drifting ships.

*Excellent work on the drop ship,* Nyx said. *Your team has adapted to the Valkyries quite well.*

"I couldn't have done it without you," Alex said as he approached the first MBS. "I'm extending the recovery line."

*Copy. Preparing to engage the electromagnet.*

Alex felt the connection as the magnet snapped onto the Destroyer. It was odd to see the thickly armored battle suit, with tank treads and bulky weapons, drifting helplessly through space. He was drifting in the same direction as the MBS, only faster. He gave his stern thrusters another boost as he began reeling the battle suit in.

"Retracting the recovery line," Alex said.

*Once it's close, use the other line to secure it to your suit. The closer you keep them to you, the better off you'll be—just don't block the thrust nozzles.*

"Yeah, that's good advice," Alex said, feeling a prickly sensation along his back at the thought of losing control with three MBS's attached to his Valkyrie suit.

It didn't take long to gather the three drifting refugees, and Ash stayed close, offering encouragement. When he looked up, Sly and Newt were little more than tiny dots between his position and the big carrier ship. It made him feel small and lost in the vastness of space. The planet seemed impossibly large, and even though he knew it wasn't true, he felt like it was pulling him down.

*How are you doing, Alex?*

"This is different," he admitted. "No simulation even comes close."

He had to restrain himself from engaging the thrusters and sending himself hurtling toward the *Republic*.

*You're doing great. Your team is saving lives.*

"Not exactly what we trained for, but I'll take it," Alex said. "Can you show me the distance to the carrier?"

*Sending it now.*

Alex didn't have to wait. In the lower righthand side of his vision, the distance to the carrier ship appeared in kilometers. He could see the numbers counting down, and it gave him a small sliver of reassurance. It also helped not to look at the planet. The icy, white surface seemed to shimmer and beckon to him.

"Titan team," Chief Landry said over the com-link. "What's your status?"

"Newton and Lassiter are approaching the *Republic*," Ash said. "Evans and I are in transit back."

"Roger that," Landry replied. "Once you're all together, we'll open the hangar doors and lead you back inside."

It didn't take long. The rescued MBS's altered Alex's mass, but Nyx gave him plenty of warning. He slowed his approach and came to a safe stop a few meters away from

Newt and Sly. Ashton kept pace and matched his deceleration perfectly.

"Took you guys long enough," Sly said.

"We did all the heavy lifting," Ash said.

"Titan team on-station and ready for access," Alex informed Chief Landry over the com-link.

A set of double doors began sliding apart. Yellow light from within the huge ship spilled out and looked so inviting that Alex couldn't help but grin with excitement.

*Your first mission is nearly complete.*

"Yeah, don't jinx it," Alex said.

Ashton's voice came over the speakers in the Valkyrie as clear as if she were standing beside him.

"Permission to come aboard?" she said.

"Granted," Chief Landry said. "Good work, Titan team."

"Let's go one at a time," Alex said. "And spread out. We don't want any accidents now."

"I'll go first," Newt suggested.

Alex watched as Newt flew into the ship. Crossing the threshold into artificial gravity was tricky, but he managed it without too much trouble.

*Careful as you come in,* Nyx said. *Technicians and medical personnel are standing by.*

"Thanks, Nyx," Alex said as he flew into the hangar.

He made a safe landing, setting the MBS's he was towing down first, then bringing his Valkyrie down on the deck as the hangar doors closed behind him.

*Stand by. Let the technicians come in and hook onto your suit.*

"No problem," Alex said. He could feel the tension of the mission draining from him. He wanted food and a shower, then maybe he could feel normal again.

"These bulky suits aren't so bad," Sly said over the company channel of their com-link. "A few guns wouldn't hurt, though."

"I didn't join the CDF to be a glorified tow truck," Ash replied.

"We saved lives," Alex said. "That's something to be proud of."

"And we did it with style," Sly said.

"I can't get over Carthage," Newt said. "I've never seen a planet like that."

"You mean from orbit," Ash said, "with nothing but a battle suit between you and hard vacuum?"

"Yeah, that's different," Alex said. "I felt like it was pulling me down."

*That's called vertigo, Alex. Every pilot experiences it as some point. You did well not to panic.*

"I felt it too," Sly said.

"It doesn't look too inviting," Ash said. "I mean, it's beautiful from space, but it looks cold on the surface."

"Maybe being held back on the ship wasn't such a bad thing," Alex said.

He had no idea how true that statement was.

# Chapter 15

When Alex climbed from the Valkyrie, he saw the operators his team had rescued. They were lined up on a bench just inside the hangar, where technicians were seeing to their battle suits. A group of medical personnel were checking their vitals and making sure the group was okay.

Alex climbed down and was surprised when the technician, a sergeant, saluted him.

"Good job, Private," the sergeant said.

Alex snapped to attention and returned the salute. "Thank you, Sergeant."

Ash, Newt, and Sly joined Alex as they headed for the door. They walked past the group of rescued operators. They looked shaken and frightened, but healthy enough. Alex didn't recognize them, not even enough to say he'd seen them in passing. Most were older, mainly corporals and sergeants. At the end of the row, a man with gray stubble on the sides of his head and a shiny bald spot on top stood up and blocked their exit. It was a master sergeant with deep wrinkles around his squinting eyes.

"You're the fliers that pulled us out of that drop ship?" the master sergeant said.

"Yes, Master Sergeant," Alex replied.

"We're Romeo Company. We owe you our lives," the bald man said. "The least I can do is buy you all a drink at the Enlisted Club."

He thrust out a hand, and Alex shook it. The rest of his team followed suit. There were looks of gratitude on the faces of Romeo Company's eleven other members.

"We'd be happy to accept, but we're not allowed," Alex said.

The master sergeant nodded. "Well, thanks then. We owe you."

"We were just doing our job," Newt said.

The door swished opened beside them, and Chief Landry stepped in.

"Officer on deck," the master sergeant shouted.

"As you were," Landry said. "I see you've met our Titan team, Master Sergeant Brooks."

"Yes, sir. It's an honor," Brooks said. "We'd like to show our appreciation."

"You'll get your chance," Landry said. "Captain Chastain is insisting that your company get a full physical eval. But that shouldn't take long."

"Yes, sir," Master Sergeant Brooks said.

"Titan team—you're with me," Chief Landry said.

He turned on his heel and hurried out of the hangar. Alex and his friends followed. He was secretly grateful that Chief Landry was leading the way. Alex wasn't sure he could find his way back to their section of the ship on his own.

They came to a lift, and Chief Landry swiped his ID card. It opened, and they followed him inside.

"Outstanding job," Landry told them as the lift carried them up several levels. "The captain wants to congratulate you herself."

The door of the lift opened, and Landry was on the move again. Alex glanced at Ash, who had a smirk on her face. It was clear she was happy about the outcome of the mission. Alex felt more like Newt did; they had just done their jobs. He was happy that Romeo Company was safe, but he didn't feel like they were heroes.

The group hurried after Landry. No one spoke. They were in a wide corridor, and unlike the section of the ship they had been in since coming aboard the *Republic* in the Helena system, the level of the carrier they found themselves on was pristine. The deck was covered with polished black tiles. The walls were white glow panels, but there were no conduits or pipes. The corridor looked like an indoor shopping complex rather than a military vessel.

They came to a set of double doors with a narrow horizontal window. Landry turned to them and spoke in a quiet but urgent tone.

"Once we step into the bridge, you're to stand at attention," he instructed. "I'll introduce you. There's no need to speak unless asked a direct question. Okay, here we go."

He turned and held his ID to the reader beside the doors. A beep sounded, then the doors opened on a round room. There were several people inside standing at consoles that surrounded a large holographic projector in the center of the room. Shimmering in super high definition was Carthage Prime, with an exact replica of the *Republic* in orbit around her. Alex even saw a tiny dot that he guessed was the abandoned drop ship from which he and his team had rescued the operators.

There were large display screens on the far wall. Some showed the ship's systems and technical readouts. Others showed radar and a plot of the entire Carthage system. On either side of the door more officers stood, observing. A steady stream of communications from the drop ships sounded over the bridge's sound system. Alex followed Chief Landry onto the bridge. Ash was to his left. Newt and Sly stood shoulder to shoulder beyond her.

Captain Chastain was short with dark hair and a friendly face, but her eyes were piercing and direct, with dark, puffy skin beneath that made her seem old. She smiled as she stepped up to Chief Landry.

"Is this your Titan team?" Captain Chastain asked.

"Yes, Captain," Landry said, before stepping aside so that the captain could look them over.

"Outstanding work today," she said. "It's my understanding that you haven't trained in the AR Valkyries?"

"No, Captain," they all said in unison.

"Impressive. Well, I suppose it's only fitting that you get bumped in rank. You're all corporals now. With that comes access to the entire ship. I'll leave it to Chief Landry to work out what you can do and where you can go. Just remember: we're a military ship with reason to believe that we could come under attack at any moment. So, don't do anything that might incapacitate you if the call to action should come."

She stopped in front of Alex. He saw her glance at his name that was stenciled onto the left side of his chest.

"Corporal Evans," she said, using his new rank. "Vice President Loman is a friend. He promoted me to captain himself. I want to thank you for saving his life."

Alex shook his head and was about to dismiss her thanks, but she held up a hand to silence him.

"Humility is a virtuous trait, but what you did was more than just your duty."

"I was only trying to get out of that room alive," Alex admitted.

Captain Chastain chuckled. "Of course you were. He's smart," she said to Chief Landry.

"Corporal Evans has proven himself to be a talented operator," Landry said.

"Indeed," Captain Chastain said. "You have my thanks, Corporal. I will be glad to return the favor if I can. Take the rest of the day to decompress, but return to your training schedule first thing tomorrow. I have one team of FA Titans, and I plan to use them when the time comes."

"Thank you, Captain," Landry said. "We won't let you down."

She nodded, then turned back to her duties on the bridge. Landry waved for Alex and his team to leave. The door opened silently behind them, and they hurried out. Chief Landry went with them, and when the bridge door closed, he breathed an audible sigh of relief.

"Well, that went better than expected, eh?" Landry said. "I'll put in the promotions Captain Chastain issued and send someone to give the four of you a tour of the ship. That being said, there are some areas that will continue to be off-limits, the command level being one. You have no need to be in the engineering sections or the weapon control areas, for that matter. Boring stuff, anyway. You'll want to go to the upper levels—that's where the entertainment areas are. Go get cleaned up and take the tour. I'm restricting you to one drink each, and no ardent spirits. We can't have you drunk or hungover if the captain calls for you tomorrow."

"Sir?" Alex said. "Were we kept here because we aren't ready for combat?"

"Yeah, why did the rest of Echo Company get sent down and we didn't?" Ash asked.

"Don't be so quick to fight," Chief Landry said. "It's not all glorious and exciting like it seems in the movies. And no, you weren't held back because we didn't think you were ready. Captain Chastain feels an orbital insertion is the best strategy. You four are the only qualified Titan operators on board. She wanted to keep you close and use you to her advantage if we come under attack."

"You think someone would try to take out the *Republic*?" Newt asked.

"More likely they'll try to destroy whatever mining operations are set up on the surface," Landry said, leading them down the pristine corridor toward the lifts. "Corporate conflicts aren't usually so direct. Fighting a carrier would be dangerous and expensive. A small insertion team in atmosphere, on the other hand, could cause a lot of damage and be hard to track down. They might even get away clean."

"Wouldn't we see them in orbit?" Sly pointed out.

"Not if they came in disguised as a freighter, like a shipment of mining equipment or construction supplies," Landry said. "But you don't need to worry about that. Once you're called on, the objective will be clear. Until then, you can enjoy your day off, then hit your training again tomorrow, just like the captain ordered."

"Yes, Chief," they all said together.

"The lift will take you down to level two," Landry said. "By the time you're done cleaning up, your promotion will show on your ID's."

They stepped aboard the lift and turned back to face him as the doors started to close.

"Good work today," he said.

Then the doors closed, and they were headed down.

"Corporal Newton...I like the sound of that," Newt said.

"The rest of the day off sounds pretty good, too," Ash said.

"Yeah," Alex said as the lift came to a stop and the doors opened. "Now all we have to do is find our quarters."

"I think it's this way," Sly said.

"Better go the other then," Ash replied.

"Oh, very funny," Sly said, but he was laughing with the rest of the team.

# Chapter 16

Loman was in his new office. It was small with barely enough room for his desk and chair, but Loman didn't mind tight spaces. It reminded him of his early days in the company, when he was an operator in a battle suit. That seemed like another lifetime. Now he was the Executive Vice President of Security, a position that carried a significant amount of prestige that was not reflected in the tiny office he'd moved himself into. There was no room to meet with employees or sales reps. He had no windows and no decor of any kind, yet he almost felt more secure in the tiny office. All he really needed was his phone and his computer, both of which fit neatly on his desk.

His PIL vibrated. It was 0858, time for him to emerge from his lair, as he thought of the tiny office, for his meeting with manager Zan Fordham. The man was a poser and a greedy corporate climber. How Fordham had reached the rank of manager astonished Loman, but he couldn't be in charge of everything within his division, and obviously Zan had very influential friends. It was only a matter of time before word came down from above that Zan should be given a new title, along with the financial perks of being an executive. If the greedy little worm was insufferable now, how horrible would he be when he was named co-VP of security? Loman wondered.

The distance from Loman's new office to his old one wasn't far. He passed Raz at the reception desk. The big man looked odd behind the small desk, as if he were seated at a child's table. He nodded as Loman passed, raising his eyebrows as if to say something. Loman could only guess. Deliveries had been coming up constantly since Loman had given up his office. He had done his best to ignore the distraction, but when he rounded the corner, the door to the office was open and Loman could see inside.

Where Loman had been minimalist in decorating his corner office, Zan had gone all out, filling the place with exotic plants, lavish furniture, sculptures, and paintings. There was even a huge water feature made with dark stones piled up nearly to the ceiling; water fell and splashed against the rocks. The floors had been covered with simple, corporate-style carpets, but Zan had spread out thick, handmade rugs and runners. His new desk was a monstrosity, set on a platform that raised him nearly twenty centimeters above the rest of the office. He sat in a large chair covered in some type of animal skin. It was a bright, golden color with dark spots. The desk was made of dark wood with ornate carvings. Loman guessed the decor cost nearly a million credits, perhaps even more. The entire redecoration was intended to project an air of wealth and sophistication—yet it only made Zan seem small and out of place.

"We have a meeting?" Loman said.

"Yes, yes, of course we do," Zan said. It was obvious the man had forgotten about their plans to discuss candidates to replace Colonel Bixby.

There was no place for a visitor to sit near the desk. There were three uncomfortable-looking chairs in the room, along with a low-backed sofa. Two of the chairs were by the water feature. Loman could tell at a glance that anyone sitting in them would get wet. He pointed toward the sofa.

"Should we sit there?"

"Yes, that will do nicely," Zan said.

Even the man's tone of voice was different, as if he were somehow above the work they were being paid to do.

Loman sat on the sofa. It was upholstered in leather that was waxed to a high shine. He slid back, the leather creaking beneath him. Zan came around his huge desk, and Loman realized he'd done more than order furniture. The man was dressed in one of the strange, incredibly expensive, alternative business suits. It was made of shimmersilk and was actually a gown that looked like a judge's robes. It had a tiny collar and shoulder pads to make Zan appear to be in better shape than he actually was. Loman couldn't help but wonder if Zan also had some type of compression device holding in his stomach.

He sat on the chair opposite from Loman and perched right on the front edge. The bottom of the gown rose upward when he sat, revealing glossy shoes with a high polish. Zan looked extremely uncomfortable, and Loman guessed the sales professional had raved about how good the fashionable clothing looked on him, but it simply wasn't true.

"Do you have some names you'd like us to start with?" Loman asked.

"I do, yes, of course," Zan said, shifting his weight on the strange chair. It looked like a padded rail with a tiny backrest that made it impossible to lean back against without his gown hiking up even farther. "But why don't you start? I'm sure you have someone in mind."

Loman did have someone in mind, but he wasn't about to come right out and tell Zan who he wanted. The dance had begun, and the inevitable power struggle was about to become a war.

"I have a few names in mind. I'm not sure you know them," Loman said.

"I have extensive contacts," Zan said. "Let's see if any of the names on your list match up with mine."

"All right," Loman said. "As you know from your research, the colonel rank is the highest military position in the company. The primary job is to advise the VP on strategy and tactics."

"Yes, that's how I understand it."

"Captain Quana Oliphasus has the most experience," Loman said, pausing to see how Zan would react.

"Experience doesn't always equal skill," he said.

Loman forced himself to frown, but inwardly he was smiling. Manipulating people wasn't something he valued, and he certainly didn't enjoy doing it. But Loman had studied negotiation. He knew that Zan was likely to reject whomever Loman suggested first. Zan had not only reacted as Loman expected, but he'd also revealed that he had no real thoughts on the matter. Platitudes had their place, but if Zan had any real feelings about the staffing position, he would have expressed more than an old axiom. It was clear to Loman that what Zan really wanted was to thwart Loman's wishes, and all that was needed was to make Zan believe he had won the negotiation—even if he was actually lobbying for the very person Loman wanted to be the new colonel.

"All right, well, Libby Gonzalez is efficient and well-liked by her crew," Loman offered.

"Gonzalez...Gonzalez...where have I heard that name?" Zan asked.

"Captain Gonzalez is on Hagen space station," Loman said.

Once more he waited for a reaction. The Hagen space station was a refitting platform on the verge of known space. Gonzalez was famous for her dislike of the administrators. Loman knew from his research that Zan had crossed paths with Gonzalez early in his career. When the manager recalled Gonzalez in his memory, his feelings about her showed clearly on his face.

"Oh, no," he said. "She has the wrong temperament. It would never work. She's not a team player by any means. I have to insist that we find someone else. Anyone but her."

"Well, I only have one other name on my list, but I don't know that I should even mention her," Loman said. "She's deployed on a mission, and to be honest it might make waves."

Loman looked away from Zan, afraid he would burst out into peals of laughter. The manager's eyes were bulging with excitement at Loman's reluctance. It was almost too easy, and that thought brought Loman up short. Was he being played by Zan? Did the greasy little manager expect Loman to come in and try to manipulate him? Loman looked back up. Zan was trying not to smile and failing.

"Who are you suggesting?" Zan asked.

If the man was pretending, he was a marvelous actor. He looked as if he were about to burst waiting to hear the name of the candidate that Loman seemingly didn't really want.

"Well, if you're sure about Gonzalez," Loman said.

"Quite sure," Zan replied.

"Well, then, I suppose we could promote Captain Ursula Chastain."

"Why, I believe she's near the top of my own list," Zan said.

He was clumsy and had spoken too fast. His enthusiasm didn't match the occasion, and Loman would have bet his entire net worth that Zan didn't even have a list. But Loman still found himself hesitating. Was it possible that Chastain was secretly on Chairwoman Faulk's side? He didn't think so. Unlike most of the other captains, she had a strong believe in the CDF as a military institution. She believed in the chain of command and that a person should be judged by their abilities.

"I'm still not convinced," Loman said.

"I am," he said. "She's perfect."

Loman knew that Zan Fordham had never in his life even met Captain Chastain. She preferred to work instead of hobnob. Zan had spent most of his career on Helena Prime, while Chastain was rarely even in the Helena system.

"If you really think so," Loman said.

"I do. I insist."

"All right, I'll begin the paperwork," Loman said.

"My, my, we're working together well already," Zan said, trying to look smug but failing in his business gown.

"We should go out to the Carthage system," Loman said. "Captain Chastain is leading the full engagement there. It would do the troops some good to see our confidence in them, and I would like to see what progress is being made firsthand."

"Carthage?" Zan asked.

"Yes, you know we got the contract for the mineral rights on Carthage Prime?" Loman said.

"Oh, yes, I believe I did read that somewhere," Zan lied.

"It's a new planet. The southern hemisphere is a tundra, but a quick tour would be a great way for our security specialists to get to know you."

"Actually, I have some meetings here," Zan said. "I really shouldn't go running off, not so soon after arriving."

"I could go on my own, but it would be bet—"

Zan cut him off. "I really must insist that I stay. It's one of the reasons I've been brought in, you know. That way, someone is always here if we're needed."

"All right," Loman said, doing his best to sound defeated.

"Well then, if that's all," Zan said, standing up and smoothing his gown as he returned to his desk on its raised platform, "I should be getting back to it."

"Yes, of course," Loman said.

He slid off the sofa, which was so new it was slippery. He walked to the door and then stopped. He looked back. Zan was in the large executive chair, smoothing his shimmer silk gown. The office looked like it belonged on a movie set. Things were changing, but if all Loman had to do to keep his job was put up with a pretentious fool, he would make that work.

Loman left the office and walked back toward the reception desk. Raz was waiting. He looked up as Loman came into view.

"Mr. Haley," he said quietly with a slight bob of the head.

Loman stopped at the big man's desk and leaned over.

"I'm heading to the Carthage system. Can you set that up?"

"Yes, sir. When would you like to leave?"

"As soon as possible," Loman said. "And when you get a chance, let's set up a full surveillance suite in Mr. Fordham's office. Audio and visual."

"Yes, sir," Raz rumbled.

"You could monitor it from here, couldn't you?"

"Absolutely," Raz said. "When you're gone, there's nothing else to do but order lunch for Mr. Fordham. Anything in particular you're looking for?"

"No, but I don't want him giving orders. He's got no concept for what we do here. And we might just get something on record that we can use if things continue to go south with the board of directors."

"Sounds like a good plan," Raz said. "I'll see to it personally."

"Thank you, Raz. It's good to have someone here I can trust."

Loman went back to his office and ordered his AI computer to begin the promotional paperwork for Captain Chastain. After gathering his things, he headed out of the office. It felt good to be leaving Arcadia again. Perhaps having Zan around could be used to his advantage, after all. He preferred being out with his security division, not stuck in an office where he couldn't even have a drink when he felt like it. He touched the interior coat pocket, making sure his lucky flask was still there. It was, and he realized he could accomplish two goals by going to the

Carthage system: he could promote Captain Chastain and also check in on his new poster boy, Alex Evans.

# Chapter 17

After cleaning up and putting on civilian clothes, the Titan team was met at their quarters by their guide. Alex felt a thrill when he saw her. Nyx was still in her fatigues, but unlike the compression wear his team wore, controllers had more casual garb; she was in a dark navy blue outfit with white stripes on her sleeves.

"Nyx," Alex said when they opened the door and found her waiting outside their berth. "What are you doing here?"

"I heard you needed a tour guide," she said with a smile.

"Guys, this is Nyx, my controller," Alex said. "This is Ash, and Sly, and Newt."

"It's good to put faces to the names I hear on the com-link," Nyx said.

"I thought controllers didn't like knowing their operators outside of missions," Ash said. "Mine hasn't shown any interest."

"Some don't," Nyx said. "They prefer some distance, just in case...you know."

"In case we bite it," Sly said. "Makes sense to me."

Nyx started down the empty corridor, and Alex's team followed. He had to hang back as the other three crowded close to Nyx.

"Can we see where you work?" Newt asked.

"Do you want to see that?" Nyx asked.

"Sure," Newt said enthusiastically.

"Not all of us," Ash said. "We only have a day. Let's do something fun."

"We could start with lunch," Sly said. "I'm starving."

Alex wanted Nyx all to himself, but he knew it wasn't the right time. It was their first day of liberty on the carrier, and the first time they could see what all was on the big ship. Spending time alone with Nyx might have been his first choice, but he couldn't abandon his friends. And he had no idea how Nyx felt about him. Perhaps being alone wasn't something she would enjoy.

They made their way back to the lift and got inside. Alex stood next to Nyx. Never in his life had he felt such a strong desire to touch someone. It felt like she was part of his life and not just a voice in his head. He felt like she knew him, and he knew her—but he forced himself to hold back. The feelings weren't real; they were like the illusion of the huge planet pulling him down. He didn't really know Nyx more than anyone else in the elevator.

"So where are we going first?" Sly said.

"Eighth level is called the promenade," Nyx said. "It's the top of the ship. Lots of windows and observation areas."

"We've been outside," Ash said. "I doubt it beats that view."

"True," Nyx said. "But it's a nice place. Much wider than most of the spaces on the ship. And there are a few small vendors there selling food and drinks."

"Now we're talking," Sly said. "Not food dispensers, right? Real food?"

"Yeah, it's real food," Nyx said.

"How's that possible?" Newt asked. "Isn't this a war ship?"

"It's a carrier, which the Ahzco corporation uses for a variety of purposes," Nyx said. "And because the company has a lot of products, and some of those are food-related, they assign some of their employees to work the various ships in the CDF."

"That makes sense," Newt said.

"It makes me hungry," Sly added. "How do we buy the food?"

"Your ID card," Nyx said. "Our per diem is based on rank, but you earn a certain amount of credit for food and entertainment."

"Captain Chastain said we could only get one drink," Ash said.

"Yes, one alcoholic beverage is standard for most of us," Nyx said. "Sergeants and master sergeants get two per day."

"What about soda?" Sly asked.

"The only limit is your credit account," Nyx said.

"And the fact that you'll be sick when we hit the gym tomorrow if you don't show some restraint," Ash said.

The lift came to a stop, and the group stepped out onto a wide corridor. The ceiling was twice as high as the rest of the ship, and there were windows spaced at regular intervals. For an hour they strolled along, stopping at the various vendors for snacks and soda. They were like children at a carnival for the first time.

Alex's favorite place was a large observation deck. He could see Carthage below the ship and several other system planets, as well as the star they revolved around. The view made him feel as if he wasn't trapped on a spaceship, but rather in a brand-new solar system.

"Beautiful, in a way," Nyx said, looking down at the shimmering surface of Carthage Prime.

"Stark," Ash added.

"Cold," Sly said, sipping on this fourth soft drink.

"I wonder what it's like down there," Alex said.

"I kind of hope we don't find out," Newt said. "Captain Chastain said we wouldn't be sent unless there's trouble."

"None of us want that," Ash said, "but I wouldn't mind a little action."

"Yeah, I've had enough simulations to last a lifetime," Sly added.

"It's a level-two planet," Nyx said. "Breathable atmosphere, but dangerous environmental conditions."

"Most of the planet is frozen," Sly said. "Why would you want to freeze your bum off down there?"

"It just seems like a shame to simply look at it from a distance," Alex said.

"Ignore him," Ash said, giving Nyx a gentle nudge with her elbow. "He's from a level-three world. He gets a little moon-eyed over planets a person can actually breathe on."

They were all laughing, including Alex—who knew what Ash said was partially true—when the lights behind them began to flash. They all turned and saw yellow lights glowing on and off in the emergency alert nodes.

"Yellow alert!" boomed a loud voice over the ship's speakers. "Yellow alert! All personnel return to your assigned areas. This is not a test. All personnel return to your assigned areas and stand by for instructions."

"Yellow alert?" Newt asked as they hurried back across the promenade toward the lift that would take them back to their assigned area.

"There must be another ship in the system," Nyx said.

"So much for our day off," Ash said.

"You're the one who wanted action," Alex pointed out.

"Sorry about the tour," Nyx said, as they stepped into the lift.

"Raincheck," Alex said.

"Yeah, we'll have to do this again," Sly said. "I'm still hungry."

"You're always hungry," Ash complained.

The elevator carried them down several floors. When the doors opened, Alex saw more people dressed like Nyx. He felt a twinge of disappointment at the thought of being separated from her again.

"This is my level," Nyx said. "I'll talk to you all again soon."

"It was nice meeting you," Newt said.

"Yeah, don't be a stranger," Ash added.

Nyx stepped off the lift and hurried away. Alex leaned against the wall as the doors closed, and the elevator continued downward.

"Well, she's cute," Ash said. "I mean, if you're into that kind of thing."

"I think my controller's a dude," Sly said.

"Why does that matter?" Newt asked.

"It doesn't, I'm just saying," Sly said. "I guess I'll ask."

"I think Alex is the only one who got a real person," Ash said. "My controller is a robot with no emotions."

"I met Nyx before we were partnered together," Alex said.

"Really?" Sly asked. "Man, the odds of that happening are astronomical."

"We were in the admin waiting room at the same time," Alex said. "It probably wasn't an accident."

"Not a chance," Ash said. "Someone's setting you up for success, Ace. I guess we're just lucky we're along for the ride."

Alex wasn't sure if he detected a note of resentment in her voice, but as the doors opened, he felt like Ash was angry. And perhaps she was right—maybe he was getting special treatment, but he hadn't gone looking for it.

"We should get out of these street clothes and back into fatigues," Sly said.

"Lead the way," Newt said.

Back in their quarters, which seemed odd with only a few people in the big room meant for an entire squad, they changed quickly. Ash, normally not modest, took her clothes into the bathroom. Alex was in his private room but left the door open as he changed. Sly stepped into the doorway as he pulled on his compression wear.

"What's eating her?" Sly asked.

"Ash?" Alex said.

"Yeah. Is she mad about something?"

"I don't know," Alex said. "Maybe she thinks I'm getting special treatment."

"Oh, and she's not?" Sly pointed out. "Does she really think any of us would be here if not for you? It's just the luck of the draw, man."

"Maybe," Alex said. "I've had a few breaks go my way, or I wouldn't be here at all."

"Exactly," Sly said. "You didn't ask for special treatment."

"Do you think Nyx is a better controller than yours?"

Sly shrugged. "Who knows. I don't have a problem with mine. He's all business. I think if anything, he doesn't like me."

"You're an acquired taste," Alex teased.

"Not everyone can handle my greatness," Sly said. "Maybe Ash just likes being the only girl in the group."

"I kind of thought she didn't want to be thought of as a girl," Alex said. "I mean, I just think of her as part of the team."

"Yeah, me too, but maybe that's the problem. Maybe when we're off duty, she wants to be more than just a teammate."

"That's crazy."

"I've heard of crazier things."

Alex was adjusting the tight-fitting compression shirt when his Flex PIL beeped. Sly's beeped at the same time. He looked at the device, which instructed him to report to ready room 108. There was even a small diagram that showed the layout of their level of the ship. A blue dot showed his position, and a yellow line showed the directions they were to take.

Alex snapped the PIL onto his left forearm and walked out of his room. The rest of the team were waiting.

"Everyone got the message?" Alex asked.

"Ready room 108," Newt said with a nod.

"All right, you two head out," Alex said to Newt and Sly. "Ash and I will catch up in a sec."

"Sure," Sly said.

They left the room, and Ash looked at Alex. There was no doubt in his mind that she was upset, but he had no way of knowing why without asking. He suddenly felt self-conscious and thought about just hurrying out after his friends.

"What?" Ash demanded.

"Look, I can tell that you're mad," Alex said.

"Yeah, it's pretty obvious," she snapped.

"So...what's the problem?"

"There's no problem. Can't I have feelings? Sometimes a person just gets upset. I don't need to stand around and talk about it."

"Did I do something wrong?"

"Oh, sure, if I'm upset it must have something to do with you, Ace. Maybe you shouldn't believe every foolish thought that flitters through that little brain of yours."

She stepped closer to him. With her short hair and athletic build, he'd never really thought of her as anything other than a teammate. Ash was fast, capable, and fearless. Alex was team leader, but Ash could have been, just as easily. Her only fault was that she took too many chances.

"I didn't mean to make things worse," Alex said. "I just thought that if you needed to talk—"

She burst out laughing. He felt his own anger starting to rise up.

"You thought I'd talk to *you*?"

The question cut like a knife.

"I'd be the ace on this team if not for someone helping you out at every turn," Ash said. "Maybe Oggy was right about you."

"Watch yourself," Alex said angrily.

Ash held her hands up in a false surrender. "Sorry, I didn't mean to hurt your feelings."

She stormed out of their quarters, and Alex could do nothing but watch her go. He felt sick. Nothing was resolved, and they were both angry. It was not the way he wanted to feel going into a combat mission, but there was nothing left to do but follow her. He glanced at his PIL, got a sense for where he was headed, then hurried to catch up with the others.

# Chapter 18

Ready room 108 was exactly what it sounded like: it was a room for operators that had everything they needed before a mission. Alex's Titan team wasn't the only group in the room. Romeo Company was there as well. Alex and Ash had jogged through the corridors and caught up to Sly and Newt. The four of them went into the ready room together.

"Chief Landry asked me to get the four of you settled," Master Sergeant Brooks said.

"Yes, Master Sergeant," the four Titan operators said.

Alex thought the ready room looked like a locker room for a sports team. There were lockers and padded benches on one end. A food and drink dispenser took up part of one wall, and three rows of rocking stadium seats faced a large display screen on the far end of the room.

"You four will take these lockers," Master Sergeant Brooks said. "Just swipe your ID, and they'll be assigned to you."

Alex held his ID up to the reader. It beeped, scanned his face to confirm his identity, then popped open.

"If you get called into action, you can store your personal items there," Brooks continued. "If something happens to you, it all gets bagged up and sent to your next of kin."

"Now there's a cheery thought," Sly said.

"Yeah, that's what we signed up for, right?" Brooks said. "You can't have the action without some danger."

Ash looked at Alex. He couldn't tell what she thinking, and he was too afraid to ask. The last thing he wanted was to get into another argument with her in front of Master Sergeant Brooks and the entire Romeo Company. Fortunately, she didn't say anything—she just looked away as if she were disappointed.

"When there's mission info, we'll get it on the big display," Brooks said, pointing to the rows of seats. "Otherwise, we just hang out here."

"That food dispenser work?" Sly asked.

"You're hungry already?" Newt said.

"Do you have to ask?" Sly replied.

Alex sat on the padded bench and leaned back against his locker. It had been a long day and showed no signs of getting any shorter. The days on a star ship were marked on the clock, but otherwise there were no differences between night and day. Master Sergeant Brooks sat beside him.

"You the kid that saved VP Haley?" Brooks asked.

"Yeah," Alex said, watching as his three teammates got snacks from the food dispenser across the room.

"How'd that go down?" Brooks asked.

"I just happened to be there," Alex said. "My CO and Colonel Bixby had the whole thing planned."

"To kill the VP?"

"Yeah," Alex said in a low voice. "Chief McKinna was harboring a grudge about something. I think the colonel was hoping for a promotion."

"Damn, and they say being an operator's dangerous," Brooks said. "I'd rather face an enemy combatant than worry about some climber stabbing me in the back just to steal my job."

"I agree," Alex said.

"Still, taking out two guys by yourself is saying something," Brooks said. "I heard some crazy story about a flask."

Alex told him how the entire thing happened: the way McKinna reacted to Alex throwing the flask at him, how the shock blast ricocheted from the metal and incapacitated the chief, Alex's use of the chair that broke Colonel Bixby's arm, and how the traitor got a shot off that winged Loman Haley.

"It was all over in a matter of seconds," Alex said.

"That's the way most fights go," Brooks said. "That's why we train so much. In those few seconds when action really counts, you can't stop and think about what to do. You have to just react."

"Telling war stories again?" Ash said, slumping down beside Alex with a sandwich and a disposable cup of orange-flavored energy drink.

"Yeah, something like that," Alex said, trying to sound casual.

"You have any idea what's going to happen down on the planet?" Ash asked Master Sergeant Brooks.

"Right now, a lot of people are cursing their bad luck down on that ice cube," Brooks replied. "There won't be a lot for our people to do while the workers set up the base camp and start drilling for core samples."

"What about the ship coming in?" Newt said. He and Sly were standing in front of Alex, Ash, and Master Sergeant Brooks.

"Has to be a ship registered to another company," Brooks explained. "Most supplies are brought in on freighters, but specialized equipment for the colony being built could come in on a company-specific ship."

"Or a strike team," Ash said.

"That too," Brooks said. "But it's a bit early if you ask me. Most of the corporate types don't like to spend money if there's no guarantee of a return. I suspect they'll wait until they know we're onto something."

"You think it's possible they have people coming into the system on that ship though?" Newt asked.

"My guess is there are several teams from various companies already on the planet," Brooks said. "It's not unusual to go in acting as construction workers or roughnecks, until we get the word to go into action."

"You've done that?" Sly asked.

"Sure, I've been in the CDF for almost two decades. I was finishing up my final enlistment period when we got called to the *Republic*."

"You're quitting?" Ash asked.

"Retiring after twenty years isn't quitting," Brooks said. "Most operators transfer or take a training job after twenty. The company is pretty generous to those of us who make it that long."

"What were you going to do?" Alex asked.

"Take the pension. I've got family on Berring Four. They run a commercial fishing business, and I thought I'd give that a try—after spending a while laying a sandy beach in the tropics."

"Now you're talking," Sly said.

"Won't you go crazy from boredom?" Ash asked.

"Look around, corporal. A ready room is the most boring place in the galaxy," Brooks replied. "I've had twenty years of learning patience. When the drop ship crapped out on us, I figured it was just my luck. My controller kept saying help was on the way, but I didn't believe it. I figured they were just trying to keep us calm before we were incinerated upon entry. A few months from retirement, and I go down in a faulty ship without even a fighting chance. But then you hotshots showed up and gave me a second chance. So when my term is up, I'm making the most of it."

"Can't say I blame you for that," Sly replied.

"I don't think I could give it up," Ash said.

"The military life?" Alex asked.

"The action," Ash said. "I'd rather be a shooting star than a dull ember just biding my time and squeezing out as many boring years of this life as I can."

"Different strokes for different folks," Master Sergeant Brooks said. "For me, the best part of the CDF was always my squad mates."

Alex agreed. He wasn't opposed to action, but the real pull was belonging to something where he could work with good people for a common goal. He had nothing against making money or adventure, but when it came down to it, what he loved about the CDF were the three people on his team.

Before anyone else could speak, a voice sounded from a set of speakers built into the ceiling of the ready room.

*Titan Team, please gather in the briefing area for instructions.*

"Sounds like you're up," Brooks said. "Maybe you'll get your chance to see some action, Corporal Timmons."

Alex shook hands with the master sergeant. "Thanks for the help."

"Always," Brooks said. "Good luck. If you need anything, just let me know."

Alex and the rest of his team sat in the front row of seats. Alex was happy to find that the seats were comfortable and rocked back a little. There was even a cup holder and a small, retractable table for taking notes or setting gear on. Alex had nothing but his PIL, but the others all had drinks and sandwiches. They settled in, and suddenly Chief Landry's face appeared on the large screen.

"Sorry to cut your day short," Landry said. "But Captain Chastain has an assignment for you. As you're aware, a Zen Tech ship entered the system less than an hour ago. They are approaching the planet and should be in orbit in less than eight hours. Their current trajectory would have them entering orbit on the far side of the planet."

"Where we can't see what they're doing," Ash pointed out.

"Exactly," Landry said. "So, we are going to begin a rotational watch of six-hour shifts. This is a surveillance op. I don't want any heroics going on. Odds are good that this is nothing more than a delivery ship bringing in equipment for the colony being set up in Tunis. But we can't be certain, so you'll take turns going out, holding an orbit with a clear view of the dark side of Carthage Prime. Any questions?"

"When do we go?" Alex asked.

"Travel time to the coordinates assigned by Captain Chastain shouldn't be more than an hour. So, you'll need to leave an hour before your duty watch begins. Alex, you'll go first, at 0200. I've sent the rotation to your PILs. Satellites have not been approved, so you'll drop a coms buoy on your way to the assigned position to ensure that there's no interference in communications."

"Roger that," Alex said, mentally calculating how much sleep he could squeeze in before he had to leave for his shift.

"Anything else?" Chief Landry asked, but there were no more questions. "All right, check your PILs for orders, and be careful out there."

The picture disappeared on the display screen. Alex felt his PIL vibrate on his arm and knew it was the message from Chief Landry. He stood up.

"I'm going to get some sleep," Alex said.

"Surveillance? Really?" Ash said.

"Beats simulators," Sly said.

"Barely," she grumbled.

Alex didn't feel like trying to get to the bottom of Ash's complaint. She was unhappy, and while he cared, he didn't have time for a long talk. He would be in hard vacuum for at least eight hours, and he'd already been awake a long time. If he was going to get any rest before his shift, he knew he had to do so quickly.

"Your team is going out?" Master Sergeant Brooks asked as Alex walked across the room.

"Yeah, surveillance duty," Alex said. "I need to get in a nap before I head out."

"There's a sleep kit in your locker," Brooks said. "Grab an empty spot on the bench and get what you need."

Alex had wondered where he might try to rest. He had considered the chairs in the briefing area, but they didn't recline. There was plenty of empty space on the padded benches. It wouldn't be great for a full night's sleep, but for a quick nap it would work. His only other alternative was to walk back to his quarters, and Alex feared that something might make him late for his shift.

At his locker he held up his ID, let the lock scan his face, then opened the door. On the upper shelf was a small packet. Inside were sanitary wipes, caffeinated mouth refresher strips, a sleep mask, and ear plugs. He took the mask and ear plugs and put them on. The ear plugs were small but blocked the sounds around him almost completely. He sat on the padded bench, then pulled the mask from his forehead down over his eyes. It was like being in a dark room, except that he knew he wasn't. He curled up on the bench, which was surprisingly comfortable, and fell asleep.

# Chapter 19

He woke up five hours later when his Flex PIL vibrated on his arm. His body was stiff after hardly moving while he slept. The bench was comfortable but barely wide enough to lay on. He had been worried about rolling off the bench, and that concern had made him tense. He pulled off the sleep mask and found the room to be quiet and dim. Most everyone on the locker side of the room were sleeping. Those that weren't sat in the briefing area, using their PILs for entertainment.

Alex pulled out the earplugs and was assaulted by the rumbling snores of several sleeping operators. He stood up and stretched. He felt more tired than he had when he had gone to sleep, but he knew he just needed to shake out the kinks. He opened his locker, put away the sleep mask and earplugs, picked up one of the caffeinated mouth refreshers, and headed for the bathroom.

After splashing water on his face and drying off, he popped the little green strip into his mouth. A burning, minty flavor filled his mouth instantly, followed by a surge of energy. The strip dissolved almost instantly, but it had done its job. His mouth watered, as did his eyes, and yet he felt invigorated.

When he left the bathroom, he found Ash waiting for him. His PIL revealed the path to the hangar where his Titan waited for him. He had a few minutes before he had to report at the hangar.

"Got a second?" Ash whispered.

"Sure, why don't you walk with me?" Alex said.

They left the ready room and started down the short corridor to the hangar.

"I just want to say I'm sorry," she said.

He stopped and turned to her. He didn't have to ask what had gotten into her—the look on his face did that for him.

"I just sometimes get all twisted up," Ash said. "I'm not like the rest of you. I joined the CDF to be the best."

"You think we didn't?"

"No," she said. "Admit it. You joined to get off that horrible colony world."

"That doesn't mean I don't want to be the best."

"I know, but you don't need it the way I do. I'm driven, Alex. You know that about me. I only have one speed."

"And you think we're holding you back?" Alex asked.

"No, it's not that."

"Then what?"

"I'm jealous, okay," she admitted. "You're not better than me, but you're catching all the breaks, and I'm not used to being second place."

"It's not a competition," Alex said.

"I know that," Ash said. "That's why I'm apologizing. I'm just a little mixed up."

"You want to be team leader? Go ahead, I don't care."

"No, I don't want your pity."

"It's not pity, Ash. I want to contribute, and I want to be part of a team where I'm valued. I don't need to be in charge."

"Which is exactly why you should be," Ash said. "This is my problem, okay? I'll deal with it. You be careful out there."

She reached out and put a hand on his shoulder. There was no one else in the corridor, no one to see them or interrupt. Alex felt a sudden surge of affection for Ash—perhaps it was because she was opening up to him, or maybe it was just a combination of the circumstances. The thought of going out into space alone was frightening and made him want to connect with someone on a deep, meaningful level.

But there was Nyx, and Alex wanted to see if things could develop between them. Not to mention the fact that he was their team leader, and getting involved with Ash romantically was not a good idea. There had been some minor discouraging paragraphs in the operator's handbook about fraternizing with other members of the same squad, but there was no official rule about it. Still, he knew enough to know that they were both vulnerable at that moment, and doing something rash that they would both regret later wasn't wise.

"I will be," he said as casually as he could. "Thanks, Ash."

Her hand fell away, and he thought there was a slight hint of disappointment on her face. He turned away and headed for the hangar, resisting the urge to turn back and look at Ash again. He wanted to see her giving him a friendly smile, but he feared a look of rage, or worse still, tears. And whether he admitted it or not, if he looked back, he might accidentally give her false hope that there was a chance for the two of them to be together.

The hangar door opened as he approached, and he stepped through, relaxing just a little as it slid closed behind him. A technician approached. She was a little older, but not much, and was the same rank as Alex.

"You Evans?"

"Yes," Alex said, extending a hand.

"I'm Everyss," she said. "I take care of your Titan."

"It's nice to meet you," Alex said.

"Likewise," she replied. "Let's get you suited up and on your way."

"Sound's good," Alex said.

Everyss wore a dark blue jumpsuit. There were stains on it. Her handshake was firm, and everything about her indicated that she took her job seriously. She led the way across the hangar. They walked between large, dangerous-looking mechanized battle suits. Despite the trepidation of going into outer space alone, Alex couldn't help but feel fortunate. He was just a kid from a no-name planet, and somehow he'd made his way into the pilot's seat of the most incredible fighting machines in the galaxy.

They came to a row of tall, human-shaped battle suits. The closest one had his initials printed on the chest piece in a dark gray color: ACE. Everyss walked around the MBS, giving it one final visual inspection as Alex climbed the portable steps that had been rolled up beside the battle suit. He had flown Titan training suits, but this was the first time he was going out in an actual FA Titan MBS.

"You can get in," Everyss said. "Everything looks good. You've got a full battery charge. I understand this is a surveillance op, but I've loaded you up with heat-seeking, hard-vac warheads. Just in case."

"Thanks," Alex said.

"I believe in being prepared," she said. "Better to have them and not need them than to need them and not have them."

"Copy that," Alex said.

He felt like he had scored a good technician to keep his Titan in good working order. It made him wonder if someone really was giving him special treatment. His mind went immediately to Loman Haley, Executive VP of Security. Haley certainly had the pull, but Alex wasn't sure why he would go out of his way to help Alex. In fact, Haley had brought him in for questioning. It was a mystery he would have to wait to uncover. He had a mission to do, and as he climbed into the Titan his mind shifted to the task at hand.

The FA Titan seemed brand-new. Every battle suit Alex had been in so far had had a smell. Usually it was sweat or body odor, although sometimes it was more mechanical in nature—hot wiring, oil, or the musty smell of enclosed spaces surrounded by metal. Yet this Titan just smelled new. His feet slipped easily down into the leg pieces and found the flexible pedals with their inverted stirrups.

"We ready?" Alex called out to Everyss.

She gave him a thumbs-up, then pushed the portable stairs away. Alex couldn't help but grin as he pressed the activation button, and the suit closed in around him.

# Chapter 20

Nyx was at her station, waiting patiently for Alex to come online. When he did, she felt a thrill of excitement.

"Hello, stranger," she said.

"Hi, Nyx. How are we looking?"

"Green across the board. I'm sending word to the bridge that you're ready for launch."

"Chief Landry said something about a communication buoy."

"It's loaded into the special ordinance compartment on your suit," Nyx explained. "We'll launch it at the halfway curve."

"Roger that. I'm all set on my end."

Nyx hit a button that opened the command channel. Her tiny headset picked up her voice perfectly and transmitted it to the officers on the bridge.

"Republic command, this is controller NX18. Titan One is ready for launch. Standing by."

"Copy, controller NX18. Moving Titan One to the launch platform now."

Nyx switched back to her direct link with Alex.

"You should be moving to the launch hangar," she said.

"I am. Anything I should know?"

"No, it's just a simple launch like before. Once the doors open, you'll be propelled out and free to operate the Titan as you see fit."

The launch procedure took less than five minutes. The *Republic* was the only ship in orbit, and there was no need for excessive caution. The outer bay doors opened, the magnetic shield was lowered, and Alex was gently cast out of the ship's artificial gravity into open space.

"You're clear, Alex."

"Roger that. Firing thrusters now."

Nyx kept close tabs on the Titan's systems. An eight-hour op was well within the safe range of the mechanized battle suit's power. Being in a weightless environment actually prolonged the Titan's power capacity. Alex could operate for well over fifty hours, especially in a non-combat mode. Still, if a single system malfunctioned, he could be killed or stranded in space. The very thought of it made her shiver.

"You're on course," Nyx said. "Speed is good."

"Just a walk in the park...not that I would know. We didn't have parks on NP8261."

"We didn't have a park on the space station I grew up in, either," Nyx said. "But I did take walks through the hydroponics module."

"My mother was a botanist's helper when I was growing up. We didn't have much, but we always had fresh vegetables to supplement the processed protein rations the company sold."

They kept up a steady banter as the time passed. It took Alex half an hour to reach the drop point for the communication buoy.

"It's automated," Nyx explained. "Just a simple amplifier. Whatever signals you send will be picked up, boosted, and sent on toward the *Republic*."

"I thought satellites weren't approved here yet," Alex said.

"They're not—which is why your team is being used instead of a surveillance satellite."

"But isn't the buoy a satellite?"

"Technically no," Nyx said. "It's too small, with only one real function. It doesn't even have propulsion capabilities."

"Won't it just get pulled down and burned up in atmo?"

"Yes, it will. But that will take weeks, maybe longer. And eventually it will disintegrate and leave no evidence behind."

"That's a little shady."

"Maybe," Nyx said. "We aren't technically breaking any laws. The satellite ban is in place because the planet doesn't have adequate orbital tracking. Satellites would be a danger to ships bringing in vital supplies, but our little buoy is too small to cause damage to a space vessel. And it's engineered to break apart on contact."

Alex launched the coms buoy and continued around the curve of the planet. Nyx could still get a reading on the suit's systems, but Alex was effectively out of sight. The *Republic's* sophisticated radar system couldn't pick him up on the far side of the planet. Half an hour later, he was in position.

"What now?"

"Now we wait," Nyx said. "It shouldn't be long before you pick up the Zen Tech ship."

Nyx optimized the Titan's systems without explaining it all to Alex. His job was to be the spy, hers was to make sure the officers on the *Republic* got the information from him. The FA Titan was a versatile MBS, the most effective combat mech in the CDF's fleet, but also the most difficult to operate. Yet combat was just one role the Titan could play; it was also an effective spy when the need arose. As Alex's controller, Nyx could narrow the suit's outward-bound transmissions into a tight beam of information, which she directed straight toward the buoy. She could not only hear his reports, but she had full readings of the suit's systems and could display the exact same visuals that Alex saw himself. His eyes were useless sealed up inside the Titan battle suit. There was no window —all visuals were picked up by the suit's tiny cameras, and the digital feed was translated by the INC chip into visual representation by his brain. The INC also replicated that information and sent it back out of the Titan to the controller. Nyx made sure she could see what Alex was seeing and that the senior officers on the bridge of the *Republic* had full access, as well.

So far, there wasn't much to see. Alex was on the dark side of the planet. A glowing line marked the far edge of Carthage Prime. Alex and Nyx watched that glowing line for the arrival of the Zen Tech ship. When it came, it was like a shadow.

"She's killed her running lights," Alex explained. "I can't keep visual track in the darkness on this side of the planet."

"No worries," Nyx said, typing away at her console. "I'm bringing up thermal vision now."

The image on Nyx's screen and in Alex's head changed. The dark side of the planet began to glow a deep purple. Space was still black, but the Zen Tech ship was a red blob with yellow and white lines at the engine exhaust ports.

"Wow," Alex said.

"We have a strong visual," Nyx added. "We should be able to keep tabs easily enough."

The ship settled into orbit and seemed to come to a complete stop. For several hours, nothing seemed to happen. Whatever the officers on the rival ship were doing, they were taking their time. Eventually, when Alex's shift was nearly over, a smaller blob left the Zen Tech ship and headed for the northern hemisphere of the planet.

"Looks like they're delivering goods to the colony," Nyx said.

"Yeah, but why hide out on the dark side of the planet if you're just making a delivery?"

"Probably because we were here first," Nyx said. "They're a direct competitor, and they don't want us to know what they're doing any more than we want them knowing what we're up to."

"But they already know, right? We bid for the planet's mineral rights, and that was public."

"True, in this case they know. Which is why we aren't being more secretive."

A few minutes later, Sly arrived to relieve Alex. They talked about what had happened, and then Alex began his journey back to the *Republic*.

"Feels good to be moving again," Alex said. "Doing something is better than nothing in my book."

"Watch duty is usually boring," Nyx said. "You handled it well."

"There was something to watch for at first. And at least we could talk. That helps."

Nyx felt a tingle deep inside. Was Alex flirting? She couldn't tell. Real life was nothing like the holo-films, in which men and women were smooth-talking and confident. Her experience was much more awkward and difficult. She liked Alex. A controller falling for their operator wasn't unheard of, but there was a danger to falling in love with someone who put their lives on the line. Some controllers were never the same after their operators died in action. Nyx wanted a long and distinguished career in the CDF. She always imagined that love and family would come later in life, probably from somewhere outside of her work. But the more time she spent working with Alex, the closer she felt to him. Their few times together in person were the highlights of her short professional life.

But she was a novice at love. There were signals and implications that were like a foreign language to her. She needed a translator, but she was completely on her own. And she knew she was on dangerous ground with Alex. If she fell in love with him but he didn't have feelings for her, it could ruin their working relationship. If she could no longer work with Alex, she'd have to request a new operator—and controllers requesting new operators were shuffled to the end of the waiting list. She might get stuck on a small orbital station on a sleeping world on the edge of Ahzco's galactic territory, where nothing ever happened. She could be paired with an operator in a Defender or Patroller MBS. She didn't think she could be happy with such a simple battle suit and playing a small role after being paired with Alex in the elite FA Titan. Basically, she was risking her career by even entertaining the idea of a romance with Alex.

She would have to tread carefully. Risking her career wasn't smart, but neither was manipulating her emotions. There was more to being a controller than she had imagined, yet she was determined to be great. Nothing could interfere with her ambition—not even Alex. It was a painful thought, but she refused to budge. Her dreams were more important than any boy, and she was determined to see them come true.

# Chapter 21

Alex reached the *Republic* with no difficulties. The Titan MBS was like a second skin once his INC was synced with the battle suit's computer controls. He didn't feel claustrophobic or even tired. The only unpleasant part of his tour was the boredom. Coming back around to the light side of the planet was satisfying. On the dark side, a million stars were visible in the great void of space, but on the light side the beauty of Carthage Prime held his attention.

He passed through the artificial gravity barrier and came down on the Titan's feet inside the launch hangar. In his absence, the drop ships had returned. He came into the *Republic* between two of the slick vessels used for ferrying operators into combat zones. They looked powerful, but bloated and heavy. The FA Titan, on the other hand, was light, sleek, and powerful in its own right. Alex absolutely loved being a Titan operator. He wasn't anxious to get into a fight, but he looked forward to seeing what his team could do in the powerful battle suits.

After striding across the launch hangar, he made his way into the MBS hangar. He was met almost immediately by Everyss, who waved him back to the harness that would support and recharge the suit as soon as he was out of it. She hooked the harness onto the battle suit with swift efficiency and then rolled the portable stairs up close beside him as he opened the Titan.

"How was your first time out?" Everyss asked.

"Perfection," Alex admitted. "The suit is perfect."

"I'll take that as a compliment," she said. "I'll have it recharged and ready, Corporal."

"Thank you," Alex said.

His stomach growled as he left the hangar. He retrieved his PIL from the locker in the ready room. The other operators had mostly moved on. There were two messages on his PIL. One was from Chief Landry, giving him permission to return to his berth and use the facilities in the operator section of the ship. The second was from Ash. She and Newt were in the chow hall waiting for him.

He was slowly becoming familiar with the winding passageways of the spaceship. He found his way to the chow hall without using the map on his Flex PIL, which he had snapped onto his forearm. He walked into the nearly empty chow hall and saw his friends at a table, waiting on him. After retrieving a bowl of pasta that came with crackers and a container of steamed broccoli, he joined his friends at the table.

"How was it?" Newt asked.

"Sort of like a simulation," Alex said, "but longer."

"That sounds dull," Ash said.

"What can I say—it's surveillance," Alex said. "Odds are, the Zen Tech ship is just delivering supplies."

"Boring," Ash decided.

"Is it hard being out alone?" Newt asked.

"Not really," Alex said. "You've got your controller to talk to."

"My controller doesn't talk," Newt said. "He spits out information like a computer. I think AI has more personality."

"Mine's a barrel of monkeys," Ash said sarcastically. "It's like flying with my mother. She's constantly telling me to slow down."

They chatted while they ate. Newt had the third shift, and Ash was up after that. Once they finished eating, Newt headed off to the ready room, while Ash went to their quarters to get some sleep. Alex decided to go to the weight room. It took a few minutes of trial and error to figure out the controls on the circuit machine, but once he had it set up, he powered through a full workout. After hardly using his muscles at all in zero-gravity, it felt good to push himself. He left the gym tired, sweaty, and happy. He was living a life he'd never imagined possible. Not only had he left the dreary colony on NP8261 far behind, but now he was actually an operator in the CDF. After spending the last eight hours in space operating an FA Titan, he couldn't imagine anything better than being in the Corporate Defense Force.

He returned to his berth to shower and get some rest. Ash was in her bunk. She had dialed up the opacity of the transparent door to her recessed sleeping pod. It blocked light and made it impossible to see who was inside the pod or what they were doing. Alex guessed she was sleeping, but he couldn't say for sure.

After taking a shower, he stretched out on his bed in the small private room he'd been assigned. The room was a lot like his bedroom growing up, only with less clutter. He wondered if he would be on the *Republic* long enough for him to add a few personal touches. He activated his PIL and checked for messages. There were none. Being at the edge of open space, transmit times for messages were longer than before, even on Ahzco's company network.

With no news from his parents, he felt a pang of loneliness and browsed through his pictures of them. There weren't many on his PIL, and he wished he had taken more before leaving NP8261. He had hoped to see them once he completed training. He couldn't help but wonder what Skandia Seven was like. Alex had never been to a level-one planet. His condition for joining the CDF was a transfer for his father, and Loman Haley had even included a bonus that allowed them to purchase a small home. He typed out a quick message telling them he'd been promoted to corporal but leaving out any details of the mission he was on. The last thing he wanted was to have them worrying about him.

He checked the company site and saw that his promotion came with a bump in pay. His banking account could grow while he was deployed on the *Republic*. His ship credits accumulated since he didn't get up to the entertainment levels often, although it did cross his mind that he could go up and meet with Nyx sometime. He wondered what that would be like. Would his team resent it? He had dated a time or two growing up, but it was never really serious. The girls were more like friends than love interests, and the dates were really about just going through the motions—more of a social activity than an actual romantic encounter.

There was too much pressure to even consider going up for a while. The threat alert had been dialed back to orange, but there was still a chance that the Zen Tech ship could attack them. He didn't want to be six levels up watching a holo-film if the ship were attacked and his team was called into action.

He read for a short while before setting his PIL to wake in him eight hours, then put it on standby cuffed on his forearm. He turned the lights off and lay in the darkness, wondering what Nyx was doing, as he drifted off to sleep.

A week went by, and Alex began counting the days according to his shifts on surveillance duty. He adjusted to the routine easily enough: breakfast with Sly and Newt, his watch shift off the ship, then back for dinner with Ash and Newt. Some days he went for a long walk after dinner or hit the gym to work up a good sweat. He almost always spent an hour reading before bed. One thing his credit account afforded him was the ability to purchase books from the online bookstore of his choice. He soon had a virtual library of books waiting to be read.

His work was boring at times, and isolation was hard to avoid. His team had created their own routines, and while they spent time together every day, he felt like there was distance between them. His relationship with Nyx was growing, but he felt as if there were barriers between them, too. He had been thinking of inviting her to have a meal on the entertainment level with him, but something about her demeanor had changed. It was hard to be certain, though, since he heard her in his head as if her voice was actually his own inner monologue. He talked to Sly and Newt about his feelings, but not Ash. Their relationship had cooled since the yellow alert. Everyone seemed to be moving away from Alex, creating intentional distance. He didn't know if it was because of him or simply to avoid being hurt, but it made him feel like something was wrong.

In the end, he decided just to focus on the work and his routine. There was no need to shake things up. On the eighth day, shortly after Ash had gone on watch, Alex was awakened by a ship-wide announcement.

"Yellow alert. I repeat, this is a yellow alert. All personnel report to their stations."

At the same time, Alex's PIL vibrated on his arm. He was struggling to wake up as he activated the PIL and looked at the message: *Titan team report to ready room 108.*

He got to his feet, stretched, then pulled on his compression fatigues. He was still tugging at the tight-fitting clothes as he hurried down the corridor. He made his way to the ready room and found his friends, including Master Sergeant Brooks, waiting. The NCO waved him over to the briefing section where everyone else was gathered. Chief Landry was already speaking via the large display screen.

"...have set up operations on this plateau, at the northern end of the Cipius mountain range. The operators on the ground have two primary objectives. First, protect the miners drilling for ore, including the expeditions to surrounding sites. And second, maintain passage from Tunis to the base of operations..."

"What's going on?" Alex whispered to Sly.

"The ship we've been watching sent drop ships to the southern hemisphere," Sly whispered back.

"...land mass is massive, with most ground water frozen, creating one super continent in the southern hemisphere," Chief Landry continued. "Odds are high that the landing parties we have observed are merely there to poach ore, but they could be combat forces, and if so, we have to be ready to intervene. To that end, Romeo Company will board a drop ship tasked with slipping into atmo and doing an aerial reconnaissance of the Zen Tech vessels. Master Sergeant Brooks, your squad should be ready for immediate deployment in the case of an attack."

"Roger that, Chief," Brooks replied. "We'll be ready."

"Titan Team, all further recon missions are canceled until further notice," Landry said. "You're to be in a state of readiness at all times. If combat is initiated, you will make a precision entry from orbit and bring the full weight of your FA Titan team to bear wherever you're needed. Any questions?"

"No, Chief," Alex said.

"Very good. Stand by for further orders." The screen went black as the transmission ended.

"All right, you heard the man," Master Sergeant Brooks shouted at his squad. "Romeo Company, get your gear ready and report to the MBS hangar. I want everyone suited up and ready to rock in fifteen minutes."

The squad rumbled past Alex and began getting ready. There was a mix of excitement and frustration. Being suited up but clamped into a drop ship was not Alex's idea of fun. He could only guess how Romeo Company felt about it after their last experience. Who knew how long they would be confined in the drop ship?

Alex sat down next to Sly and Newt. He needed one of the refresh strips with its jolt of caffeine, but he decided to wait until Romeo Company had cleared out.

"Sounds like Ash may get some action, after all," Newt said.

"Yeah, maybe," Alex said. "Do you guys have everything you need?"

"I wouldn't say no to a quick shower," Sly said. "I'm getting ripe."

"We know," Newt said.

"Go get it," Alex said. "Odds are high that this is the only free time we'll have for a while."

"Thanks," Sly said, slipping past Newt and Alex.

"When was the last time you slept?" Alex said.

"I got in eight hours," Newt said. "If you want to crash, I'll make sure Sly gets back here."

"Okay, thanks," Alex replied. "You wake me if there's any news at all."

"Sure, Ace, no problem."

The ready room cleared out, and Alex dialed the light down. Newt was on his PIL, and Alex slipped on the sleep mask but left the ear plugs out. If there was trouble, he didn't want to be caught off guard. His body had burned through the adrenaline that he'd felt upon being wakened by the yellow alert. He stretched out on a padded bench and was grateful for the chance to sneak in a little more rest. The sleep mask blocked the light, and he was soon able to drift off into a fitful doze.

# Chapter 22

Alex was awakened an hour later when his PIL vibrated. He pulled off the sleep mask and sat up. Ash was standing by the food dispenser, wolfing down a quick meal. Newt and Sly were standing near the briefing area. Both of them were looking at their PILs and talking.

The Flex PIL on Alex's forearm showed a message. The Titan team was being called to action. Alex felt a tremor of panic—he didn't feel ready, but it was too late to back out. He stood up, popped open his locker, and retrieved a caffeine strip. He placed it in his mouth and felt the sudden, flavorful burn followed by the jolt of energy. Suddenly his fears were cast aside, and now he felt invincible.

They had five minutes to report to the MBS hangar. Alex walked up to Ash and started pouring himself a drink.

"Eventful watch?" he said.

She nodded, her mouth full of food. "It's going down," she mumbled.

"Not without us," Alex said.

He gulped down the sports drink and turned to the others. "You guys ready?"

"Sittin' on go," Sly replied.

"Always," Newt replied.

It wasn't lost on Alex that their confidence had grown over the past week. Moving from simulators to actual missions had been good for his team. They had no idea what to expect once they launched on the latest op, but they were all excited about it.

"Let's stay that way," Alex said. "Head on a swivel. We work together as a team."

"Roger that," Newt said.

"Man, I'm pumped," Sly said.

"Ready," Ash said, swallowing the last half-chewed mouthful of her hasty meal.

"All right, Titan team—let's go," Alex ordered.

He wasn't their superior, but every team needed a leader. The four Titan operators were more than just colleagues; they had developed a tight bond and genuine friendships. Alex was excited to be working with them again, even if it was on a combat drop. This was what they had trained for and what they knew was coming. They all wanted to get their first fight out of the way, along with the crazy nervousness that came with it.

They walked to the MBS hangar together. There was a noticeable absence of battle suits, which Alex guessed Romeo Company had taken on their drop ship.

"How long was I asleep?" Alex asked.

"About an hour," Newt said. "Romeo Company departed forty minutes ago."

"Ash just got back," Sly said.

"Just in time," she replied.

"It's good that you're here," Alex said as he climbed up into his FA Titan battle suit. "Everyss, will Ash's suit have enough power?"

"We swapped out the power supply," Everyss said as she made a few adjustments to his Titan, "and changed the munitions load on all your battle suits."

"What are we carrying?" Alex asked.

"Air-to-ground missiles, along with laser and soft-alloy projectiles," Everyss said. "Don't wreck my tech, flyboy."

"Yes, Corporal," Alex said with a grin.

She gave him a thumbs-up. They were the same rank, and giving him orders wasn't her job, but he knew it was her way of wishing him luck. He snapped off a quick salute, then activated his battle suit.

*Hello, Alex.*

"Hi, Nyx, what do you know?"

*The same as you at this point. I don't think the Zen Tech forces are poaching.*

"What makes you say that?" Alex asked.

*I took a stroll and eavesdropped on the other controllers. Sounds like they're getting ready for a fight.*

"Well, that's what we're here for, I guess."

There was a pause. The harness that Alex was hanging in began to move toward the launch bay. Chief Landry's voice came through the Titan's communication system.

"Heads up, team, let's have a comms check," he ordered.

"Titan One, I read you."

Newt was Titan Two, Sly Three, and Ash was Titan Four. They all checked in over the command channel. The harnesses released and the inner doors began to open, revealing space and the white gleam of Carthage Prime down below.

"We have a preliminary sit rep from the planet," Landry began to explain. "Radiation readings indicate that at least some of the drop ships from the Zen Tech ship carried kamikazi drones."

"Beautiful," Ash said.

"They're not attempting to drill or steal ore. This is an attack, but we don't have good radar. The drop ship is circling the plateau where our people have set up camp. Your mission is to find those drones and take them out."

"Air strikes, Chief?" Sly asked.

"Absolutely. Maybe we'll get lucky and they'll be bunched up. Those drones carry heavy warheads. You get one close to the others, and it could set off a chain reaction."

"Wipe them all out," Ash said. "Oh, yeah."

"You have to find them first," Landry said. "Be careful. The atmo on Carthage can be choppy."

"Roger that, Chief," Newt said.

"Keep one more thing in mind," Landry said, his voice deadly serious. "If even one of those drones gets away, it could wipe out our entire operation down and odds are, there's more than just the drones. Watch your six, but don't let them get past you. Every employee on the ground, even the other operators, are counting on you."

"We won't let you down, sir," Alex said.

"Good luck, Titan team. Launch is in thirty seconds."

"Follow your controller's instructions," Alex said. "We'll make our search from ten thousand meters. If you see any sign of the drones, you report it. Let's be smart about this."

The members of his team all agreed. The magnetic shield dropped, and the ship's auto-launcher propelled him gently out of the bay, through the artificial gravity barrier, and into his first combat mission.

# Chapter 23

Moving through space had its challenges, but dipping into the atmosphere of a planet felt to Alex like he was being shaken by a giant. Gravity had a firm grip on him, pulling him down, while the friction from the air battered him. The Titan battle suit absorbed the heat, converting it to usable power that fed into the suit's already fully charged power cell. Alex had flown in atmosphere many times, but he'd never made planetary entry except on simulators. The difference was shocking. He had to trust the battle suit and wait for the repulsers to slow him enough that he could take charge again.

*Approaching ten thousand meters.*

"Thank you," Alex said. "How far are we from the base camp?"

*About two hundred kilometers southeast. You should be able to follow the mountains north straight to the camp if you need to.*

"If the drones are in those mountains, they'll be much harder to spot," Alex said, before activating his team's channel on the com-link. "Newt, if the kamis are in the mountains, we have to find them."

"I had that thought myself," Newt replied.

"Why don't you and Sly do a careful recon of the mountains. Ash, you head east over the mountains and see what's beyond them. I'll search this side."

"Copy," Ash said.

He turned to his left and began scanning the ground far below for anything that might indicate movement. Somewhere across the vast, icy landscape, there were kamikaze drones and probably rival operators in Zen Tech battle suits. It seemed strange that his training hadn't included a lot of information about other companies' battle suits. Most of what he knew, including the devastating power of the kamis, was from simulations. He wouldn't know what the Zen Tech operators were in or what their capabilities were until he saw them, and then only if he recognized the battle mechs they were in.

"Let's make sure we maintain communications," Alex said.

"We'll let you know when we find them," Sly said. "First sighting wins the prize."

"What prize?" Newt asked.

"Free dinner," Sly said. "Out, not in the chow hall. Don't tease me like that."

"I'm game," Alex said.

"Sure, why not?" Ash added.

"Okay, but no cheating," Newt said.

Once Alex leveled off, the air seemed much smoother, but there were still pockets of chop. Where the thermal updrafts came from, Alex had no idea. The ground far below was covered in white. The Titan's visual feeds dimmed to keep the glare from overwhelming everything. It wasn't easy to make out the details on the ground, but he had one advantage: the drones, which were the size of cattle, would be moving. They rode on cushions of air, which might or might not kick up the powdery snow on the surface of the planet's southern hemisphere. There weren't many trees—just short, shrubby flora that could survive the harsh environment.

Alex was beginning to circle back, still looking for any signs of the corporate raiders or their drones, but he wasn't having any luck. He wondered if he was too high. The Titan's optics could zoom down and allow him to get a much closer view of the ground, but he feared that the drones might have some sort of camouflage.

"I've got movement," Alex said.

*I'm zooming in.*

"I'm pretty sure it's just some animals," Alex said.

*Better safe than sorry,* Nyx replied. *They're heading straight for the mountains.*

Alex knew that anything moving west was heading for the mountains, and that didn't really indicate anything of substance for their search. Still, he agreed with Nyx that it was better to be cautious. This was his first mission, and the last thing he wanted was to make a careless mistake.

The optical feed zoomed down. To Alex it seemed like he had suddenly dropped down to just a hundred meters above the ground. The movement was indeed animals of some sort. Their shaggy, gray fur was covered with snow. They lumbered slowly across the tundra.

*Looks like you called it.*

"We still have a lot of ground to cover."

He continued the search, but it wasn't long before Ash made contact via their com-link.

"Alex, I have something."

"You've spotted them?" Alex asked.

"Negative, but I have what looks like tracks," Ash replied.

*There are a lot of animals on Carthage Prime,* Nyx reminded Alex.

"We just saw a herd of animals," Alex said. "You sure they're not just animal tracks?"

"These tracks are straight as an arrow," Ash replied. "That's not the problem."

"What is?" Alex asked.

"The problem is that they're headed north, not toward the base camp."

That did seem odd. His first thought was that perhaps they were just maneuvering around the mountains. The Ahzco team had set up on a plateau at the northern tip of the mountain range.

"All right," Alex said. "Ash, follow the tracks. I'm heading back your way."

"Roger that—following the tracks north."

*Are we sure they're moving north and not south?*

"I don't know," Alex said. "Why don't you search the terrain and identify where they might be headed on the far side of the mountains. I need to report to Chief Landry."

Alex shifted com channels with a thought, the way one might glance from a device in their hands to another part of the room. Being synced to the powerful computer inside the Titan MBS gave him a feeling of strength and power unlike anything else. He wasn't just connected to the suit; he had full control of its amazing capabilities.

"Chief Landry, this is Titan One," Alex said.

"We read you, Titan One. Go ahead."

The communications officer's voice sounded slightly muted over the Titan's internal speakers. Alex knew it wasn't Chief Landry, but that didn't matter. As long as the senior officers on the *Republic* were getting his message, he felt confident he was doing the right thing.

"Titan Four has found tracks heading north. We're investigating the possibility that it is the Zen Tech forces."

"We have her visuals and concur," the communications officer replied. "You may proceed, Titan One."

"Roger that. I'm moving to join Titan Four. Evans out."

He was flying back toward the mountains, but he had a long way to go still.

"Nyx, how far out is Ash?"

*Approximately eight hundred kilometers.*

"All right, I'm increasing speed," Alex said. "Are Newt and Sly still over the mountains?"

*Affirmative, but south of your current trajectory.*

"Good deal," Alex said.

The Titan battle suit shifted slightly. The weapons, like arms on either side of the Titan's body, recessed into the suit's exterior armor. The result was reminiscent of a diver holding their arms tightly to their sides. Booster engines added thrust, and the suit gained speed, nearing the sound barrier.

*Alex, I see no targets north or south.*

"Maybe they're angling around the mountains," Alex suggested.

*That doesn't really make sense, either. The plateau stands above the surrounding ground to the north and west, but on the eastern side it's a gradual descent.*

"So maybe they're going to turn north?"

*According to Ash's position, she's already north of the mountain range.*

It didn't make sense. Alex knew Zen Tech might want to steal the valuable ore from the Ahzco miners, and perhaps even set up their own operations on the planet. The world was certainly big enough for multiple mining interests. Ahzco had a contract for the mineral rights on the southern hemisphere of Carthage Prime, but possession was nine tenths of the law. The only real way to get a rival off the planet would be to fight them off. But if Zen Tech merely planned to begin mining on Carthage Prime, why send kamikaze drones? It was obviously an attack force, but they were going the wrong way. It didn't make sense.

*Oh my god,* Nyx said. There was a tone to her voice that caught Alex off guard.

"What is it? What's wrong?"

*They aren't here for us.*

"They're not?"

*No, Alex. They're headed straight for the colony—Tunis.*

Alex switched to his team channel without conscious thought. "Ash?"

"Yeah, I'm here," she replied.

"Any sign of them?"

"Negative. Maybe I was wrong and they're headed south."

"I don't think so," Alex said. He felt a lump forming in his gut. He switched effortlessly to his link with Nyx. "How far are we to the colony?"

*Checking...twenty-five hundred kilometers, Alex.*

He knew the maximum speed of the Titan was fourteen hundred kilometers per hour. That put them ninety minutes from the city.

"How long have the Zen Tech forces been on the ground?"

*Already calculating. Best estimate of their land speed would have them arriving in just over two hours.*

"We can get there first," Alex said. He switched back to his team channel. "Everyone, the raiders are headed for Tunis, not our mining operation," Alex said. "Head north right now. Maximum speed."

"Copy that, team leader," Newt said.

"Wait a second," Sly said. "Why would Zen Tech attack the colony? We probably only have a small presence there. It's mostly settlers and merchants."

*Control,* Nyx said. *If they control the colony, they can cut off our supplies and make it nearly impossible to mine the ore on Carthage Prime.*

"Strategy and Tactics," Alex replied. "They're cutting off our supply train, Sly. The environment is too harsh for our miners to survive without access to the city in the north."

"But the people in Tunis aren't employees of Ahzco," Newt pointed out. "They're innocent."

"You think they care about that?" Ash said.

"They don't need the settlers and merchants dead," Alex pointed out. "As long as Zen Tech controls the city, Ahzco will be forced to pull out."

"Maybe," Sly said. "But they don't have a force large enough to fight us off for long."

"Not yet," Alex said. "My guess is they have more coming very soon. And if we don't stop the attack on the city, a lot of innocent people are going to die."

# Chapter 24

"We've come to the same conclusion," Chief Landry said. "We've already sent the drop ship with Romeo Company north. Echo Company is in the city currently and will help defend it. Your job is to stop those drones."

"Roger that, Chief," Alex said. "We're en route now. Maximum speed."

"Watch yourselves," Landry said. "Those drones are dangerous. Maintain safe distances when you engage. If you get caught in their blast radius, it could damage your MBS."

Alex felt a shiver of fear run down his back, but he set the fear aside, just as Master Sergeant Grossman had taught him. He was in superior battle armor with flight capabilities. There was no reason to fear the drones.

The Titan team all signaled their acceptance of Chief Landry's warning. Alex could see Ash in the distance. Newt and Sly were following behind, each well-spaced but pushing ahead with all the power they could muster. Below them, the frozen ground was slowly giving way to softer areas. They crossed over a river that wasn't completely frozen. It looked black, like a tiny capillary cutting across the snowy landscape. In places the ground was visible, and far to Alex's left he could make out a large body of water.

*Forty minutes and you'll reach the city,* Nyx said. *You should catch sight of the Zen Tech operators soon.*

Alex was about to respond, but Ash's voice over their team channel spoke first.

"I see them," she said.

"Winner, winner, we owe a free dinner," Sly said in a sing-song voice.

"Looks like forty MBS's or so. It's hard to be certain," Ash said. "They're kicking up a snow cloud."

"We have them in sight now," Alex said to Nyx before switching channels. "Newt, you stay with the MBS's. I want you well out of their range, but keep tabs on them."

"You got it, team leader," Newt said.

"Ash, any sign of the drones?" Alex asked.

"Not yet," Ash said.

"Okay, we keep going straight toward Tunis until we spot them," Alex said.

Alex could see the snow cloud. It was like the dust on Helena Prime, only white and heavier, and it didn't stay in the air as long. Alex could make out the dark shapes of the ground-based MBS's. They looked like Zen Tech Hunter-class battle suits, but it was impossible to tell from ten thousand meters up. He could have used the Titan's optical zoom to get more details, but instead he continued scanning in search of the drones.

"If they've painted the kamis white," Sly said. "They'll be hard to see against the snow."

"Keep trying," Alex said. "We don't quit because something's hard."

Ten minutes later, the drones were visible. A large group of small hovercraft, they looked like dots far below. Fortunately, they were bunched together.

"Should I engage?" Ash asked.

"No, wait for me and Sly to catch up to your position. We'll hit them in a cross-fire."

"Ace, there are at least a hundred of them," Ash said. "Half that many could destroy the entire colony."

"You've got eyes on them, Ash," Alex said. "Call it in."

*You'll be at her position in sixty-eight seconds at this speed.*

"Thanks, Nyx," Alex said.

"Republic, this is Titan Four. I have eyes on the kamikaze drones," Ash said.

"We read you, Titan Four," came the reply from the starship in orbit above the planet. "Titan Team leader will coordinate the strike."

"Let's go with soft-alloy rounds," Alex said. "Ash, you've got point. Sly, you take the east flank. I'll go west."

*Spinning up soft-alloy projectiles, fully automatic. You're two hundred kilometers from Tunis. The drones are half an hour from the city at their current speed.*

"Now's the time to stop them, then," Alex said, angling down and to his left. "Sly, what's your position?"

"Almost there, Ace," Sly responded. "I just need a few more seconds."

"They're on to us," Ash said. "The horde is starting to break apart."

Alex could see what she meant. Just seconds before they had been moving in close proximity to one another, but they were starting to spread out.

"Hit them now," Alex said. "Before it's too late."

Ash's cannon opened fire. Tracer rounds showed the barrage of projectiles raining down onto the drones. Alex wasn't prepared for the explosions. They blossomed like huge, fiery pillars shooting upward and crowned with dense, black smoke. There were multiple explosions, but the drones were spreading wide in an effort to avoid Ash's gunfire.

"Here we go," Alex said quietly.

He squeezed the trigger on the right-hand joystick. His own barrage of soft metal bullets shot out. They were heavy but aerodynamic, with small fins that helped them fly true. Alex aimed high and let the planet's gravity pull the projectiles down in a gentle arc.  The first bullets missed, but Alex quickly adjusted his aim. Explosions bloomed, and the sound rolled out toward Alex like distant thunder. He was hovering fifteen hundred meters above the ground. The drones were spreading out, trying to avoid the incoming fire from the Titans. The smoke was beginning to block their ability to target the drones.

Sly came in from behind the drones and rained fire down onto the group. Those bunched together were caught in the explosions, creating a domino effect, but out of the chaos nearly a quarter of their number escaped. They spread out, creating distance between them and forcing the Titan operators to target them individually.

"Switch me to lasers," Alex said.

"They're speeding up," Ash called out.

*I think the air-to-ground missiles would be more effective.*

"We have a limited number of missiles, and we still have to deal with those Hunters," Alex said. "Stick with the lasers."

*Roger that.*

"Take them out one by one," Alex said. "We can't let any get to the city."

"Roger that, team leader," Sly said.

*Laser cannon is charged and ready.*

"Thanks, Nyx," Alex said. "Sly, get high enough to keep them all in sight."

He fired at the nearest drone, but its armor was magnetically shielded. The beam of red light, visible to Alex via the Titan's enhanced optics, bounced off the drone.

"They've got shields," he said.

"Switching to missiles," Ash said.

She fired seven missiles in rapid succession. Alex saw them flying like tiny rockets, leaving pinstripe contrails in their wake. They spread out, each one targeting an individual drone and taking them out in spectacular fashion.

"You were right, switch me to missiles," Alex said to Nyx. He expected her to gloat, or at least tease him a little, but Nyx was all business.

*Air-to-ground missiles are ready. Fire as they lock onto their targets.*

Alex could have let the targeting software communicate with his brain directly, but the information was overwhelming. He held it back, just taking note when a drone was locked on. He fired his own missiles, six in all. Sly was sending down more as he rose up through the air. The drones were running fast, picking up speed as they charged across the snowy ground. But they couldn't outrun the missiles. Alex had to fly back to avoid the first and closest detonation. He felt the shockwave rock his Titan, but he knew he wasn't in danger of taking damage.

*That was close.*

"Yeah, those drones pack a punch," Alex said. "Newt, what's your status?"

"I can see the explosions," Newt said. "Mostly the smoke. The Hunters have slowed, but they're still proceeding, just with more caution. They're spreading out in a long line. A few have tried to target me, but I'm up to thirty thousand meters and they haven't fired yet."

"Do you have a solid number?" Alex asked.

"Forty-eight," Newt said.

*There are two more drones*, Nyx warned him.

Alex gave pursuit and took them out with missiles, as Ashton finished off the final drone.

"Looks like we're clear," Sly declared.

*There could be more hiding in the smoke, biding their time.*

"Good point," Alex said. "Sly, you stay here. Watch for anything moving. Ash, you mop up any that might be hiding in the smoke."

"Copy that," Ash said.

"Don't forget there are MBS's moving this way," Alex warned his team. "If they have ground-to-air missiles, you go high as fast as you can. Don't engage until you hear from me. I'm heading to the colony to coordinate the defense with Romeo Company."

"Do your thing, Ace," Sly replied. "We've got this."

Alex hated leaving the others behind, but he was confident they had things under control. He wouldn't be out of contact, just out of sight. He needed to find out how Romeo Company planned to defend the city against forty-eight enemy MBS's and how Alex's team of four FA Titans could best be deployed to help.

It took several minutes to reach the colony once Alex got the Titan back up to top speed. He began a long, spiral descent that gave him a good view of the colony. Alex didn't know much about Tunis, but it appeared to be built right on the snow line. One side of the city was surrounded by dark green grass, but the other had a light dusting of snow. There were trees on the outskirts of the hastily constructed village. One end of Tunis was lined with reinforced landing pads, and Alex saw several cargo ships lined up in the spaceport. The colony itself was built in sections. There were warehouses next to the spaceport—large, nondescript buildings built to hold goods from building supplies to toys and games. Next to the warehouse district was an industrial space. Solar and wind power was being harnessed, water was being filtered and recycled, and there were even large-scale fabricators operated by powerful computers to create custom parts and materials needed by the colonists. A river separated the colony right down the middle. The housing, shopping, and entertainment sections were on the opposite side of the river from the spaceport.

Alex saw the drop ship offloading the MBS's from Romeo Company onto one of the large landing pads. He opened his com-link to the command channel and radioed to Master Sergeant Brooks.

"Titan One calling Master Sergeant Brooks of Romeo Company. Do you read?"

"I have you five by five, Titan One," came Brooks' familiar voice.

"We've taken out the kamikaze drones," Alex said. "But there are almost fifty Zen Tech Hunters headed your way."

"We just got the word," Brooks said. "Romeo Company is taking the lead in defending the city. Echo Company is being rallied, but that still leaves us outnumbered two to one."

"Tell us how we can even the odds," Alex said.

"The best way to protect the city is to take out the Hunters before they get here. Those bastards have a long reach, though. Primex ground-to-air missiles can reach up to seventy-five thousand meters, and their laser cannons pack a punch. Is there any cover between us? What's the ground like?"

"Flat, snowy—there aren't even any trees to the south, Master Sergeant," Alex said. "It's all open country."

"That just figures," Brooks said.

Alex could see the master sergeant's AT Interceptor leading his platoon from the airfield. There were three Interceptors, tank-like hovercraft, and nine Destroyers that trundled along on treads with twin cannons and thick armor.

"What can you tell me about Echo Company?" Brooks asked.

"Three Interceptors, two Destroyers, four Minotaurs, and a Medic," Alex said. "We're part of Echo Company, and this is our first combat engagement."

"Who's in charge?" Brooks asked.

"That would be me," Master Sergeant Geller said over the com-link. "Master Sergeant Kay Gellar. We're suited up and ready. We'll meet you on the south side of town."

"Outstanding," Brooks said. "This is shaping up into a decent fight. Let's combine our Interceptors and Destroyers at the center of the line. The Titans and Minotaurs can work the flanks"

"Works for me," Gellar said.

Alex had to wait for the land-based MBS's to maneuver through the city and converge on the south side of the colony. There was no time to build defenses. The

Free Trade Association had founded the colony, but they had no military, and the city was constructed without thought for any type of protection. Corporate raiders were always a threat, but they usually only attacked other large business holdings. The planet was too far away from the highly populated civil worlds where attacks on the innocent would be punished. On the edge of humanity's galactic expansion, only the strong survived.

"We've cleaned out the kamis, Ace," Ash said. "What now?"

"How far out is that group of Hunters?" Alex asked.

"Still a hundred kilometers, team leader," Newt said. "The colony will be in range in half an hour at their current speed."

"Great," Alex said. "We're outnumbered and out of time."

"What's the matter, Ace?" came a snarky voice Alex hadn't expected to hear. He was still circling the colony, and Oggy was part of Echo Company below him. "Are you afraid? Leave the fighting to us. You should go back to the ship and keep the simulators running."

"Can that chatter, Oggy," Gellar snarled. "No one speaks unless they are asked a direct question or reporting actionable intel."

"Yes, Master Sergeant," Oggy replied.

Alex smiled. He didn't want to be petty, but it made him happy to hear Oggy put in his place.

"All units, all units," a new voice broke in. Alex recognized Captain Chastain's calm diction. "We are now at red alert. Zen Tech vessels have entered the system. Stand by for further orders."

Alex waited, wondering what was happening.

"Nyx?"

*I'm checking it,* she replied. *Looks like three ships. A carrier like the* Republic *and two escort ships.*

"Dang," Alex said. "That seems excessive."

*They'll outnumber us in orbit and on the ground. We might have to retreat.*

"You mean leave the planet to Zen Tech?"

*It's possible. They have the numbers, and we can't afford to lose this many CDF assets.*

"Doesn't feel right to run," Alex said.

*They just want the planet's resources.*

"Which we've already paid for."

*The brass will find a way to get their money back.*

"And what about our pride?"

*It's not worth dying for.*

Alex knew she was right, but until he was told to run, he was going to fight. And a plan was already forming in his mind.

"Master Sergeant Brooks, Master Sergeant Gellar," he said on the open channel of his com-link. "What if we try this?"

# Chapter 25

Alex was hovering just below eighty thousand meters, barely under Carthage Prime's thermosphere. Nothing was visible on the ground—just the dazzling reflection of light from the snow and ice. Alex could see the curve of the planet, and despite the daylight, he could see stars overhead.

"Are you ready?" Alex asked.

*Almost. Even computers take time to crunch equations this big.*

Master Sergeant Brooks had agreed with Alex's plan. The problem with attacking the Zen Tech Hunters was their long-range weapons. There was no way to hit them without coming under their return fire. Instead, Alex had designated an area far enough from their own MBS's but large enough that munitions would have time to reach them. The controllers had changed the programming on the Titans, allowing Alex and his team to dump their supply of air-to-ground missiles. The computers were calculating the time it would take them to fall down to the troposphere where they would be activated, hopefully directly over the Zen Tech Hunters. Their heat-seeking directional guidance would send them hurtling toward the enemy. It was all theoretical and would use up all their missiles, leaving them only the short-range projectiles and laser cannons. Still, it would strike the first blow in the fight without risking any of the CDF operators. If they could succeed in taking out half of the Zen Tech Hunters, it would even the odds.

"I'd rather fight them directly," Ash said. "We're much faster than they are."

"You're not faster than a missile," Newt said.

"You'll get a chance," Alex insisted. "But let's give this a shot."

*Almost ready. Prepare to drop munitions.*

"Roger that. Get ready to drop your payloads," Alex said.

*Now!*

Alex knew the other controllers would have given their operators the same order. He willed the missiles to fire, squeezing the trigger on his left joystick. There was no sound. The missiles, which rotated through a compartment and into the launch nozzle, dropped out in a stream of deadly firepower. There was no exhaust, no contrails. The missiles fell away from him, pulled by gravity through the planet's atmosphere toward the targets far below. When the last missile dropped, an alert warning went off inside the Titan.

"I'm out," Alex said.

"Me too," Ash replied.

"And me," Sly added.

Newt still had a full complement of missiles and was taking longer to disgorge his supply.

"Ash, get moving. I want visual confirmation, but don't get too close. I don't want you coming under fire."

Ash had taken off before he finished giving her the order.

"I'm done," Newt said.

"All right. Sly, you're with Ash on the eastern flank. Newt, you're with me."

"Roger that, Ace," Sly said.

They all began a slow, arcing descent toward the line of defenders.

*Missiles passing ten thousand meters. Activating munitions now.*

The Hunters were spread out in a long line. They weren't in a perfect row—the uneven terrain made that impossible—but they were in good formation. Alex zoomed in his optics as far as they would go, trying to maintain enough distance from the raiders to keep them from firing at him.

The Zen Tech operators realized the danger they were in and began firing in hopes of destroying the missiles before they could reach their targets. Laser blasts and projectiles were hurled upwards, hitting some of the missiles, which exploded harmlessly in the air. Alex felt a knot form in his gut. What if they wasted all their missiles and the attack was a complete failure? He thought for a moment that he might be sick, and he wondered what would happen inside the Titan battle suit if he were to vomit.

Fortunately, he didn't find out. The first of the missiles to hit the targets did so in devastating fashion. The entire attack happened quickly. Explosions made the ground tremble and billowing smoke made it hard to see as over a hundred missiles hit the ground in the space of a few seconds. Then everything was quiet.

"What happened?" Master Sergeant Brooks said. "Who has eyes on the impact zone?"

Alex could see part, but not all of the area. What he could see was obscured by black smoke. He was just about to respond to the request, but Ash beat him to it.

"I'm moving in," she said.

"Careful," he warned her, but Ash was fearless. She wasn't a fool, but caution simply wasn't in her nature.

Alex flew upward, trying to see through the smoke. The good news was that the Zen Tech advance had stopped. Alex had expected to see several of the Hunters charge through the smoke into the open ground on the other side, but none did. It made him nervous.

"Looks like there's some movement down there," Ash said. "A few survivors."

"My team will finish them off," Oggy said. "Minotaurs, move in."

Alex saw the Fast-Attack Minotaurs charging forward at full speed. The battle suits on six wheels kicked up large amounts of snow behind them like white tails.

"Romeo Company, hold your positions," Master Sergeant Brooks ordered.

Alex waited for Master Sergeant Gellar to call Oggy back, but she was silent. The Minotaurs were fast, but they had a lot of ground to cover. Smoke was clearing in some areas, and Alex could see that a few of the operators in the Zen Tech Hunters were alive. Their battle suits were ruined, but a few of the men and women inside them had survived. There was a small amount of pride in knowing that his plan had worked, but another part of him felt sick. One operator that he could see through the smoke was covered in blood as he crawled from the wreckage of his MBS.

"Master Sergeant," Alex said. "It might be better to hold back the Minotaurs."

"Are the Hunters regrouping?" Brooks asked.

"Negative. Looks like we managed to get them all," Alex said.

"Good work, Titan team," Master Sergeant Gellar said.

"Thanks…it's just that I had an idea," Alex said.

"What do you have in mind?" Brooks said.

Alex was struggling to come up with an idea that would be a good reason not to slaughter the operators. His airstrike had stopped the Hunters, and he had no doubt that most had been killed in the attack, but it turned his stomach to think of Oggy and his friends murdering the survivors. There had to be a reason to keep them alive.

*Use them to lure the Zen Tech forces into a trap.*

At first Alex wasn't sure if the voice in his head was Nyx or if it was an original idea of his own. But he knew instantly that it was a good one.

"I was just thinking, with the Zen Tech forces arriving in the system," Alex said, "if we capture rather than kill the prisoners, we might be able to lure their forces down to Tunis and ambush them there."

For a moment there was silence over the com-link. When Master Sergeant Brooks spoke, it wasn't to Alex.

"Minotaurs, hold your positions and wait for orders," Brooks said. "*Republic*, are you reading us?"

"Loud and clear, Romeo Company," came the communications officer's voice. There was some static, but it was easy to understand. "Captain Chastain is considering the plan."

"There are plenty of areas to hide," Alex went on. "The warehouses next to the landing platforms would be perfect. We lure their forces down to the surface and take them out while they're disembarking."

More silence followed. Alex felt tense as he wondered whether they were really considering his plan or just scoffing at it. When Captain Chastain's voice came over the com-link, Alex felt both gratification and panic.

"This plan only works if we sell it," she declared. "That means having the units in the field stay close to the base camp the miners have built. And the *Republic* would have to leave the system. You'll be completely on your own in Tunis."

"Roger that, Captain," Master Sergeant Brooks said. "I think we can make it work."

"You are authorized to proceed," Chastain said. "All future communications will be mission-specific, just in case Zen Tech found a way to break our encryption."

"Copy, we will proceed," Master Sergeant Brooks said. "Romeo Company out."

Alex felt a wave of relief, but also concern. He might have saved a few lives, but how many more would be killed in the ambush?

# Chapter 26

Nyx felt a thrill of excitement. Her idea had been accepted by Alex, the operators on the ground, and the senior officers on the ship. As soon as Captain Chastain ended the radio communications with Romeo Company, she sent an order to the controllers on board the *Republic*.

"As many of you know, we are undertaking a courageous plan to ambush the Zen Tech forces, who are at this very moment moving toward Carthage Prime. To carry off the ruse that we have been defeated, the *Republic* will leave the system. A select group of controllers will travel to the base camp with me and set up MBS control on the ground. It will be difficult and dangerous, but our operators can't be left stranded once the *Republic* is out of the system. If you are selected, please report immediately to the drop ship in hangar 3."

Almost immediately, her PIL beeped with an incoming message. She checked the screen and saw that she had been selected. It was exciting, but also frightening. Nyx West was the kind of person who wanted to make a difference but preferred staying behind the scenes. It was part of what made her such a good controller; she could take an active part in the mission while not actually being in danger. Nyx didn't think she was a coward, but physical abilities weren't her strong suit. She was an introvert at heart. The thought of leaving the large carrier ship to go down to the surface of the planet made her feel more than a little shaky.

"Alex," she spoke into the tiny mic beside her jaw that was part of her controller headset.

"I'm here," he replied.

"I just got called up," she said. "I'll be taking the drop ship down to the base camp."

"Okay." There was concern and a little bafflement in his voice. "Is that safe?"

"Not really," she replied. "If our plan fails, we'll be stuck on Carthage Prime with a lot of hostile Zen Tech people."

"Then we won't let it fail, Nyx."

She felt tears stinging her eyes and a lump in her throat that made talking difficult. Never in her entire life had anyone made her feel as safe as Alex just had. All her thoughts about setting her feelings for him aside suddenly seemed so foolish. There were risks to feeling too much for her operator, but keeping him at arms' length wouldn't make it hurt any less if something happened to him.

"All right," Nyx said. "I'm going to have to switch over to a portable control station. It will take me ninety seconds. As long as you don't do anything crazy, we should be okay."

"I'll do my best, but no promises," he said with a chuckle.

She could see that he was airborne but just hovering. He should be fine for the minute and a half it would take her to retrieve a portable control terminal and sync it to his FA Titan.

"All right, the ninety seconds starts now," she declared.

Pulling off the headset that connected her to Alex was hard. She felt blind and worried that he would need her, but she couldn't focus on that. The portable controller consoles, or PCCs, were stored in charging racks at the end of the row of cubicles where she worked. Part of her training had been learning to use PCCs and included emergency drills. She dashed down the row. There were four other controllers ahead of her. The charging station was already open, and the controllers ahead of her each pulled a PCC free and hurried back toward their station.

Nyx had done the drills and knew exactly how long it would take to get the PCC from the racks, boot it up, and switch Alex's Titan to the PCC from her more expansive controller station in the cubical. She snatched a PCC from the rack. It was essentially a computer with three small touch screens. There was a keyboard for more advanced controller functions, and the entire apparatus was made to hang from her neck. A pad on the keyboard side sat flush against her stomach, creating a flat surface to work from that allowed her complete freedom of movement. The idea was that in the case of an attack or other emergency situation, controllers could flee to safety while continuing to help their operators.

When she reached her cubicle, she waited nearly half a minute for the PCC to come online. As soon as it did, she punched in her passcode, let the security features check her biometrics against what was stored in the network, and finally it asked her if she wanted to shift control from her station to the PCC.

"Yes," she said, snugging the little earpiece into place that acted as both a speaker and microphone.

The system came to life. One screen showed the FA Titan's system readings. Another was fed radar data from the *Republic*, and the center screen had readings for the Titan's weapons and flight features. She wouldn't have the ability to see what Alex saw using the PCC, but otherwise she could see everything she normally did.

"Alex, do you read me?"

"Always."

"Good, I'm going to board a drop ship. There might be some interference as we pass through the upper atmosphere."

"Okay. We're setting down to look for survivors. I'll be okay on my own for a while. Can you activate low-power lasers for me?"

Nyx pressed an icon on the middle screen to bring up the laser cannon's power. It was at full, and she slid her finger down a status bar that took the power to minimum level. The FA Titan was a hybrid MBS of sorts. Flight made it fast and dangerous to enemies, but it had other features, as well. Alex could run and even fight hand to hand in the battle suit. The Titan didn't have arms and hands, only gun barrels, but getting hit with one was dangerous to anyone not in heavy armor. He could walk and fire the weapon on his own. Getting airborne again or changing weapons would require Nyx's help, but if they were just looking through the rubble left by the missile strike on the Hunters, he should be okay even if Nyx lost contact.

"You've got low lasers on your left," she said, knowing his left hand was his primary. "And projectiles at full auto on your right, just in case."

"Perfect. Thank you."

"My pleasure," Nyx said.

She hurried from the long room where she worked with over a hundred other controllers out into the corridor that led to the lift. She needed to go down several levels to get to the hangar bays, which were located on the bottom of the ship. There were several other controllers waiting with her. Everyone looked nervous. Nyx couldn't help but think of the drop ship that had malfunctioned with Romeo Company on board. If that happened, she couldn't hope for rescue. The controllers wouldn't be in space suits. A breech in the drop ship's hull would mean certain death for everyone on board.

The lift doors opened, and she stepped inside. Six controllers filled the space with the PCCs, making them twice as large. The elevator descended smoothly, and when the doors opened again, they found themselves on the rugged lower level of the ship. Gone were the polished deck tiles and the bright, colorful signs of the upper levels. The deck was a dull gray grate. She could see the electrical, plumbing, and life-support pipes and conduits down below. The walls and ceiling were glow panels, but she felt certain they weren't as bright as the ones on the levels above. There was a used quality to everything she saw, and more than a little grime. Their boots echoed on the steel floor, and the tension among the group of controllers was rising.

Hangar 3 was essentially one big airlock. The door was small, and a short platform led to the drop ship. Inside, Nyx found herself with nearly sixty other controllers, a few officers, and Captain Chastain. They were seated in chairs with harness straps as the hangar was sealed off and prepared for launch. Nyx was uncomfortably close to the controllers on either side. No one looked happy, but war wasn't supposed to be comfortable. She was buckled in and had contact with Alex, who was moving among the wreckage near Tunis. Fortunately for them both, they didn't need her help with much.

The drop ship launched, and Nyx felt giddy as they moved into zero-gravity. The fun didn't last long, as Nyx and the other controllers were called to the front of the ship for Master Sergeants Brooks and Gellar.

"What's happening up there?" Alex said.

"We're making our way to the planet," Nyx said. "I'm about to join the captain. Not sure what's they're planning. How are things down there?"

"We've recovered three operators in decent shape. Most are dead or severely wounded. They seem belligerent right now, but I'm hoping that will change."

"Okay, well, at least there's hope that our plan will work."

"You should get all the credit for this one," Alex said. "It's a smart plan."

Nyx was grateful for his attitude, but she also knew that the odds were against them. If the plan failed, the entire Ahzco team could be wiped out. Even if they survived, their careers would be over. Nyx was wishing more and more that she'd just kept her mouth shut.

The drop ship didn't have separate cabins, but there were a few empty seats in the front, and Nyx joined the captain, a lieutenant she didn't recognize, and the two other controllers.

"Who has a status update?" Captain Chastain asked.

Nyx looked at the two other controllers, who were staring back at her. After a few seconds she realized they weren't going to answer.

"The Titan team is exploring the wreckage," Nyx said, her voice a little shaky. She had muted her headset so that Alex didn't have to hear everything she said. "They've found three survivors who could pull off the plan."

"Three will work," Captain Chastain said. She turned to the other two controllers. "I want them separated before questioning. We don't have a lot of time, but we have to know what they planned to do once they had Tunis under control."

"Separating them will let us know if they're lying," the lieutenant said. Nyx saw "Cooper, M." stenciled on his uniform.

"Exactly," the captain agreed. "I want Brooks in charge of them. Gellar will take charge of getting the entire group hidden in the warehouses."

The controllers nodded, then began whispering orders and typing on their PCCs. The captain looked at Nyx. Chastain had a penetrating stare that made Nyx nervous.

"Whose idea was this?"

"Both of ours, Captain," Nyx said.

Chastain nodded. "The best operators have a connection with their controllers that goes beyond the INC. This entire plan hinges on the surprise attack. It has to be perfect, and there's a good chance that some of the Zen Tech drop ships will survive. The Titans will have to hunt them down. Taking those ships out with their MBS's on board is the key."

"I agree," Nyx said.

"I'm giving you and your operator—what's his name?"

"Alex Evans."

"Yes, Evans—I'm giving you both a field promotion. He's the squad leader, but the two of you will need to take control of the Titans once the fighting begins. Get on your PCC and find good launch points outside the colony."

"You want them coming from outside the city?" Nyx asked.

"Two of them," Chastain said. "And two in the city. We need to get them more missiles too. They need something with explosive force to take down the drop ships and wipe out the MBS's inside."

"All right," Nyx said.

She sat back in her seat and unmuted her headset. "Alex?" She whispered.

"Yes?" he replied.

"We have orders. Turn the survivors over to Master Sergeant Brooks."

"He already sent word that he's coming for them with a ground transport from the colony."

"Good. We've been given a field promotion to sergeant."

"What?"

"Captain Chastain wants you fully in charge of the Titan team."

"Okay, but I didn't need a promotion."

"Just listen, we've got a lot to do."

Nyx could feel gravity starting to pull at her. It was a strange sensation, as if her body was growing heavier and being pulled down into her seat. She was glad she didn't need to type commands or do much with her PCC at that moment.

"I'm listening," Alex said.

"We've been tasked with taking out whatever ships escape the trap that Master Sergeant Brooks is setting at the landing zone. You'll need to restock your missile supply."

"And how am I supposed to do that?"

"There's only one way that I can think of," Nyx said.

"Take them from the Minotaurs."

There was something in Alex's voice that told her he was dreading the assignment. She knew he had issues with some of the operators in Echo Company, but there were four Minotaurs, and their munitions were compatible with the Titans. It was the only way to carry out their orders that she could see.

"I'm sorry, but if some of the drop ships escape, you'll need to blow them up to take out the MBS's they're carrying. Just shooting them down won't do."

"I see the logic. It won't be pleasant, but I'll do it."

"Also, the captain wants two Titans hidden out beyond the colony. I'll find a place for them to take some cover."

"It shouldn't be too hard. There are trees north of the city," Alex said.

"Good. We're on the clock, so don't take too long."

"Got it. But I really need a direct order from the captain to get those missiles from Oggy and his crew," Alex said. "They won't like it."

"I'll see about that order. Be careful."

"You too, Nyx."

She didn't have access to a satellite feed on her PCC, so she opened her PIL and brought up the global imaging of Carthage Prime that the Free Trade Association had listed online when they began to promote the new planet. She punched in the coordinates for the landing port, then began searching the features beyond that point to find locations to hide two FA Titans.

The pull of gravity increased, and the ride through the atmosphere became extremely rough. Nyx had to stop working and just hang on for a while. The turbulence lasted nearly ten minutes, and more than once she worried that the drop ship might crash. There were no windows on the vessel, and there was no way to know if they were flying normally or hurtling to their deaths. Eventually the flight smoothed out, and she could breathe easier. She had just recorded the coordinates for the two hiding places beyond the colony when Alex reported in.

"We've cleared the Zen Tech Hunters. From the looks of it, only the three we found earlier will survive. All the rest are hurt too badly."

"Roger that. Three survivors."

"Can you get me in the air again?" Alex said.

"Absolutely. Repulsers are online," she said, tapping one of the icons on the touchscreen. "Increasing power for atmospheric flight."

"Once we're back at the colony, we'll have to shut down our battle suits and figure out how to reload the missiles."

"We'll do what we can on this end," Nyx said.

Nyx relayed the information to Captain Chastain and asked about the order. She nodded. If the captain saw the rivalry between Alex and the Minotaurs as an issue, she didn't show it. Nyx leaned back in her seat and began looking for instructions on loading missiles into the FA Titan. Once Alex was out of the battle suit, she wouldn't have contact with him. That was the one drawback to her job; unless her operator was in his battle suit and synced with his Implanted Neural Control, he wouldn't hear her. She always felt like something was missing when they weren't linked. She couldn't help but hope that there would be a lot more time together in future. She just wished he didn't have to be in danger for Nyx to be inside his head.

# Chapter 27

Being back in the air again helped, but Alex was filled with a sense of dread. He had walked through the carnage that his airdrop idea had created. Almost fifty Hunter-class mechanized battle suits were destroyed, and many were nothing more than mangled bits of metal—but it was the human remains that were hardest to live with. Alex saw body parts and gore and heard the wails of the dying, who begged and pleaded for help. The memories were etched in his mind, and while he felt the need to process what he'd seen and been part of, there was no time.

Master Sergeant Gellar had already recalled Echo Company, to the frustration of Oggy and his crew of Minotaurs, who were anxious to make a name for themselves in pitched battle. After what Alex had seen on the battlefield, he didn't think they knew what they were asking for. The Titans stayed with the three survivors until Master Sergeant Brooks arrived with a ground transport. The survivors, having been captured and with no hope of escape, submitted without protest. Alex guessed they were shell-shocked and couldn't blame them. Once they were headed back to the colony, Alex took to the air and joined his team circling above the wreckage.

"It worked," Newt said.

"Did it ever," Sly said. "Forty-eight Hunters taken out before they could fire a shot at any of us."

"The best outcome we could have hoped for," Alex said. "No casualties on our side."

"Not very exciting, though," Ash said, although there was a hollow tone to her voice that made Alex think she wasn't as gung-ho to fight as she had been.

"Looks like we're just getting started," Alex said. "I have good news and bad news."

"Give us the good news," Newt said.

"We're being tasked with taking out any of the drop ships not destroyed in the ambush," Alex said. "Newt and I will be posted in the colony. Ash and Sly will be hidden on the far side of the landing port somewhere. If any of the ships try to run..."

"We chase them down and take them out," Sly said.

"Which brings us to the bad news," Alex said. "We have to get missiles from Oggy and his crew of Minotaurs before the Zen Tech ships arrive in orbit."

"Spectacular," Ash said. "So we're definitely in for a fight."

"I've asked for the order to come from Captain Chastain," Alex said.

"Like that will do a lot of good," Sly said. "Those guys are idiots."

"But they don't have a choice if the captain orders it," Newt said.

"We still have to deal with them," Ash said.

"So let's get it over with," Alex replied.

They started back toward the colony. There were no crowds cheering the CDF, who had just saved the lives and livelihoods of most of the inhabitants. The colony seemed to hardly even take notice of the group.

"Nyx, can you find out what warehouse Master Sergeant Gellar's in?"

*Roger that. Captain Chastain sent down word for the Minotaurs to share their missile supply.*

"I hope it helps," Alex said, but he wasn't optimistic.

They landed just outside one of the hangars nearest the landing pads. It was filled on both sides with large crates, and there were machines for moving heavy cargo. Alex guessed it was the central loading station for ships coming in. Ships could be unloaded, the cargo crated up, and sent off in either direction. There were big doors on both ends of the building.

Alex walked inside the warehouse and stopped next to the cargo lift.

"I'm here," he said.

*All systems are on standby for a quick response. Good luck.*

"Thanks, I'm going to need it."

Master Sergeant Gellar was nearby, giving orders to a group of locals. Alex hit the disengage switch, and FA Titan began opening up. The air that hit Alex was cold and reminded him of his old home on NP8261. He climbed out of the Titan, onto the cargo lift, and down to the floor. Master Sergeant Gellar was the only other CDF operator out of her battle suit. There was something commanding about her that was, in many ways, more intimidating than a battle suit. He walked her way as she dismissed the group of locals.

"Fools," she mumbled. "They want to keep working."

"We're just in their way," Alex said.

"If they stick around they'll most likely be killed, but you can't fix stupid," Gellar remarked. "They've been warned, but I'm guessing we'll find two or three of them caught in the crossfire."

"You think there will be a lot of that?" Alex asked.

"Hope for the best, but plan for the worst, Evans. I heard about the field promotion. Congrats. That may be a record for fastest climb through the ranks."

"I'll get bumped back down when this is all over," he replied.

"Unless it's a smashing success," Gellar said. "You've got a knack for strategy and tactics. This is a good plan."

"You don't think it's too risky? If the ambush doesn't go well, we could be in trouble."

"True, but we're not helpless here," Gellar said. "All we really need is a way to even the odds. The ambush does that. Thanks to you, we're not on a hasty retreat out of the system. I hate running from a fight."

Alex thought about his own fight that lay ahead of him. Better to face it head on, he thought.

"You know why I'm here?" Alex asked.

"The missiles?" Gellar said with a raised eyebrow. "No one likes someone taking their toys, Ace."

"Yeah, it doesn't help that Oggy already hates me."

She chuckled. "You can't please everyone."

"Do you know where they are?"

"I've got them positioned on the flanks," Gellar said. "But you can call them over here to move the munitions."

She handed him an old-fashioned hand radio. "Thanks, Master Sergeant."

"You're welcome, *Sergeant* Evans."

He keyed the mic on the radio and spoke clearly. "Minotaur team, report to the main warehouse, please. I repeat, Minotaur team, report to the main warehouse."

Working with Romeo Company meant that Oggy and his crew didn't recognize every voice giving them orders. They obeyed without question, driving their Minotaurs to the warehouse, where Alex and the other Titans were waiting.

Oggy didn't get out of his battle suit, but rather rolled right up to Alex. When he spoke, his voice boomed though the Minotaur's external speakers.

"What the hell are you doing here, Ace?" Oggy demanded, his voice echoing in the warehouse.

Ash's voice crackled over the radio in response.

"That's Sergeant Evans you're speaking to, Private McGeek," she snapped.

For a moment there was no response. Alex guessed that Oggy and his friends were confirming the promotions. The Titan team were the only operators from Echo Company to have been promoted from private.

"Whatever," Oggy said contemptuously. "What do you want?"

"You should have gotten orders from Captain Chastain. We need half your missiles," Alex said.

Sly and Newt were out of their Titans and came walking over to join Ace. He still had no idea how to move the munitions from one MBS to another, but he couldn't let Oggy know that.

"You're crazy," Tig said. "We ain't giving up our missiles to you."

"There's a fight coming," Nuk joined in. "We're going to need them."

"Thanks for pointing that out," Sly said. "Your grasp of the obvious is astounding."

"Whose idea do you think it was to ambush the Zen Tech force?" Newt said. "Ace came up with it, and the captain endorsed it."

"We still aren't doing it," Oggy said. "You wasted your ammo, and that's your fault."

"We used our ammo taking out the kami drones," Ash said. Her voice sounded small and far away compared to Oggy's booming voice from his Minotaur. "And destroying the Hunters. It wasn't wasted."

"You still have lasers," Nuk said. "We need our ammo."

"This isn't a request," Alex said. "It's an order from Captain Chastain. Disengage from your battle suits, and let's get this done before we run out of time."

Oggy's Minotaur began to roll slowly forward. Alex was too close to the MBS, but he didn't move. It crept close until it was almost touching him. Alex wondered if Oggy was crazy enough to actually run him over, but before he could find out, Master Sergeant Gellar returned.

"What's going on here?" Master Sergeant Gellar demanded. "Why aren't you transferring those munitions?"

"Private McGee is reluctant to shut down his Minotaur," Sly said.

"Turn 'em off or you'll be cleaning toilets for a year on a planet that makes this egg-shaped rock look like paradise," she ordered. "We're under threat, and you yahoos are trying to pretend you're the toughest kids on the block. You have orders, McGee. Get it done, or you won't be a team leader or an operator. You have my promise that I'll see you shipped off to the worst place possible."

"Yes, Master Sergeant," Oggy said, his voice coming through the handheld radio instead of the Minotaur's public address speakers.

Alex felt a slight sense of relief, but he still didn't know how to actually move the missiles. Fortunately, Ash came to his rescue. She was still in her Titan, and her voice came through the radio as Oggy's Minotaurs shut down their battle suits.

"I'll walk you through the procedure," Ash said. "We can load you three up, and then me."

"Good idea," Alex said.

The swap took them half an hour. Both the Minotaur and the Titan battle suits used high-yield warheads on mini rockets. The Minotaurs had forty missiles on board. Each one weighed fifteen kilograms. Alex was sweating, despite the cold temperatures of the planet, by the time they finished. When he finally climbed back into his Titan and engaged the suit, he let his body sink into the cushioned seat. It wasn't like a chair; Alex was still upright as if he were standing, but there was a small pad, like an oblong bicycle seat, that gave him support at the moment he needed it. Oggy's band of Minotaurs had returned to their posts. Ash and Sly were heading out to their rearranged coordinates, and Alex realized he was exhausted.

*Tired?*

"How'd you know?"

*I'm tired, and I can only imagine what it's like for you.*

"We got the missiles transferred," Alex said. "So that's done. Nothing left to do now but get into position and wait."

*Are you walking or flying?*

"Walking," Alex said.

He moved out, the Titan's metal fleet banging on the concrete floor of the warehouse. Behind him, Sergeant Gellar and someone Alex didn't recognize were moving among the landing pads.

*Did you hear about the explosives?*

"Negative," Alex asked, his body tensing for bad news.

*The locals had them for construction of roads through the forest and mountains. Master Sergeant Gellar bought them from the locals and is wiring the landing pad. There was some pushback against the idea of destroying the landing pads, but in the end, Captain Chastain convinced the locals that it would be better to have Ahzco build a new spaceport than for Zen Tech to take control of the entire world.*

"Yeah," Alex said. "Not much of a choice there."

He reached his designated area and turned to face the landing port. He was between two warehouses with the back of the MBS against the wall. The building had a slight overhang that would block him from view, but he could take a couple steps forward and be clear to go airborne.

"Any idea how close the Zen Tech carrier is?"

*Unfortunately not. The* Republic *is on its way out of the system.*

"So there's nothing to do but wait," Alex said.

*True enough. Think you can get some sleep?*

"I'm not sure I should risk that," Alex said, but the thought was tempting.

*Don't worry, you've got plenty of charge on the Titan. I'm shutting down everything but coms and life* support to keep you warm. I'll alert you when it's necessary.

"Are you sure?"

Absolutely. That's my job.

"You know I could never do this without you," he said.

I wouldn't want to do it without you, Alex.

"Thanks, Nyx."

Get some sleep, Sergeant. You've earned it.

He felt the Titan's systems shutting down one by one. He hoped that wouldn't cost him valuable time if he was suddenly called into action, but he knew there would be time. The Zen Tech fighters couldn't just suddenly appear at the colony. Their ships would have to make orbit and ferry the fighters down. If they didn't come en masse, the entire plan would fall apart, but Alex decided it was okay to let his superiors worry about that. He had done his part, and with nothing else to accomplish at that moment, the best thing he could do was sleep.

He closed his eyes and pondered his battlefield promotion. "Sergeant Evans" sounded good to him. Maybe they would rescind the promotion once the fighting on Carthage Prime was over, but he looked forward to rising through the ranks. There hadn't been many chances for recognition growing up, but he could look with pride on his accomplishments since joining the CDF. And when he finally got the chance to go visit his parents on Skandia Seven, he would have some stories to tell them.

# Chapter 28

The drop ship landed at the base camp, which was really no more than a few hastily thrown-together structures. Plans for more significant construction were scheduled to take place once significant ore was discovered. Two buildings were the barracks: one for the miners, and another for the operators and technicians on duty. The drop ship landed nearby and was tasked with being a fourth structure, where the controllers could help their operators using the portable controller consoles.

The third building was a multipurpose structure with a kitchen and ore-testing stations. Captain Chastain took control of the multipurpose building, making it her headquarters. The big radio transmitter was turned north, in the direction of Tunis, and several instruments were set up outside. One was a radar that would give them warning if the camp was approached by Zen Tech raiders. The other was a radiation detector that could pick up trace elements of radiation in the atmosphere.

Nyx expected to be working in the drop ship but was immediately called into the multipurpose building. Lieutenant Cooper had already established communications with Tunis and was urging them to scan the space around Carthage with their spaceport's long-range radar. The Zen Tech vessels were expected in orbit at any moment, and if they were prepared, they might send drop ships to the surface immediately upon arrival.

Technicians were busy running cables into the building and setting up monitors. It was chilly inside, with the doors opening and closing almost constantly. Captain

Chastain was pacing with her hands behind her back and her head bowed as if in prayer. Beside Nyx were the two controllers who were partnered with Master Sergeants Brooks and Gellar. Like their counterparts, one was a man, the other a woman. Both were master sergeants, just like their partners, and significantly older than Nyx. They didn't speak. All three kept their attention on their PCCs and tried not to get in anyone's way—until the man stood up.

"Captain, I have a message from Master Sergeant Brooks," he said.

"Let's hear it," she snapped, without looking up.

The controller whispered into his headset mic for a moment, then spoke loudly enough for everyone in the building to hear. "The prisoners have confirmed that Zen Tech is planning to launch a full invasion. It is believed to be a two-prong plan, although there may in fact be more objectives. The prisoners were only privy to the first elements. They were to take control of Tunis, and once that was done, facilitate a full invasion force at the Tunis spaceport."

"They're all coming down to the city?" Captain Chastain asked.

"Affirmative," the controller said. "Although it's not certain that they're coming down together."

"Even if they do," Lieutenant Cooper spoke up, "they wouldn't all land at the same time."

"How much time do we have?" the captain asked.

"Some," the controller said. "Master Sergeant Brooks is about to make contact with the carrier, assuming it's in orbit."

Captain Chastain looked at Cooper, who shook his head. "No word on that yet."

"We can't delay too long," Captain Chastain said. "The longer that carrier is in orbit, the more time they'll have to look down at the battlefield and see their Hunter mechs destroyed. If that happens, they'll land their people somewhere else, and we'll have a full-scale battle on our hands. Tell Brooks to have them begin ferrying down their MBS operators right away. Have Master Sergeant Gellar put up some blockades so that the Hunters or whatever tech they send can't easily leave the port. They'll have to play it by ear and attack when they can do the most damage. Is the Titan team ready?"

Nyx cleared her throat, suddenly feeling weak. "Yes, Captain," she managed to say.

"They have the missiles they need?"

"Affirmative, and all four are in place," Nyx said, her confidence returning.

"Excellent," Captain Chastain said. "Make sure Sergeant Evans knows that he must destroy all the Zen Tech drop ships that don't land or get caught in the explosions. That is imperative. Surprise is our only advantage, and if we don't at least even the odds, we'll have a hell of a fight on our hands."

Nyx nodded. She understood the importance of the battle, but like Alex, there was nothing she could do but wait and see what would happen. Fortunately, she didn't have to wait long. Less than half an hour later, word came back that two Zen Tech vessels had made orbit: one battleship, one carrier. Captain Chastain speculated that the third ship had moved to ensure that the *Republic* left the system.

"Master Sergeant Brooks has made contact, and the Zen Tech drop ships are scheduled to begin their deployment to the planet within the hour," the male controller said.

"Sergeant West, go find the other controllers partnered with our Titan team," Captain Chastain said. "I want them in this building when the fighting starts."

"Radar's up," Nyx heard Lieutenant Cooper announce as she headed out into the cold.

It didn't take long to find the other controllers. They were in the drop ship, and they followed Nyx back to the multipurpose building. None of them had heavy coats, and being out in the freezing weather was unpleasant. Nyx knew that if they got stuck outside, they would die from exposure. It wasn't a pleasant thought, but there had been no time to gather warm coats and heavy boots for the sixty controllers who left the safety of the *Republic* to go planet-side and assist their operators.

The operators were all in their MBS's, which would keep them warm and ready just in case the camp was attacked. It also freed up space in the barracks for the controllers to sleep. When Nyx returned to the multipurpose building, the first reports from Tunis's long-range radar were coming in.

"Eight drop ships," Lieutenant Cooper said. He was holding an old-fashioned over-the-ear headset with one hand, keeping one of the ear cups pressed to the side of his head. "Military grade. They're all on the same trajectory."

Master Sergeant Brooks' counterpart stood up again. "Confirmed. Brooks just got word from the Zen Tech carrier that eight ships were being deployed to his location. He assured them that the space pad was clear and ready to receive all eight ships."

"Outstanding," Captain Chastain said. "Zen Tech has already lost two companies and at least as many drones. If we take out eight of their drop ships, they won't have the will to keep fighting."

"It would be a devastating loss," Lieutenant Cooper said.

"They're the aggressors, and we have the mining rights," Chastain said. "Plus, we saved the FTA colony, so that's all good press for us. As long as this surprise attack goes well, we stand to gain a significant victory."

There was a feeling of quiet desperation. The entire plan hinged on Nyx's idea. She had really been just trying to give Alex a reason to spare the lives of the survivors. They hadn't discussed it, but she could hear the trepidation in his voice when the gung-ho operators wanted to rush in and kill anything that survived the missile attack. He had contributed as much to the plan as she had, and Captain Chastain had molded their crude idea into an actionable strategy with a real shot of working. All that was left to do was wait and see.

Nyx unmuted her mic and whispered, "Alex, you should wake up now."

She heard a groan in her headset.

"Can't rub my eyes," Alex replied. "Oh, this sucks."

"Sorry, but the drop ships are on their way," Nyx said.

From across the room, Lieutenant Cooper announced in a loud voice, "We're picking up the drop ships on our radar now. Eighty thousand meters and descending."

It crossed Nyx's mind that everything was happening fast now. She had been getting bored waiting before, with the tension and fear weighing down on her. She had even wished the attack would just begin so that they could get it over with—yet now that it was starting, it seemed too soon.

"There are eight drop ships," Nyx said. The other controllers were whispering away beside her. "Military grade."

"Does that mean they have weapons?" Alex asked.

"Yes, and armor," Nyx said. "You'll need to target their engines and watch out for return fire. I don't know what type of ship it is, and we can't know what type of weapons they'll have."

"All right. At least we know they're coming."

"That's right. We have the ships on radar now, so if any escape, I'll help you keep track of them."

"Roger that, and thank you. I better touch base with my team, he said. Dang, my nose itches."

She laughed. She wasn't sure if he really meant it or if he was just trying to lighten the mood. It seemed impossible that he could be trying to comfort her before flying into harm's way himself, yet she thought that maybe he was.

"Be careful, Alex."

There was a slight pause, and then she heard his voice. It sounded small and far away.

"Always."

# Chapter 29

"Titan team," Alex said. "Sound off."

"Titan two, standing by," Newt said.

"Why's it so dark?" Sly said.

"The sun's going down, you dolt," Ash said. "We're ready, Ace."

"Good deal," Alex said. "You all get word on the raiders?"

"Eight ships," Newt said.

"Military grade," Ash added.

*Be careful, Alex.*

Nyx's voice in his mind was a comfort. Even though he couldn't actually hear her voice since the messages she sent were carried through his INC and transmitted straight into his brain, he could detect the concern in her voice.

"Always," he said, trying to sound confident.

"I wish we were already in the air," Ash said.

"Yeah, that would be better," Sly agreed.

"Just stay cool, people," Alex said. "We might get lucky and not even need to engage."

"You really think that?" Newt said.

"Like Master Sergeant Gellar says, Newt: hope for the best, but plan for the worst."

"The worst would be that only one or two ships get destroyed in the initial attack," Ash said.

"We can't do more than we can do," Alex said. "The first few ships shouldn't be a concern. We'll label them all anyway—Alpha through Hotel—and assign each of us at least one. Ash and I will take two, just in case."

*Designating Alpha, Bravo, Charlie, Delta, Echo, Foxtrot, Golf, and Hotel. They're passing fifty thousand meters.*

"Thanks," Alex replied. "Any chance the other controllers have the same designations?"

*We're sitting side by side, getting a radar feed from the same unit. Captain Chastain already designated the drop ships.*

"All right," Alex said over the team channel. "Time to get ready. Make sure your Titan has all systems activated and that you are ready for takeoff. Ash, you have targets Charlie and Golf."

"Roger that," she replied. "All systems ready. I have Charlie and Golf."

"Newt, you've got Echo."

"What do I do if Echo gets destroyed?" Newt asked.

"Then you help me," Alex said.

"All right, sure, team leader," Newt said. "All systems are green, and I have target Echo."

"Sly, you've got Foxtrot."

"Foxtrot and ready to rock," Sly said.

"I'm taking Delta and Hotel," Alex said.

*The drop ships are passing twenty-five thousand meters.*

"Thank you, Nyx," Alex said. "All right, make sure you've got ears open on the command channel. No unnecessary chatter."

They all acknowledged his order. Alex felt strange giving his friends orders. In his eyes, they were equals, but someone had to coordinate their efforts. He wouldn't have minded if it had fallen to someone else, but for the moment it was his responsibility. He had done everything he could to get them all ready. All that remained was to wait and see how things unfolded.

Master Sergeant Brooks called for radio silence when the drop ships reached twenty thousand meters. Alex was looking up and had the Titan's optics zoomed in. The sky was a soft pink color as the sun set. He hoped it wouldn't become fully dark until after the attack. The lack of light would only make things more difficult, and he didn't want any accidents.

At ten thousand meters the ships came into view. Alex had no idea how high they were, but he was sure they were still very far away. They were descending in a regulation spiral. The sight of eight war ships approaching made him nervous. If they knew about the ambush, they could strike first, from the air, and wipe out the Ahzco forces. Alex thought that perhaps Ash and Sly would survive. He almost wished that Newt were in the colony, hidden among the warehouses the way he was. But it was too late to change anything.

Soon he could hear the whine of engines. What surprised Alex the most was that he also heard—or felt—the EM waves from the ships and perhaps from the Zen Tech battle suits, as well. Their technology was different from Ahzco's, but it all used power the same way, and each of the advanced fighting machines used computers to help operate the sophisticated devices. He wanted to ask his friends if they heard it as well, but he didn't break radio silence. The drop ships were getting close—only a thousand meters up and still descending. If they were planning to attack, they would have to break formation soon.

As the lead ship descended to five hundred meters Alex could tell the vessels were spaced several hundred meters apart. He hoped that maybe, just maybe, they would land and wait to deploy the MBS's they carried on board, but he doubted it. The first ship slowed slightly as it hovered over one of the landing pads. Then it came down as the next ship began to move into position.

They're buying it, Alex thought to himself. He realized they had a chance—a real shot at making the ambush work. The second ship, Bravo, landed, and Alex felt himself mentally urging the others to descend. It landed just as the first ship opened the large hatch on its side. Alex couldn't see it from where he was hiding. The MBS's on board, Zen Tech's state-of-the-art Viper-class battle suits, came gliding out. They looked like coiled serpents with their heads raised, ready to strike. The third ship had just landed, and the fourth was hovering twenty meters above its designated landing strip when the first explosion ripped through the Alpha ship. It blew apart, sending shards of concrete and metal flying in all directions. The ground shook from the explosion, and a fireball flashed upward as black smoke billowed up.

The hidden Ahzco MBS opened fire on the vipers as the second landing pad exploded. It was a sudden and complete shift from calm to chaos. The third pad blew, and then the fourth. The ship designated Delta was only fifteen meters up and tried to pull away, but the blast from below engulfed the ship. It went down but didn't explode. The Vipers inside were set free, and after getting free of the drop ship, began to fight back.

"Go, go, go," Alex said. It was an order to his fellow Titans, but also to Nyx.

He walked forward two strides so that he was in between two massive warehouses with nothing overhead. The repulsers kicked on and the thrusters fired, shooting Alex straight up in the air. The four remaining drop ships were scrambling. Echo and Foxtrot were close to the carnage and trying to pull away. Both ships were under fire from Ahzco forces on the ground. Alex saw missiles racing up. Echo was too slow and exploded over one of the warehouses. It crashed down, bursting through the roof of the building and breaking apart. Alex was sure that a fire had started in the warehouse and hoped there was nothing explosive or flammable inside.

Foxtrot was running and had outpaced the fire from the ground forces. It was skimming the treetops and never saw Sly slip up from behind and fire two missiles at close range. If he hadn't kept ascending, his Titan would have been caught in the backlash. The missiles impacted the drop ship's exhaust and sent fire billowing out, just a second before the entire ship exploded.

"Foxtrot's down," Sly said.

"Echo too," Newt said.

But Golf and Hotel were turning, their guns pointed down toward the ground troops. Alex raised his left arm, pointing toward the approaching ships, and fired missiles. A chattering of automatic projectile fire roared from the drop ships as both pulled up and apart from each other. Chaff filled the air above the fight, and the missiles were fooled, shooting through the smoke and detonating on the far side over the forest.

"They're running," Ash said.

"Not for long," Alex replied. "Newt, you're with me. Sly, stick with Ash."

"Yeah, try and keep up," Ash said as the four FA Titans raced after the drop ships in the twilight of Carthage Prime.

# Chapter 29

The Titans were fast not because they had large engines, but because they weren't as heavy as a traditional ship—but the military-grade drop ships from Zen Tech weren't slow. They had massive engine capacity that could take them out from the surface of a planet and into outer space. Alex saw the drop ship drop low and knew that if had a chance, it would deploy the Viper MBS's. That was their main objective: once the operators were out of the ship, it would turn and fight. He couldn't let that happen.

"Missiles, Newt," Alex said.

"Roger that," his companion replied.

They fired two missiles each. Alex saw the contrails as the rockets shot toward the drop ship. The ship dropped a thermobaric warhead and used its repulsers to push the large vessel into the sky. The bomb detonated on the ground and sent a wave of fire rolling across the rugged landscape. The Titans' heat-seeking missiles were drawn to the fire and exploded on the ground, sending up fountains of charred topsoil, black smoke, and steam from melting snow.

The drop ship twisted in the air and faced the Titans. Alex and Newt took off in different directions as two missiles were launched toward them.

"Nyx!" Alex said.

*Deploying flares. Pull up!*

In many circumstances, Alex could control the Titan's functions without help. His INC gave him full control of the MBS, but when he was under fire, all he could focus on was flying. Nyx had to do the rest.

"Don't lose the drop ship," Alex said.

He was taking a page out of the Zen Tech pilot's playbook. He dropped low to the ground and skimmed just meters above the surface. He was familiar enough with the terrain to know that south of the city, the land spread out in a long, flat plain.

*The flares worked!*

Alex was about to respond when an explosion not far away stole the words from his mouth. There was a tightness in his chest, and fear clawed at him like a wild animal stuck in a trap.

*The drop ship is attempting to land again. She's two kilometers ahead of you. Switching to night vision.*

Twilight had quickly shifted to full darkness. There were stars overhead but very little ambient light on the surface of the planet. Fire from the attack was far away, and the colony had very little outdoor lighting. Yet with night vision, Alex could suddenly see everything. The image in his brain was slightly different—a monochrome image, but sharp. He could see the drop ship descending. He needed to get the vessel higher so that when he took it out, the crash would kill the operators inside. He raised his right arm and pulled the trigger on the Titan's joystick. A stream of soft-alloy projectiles went screaming toward the ship. Some hit the thick armor, doing little damage, and others hit the ground. Alex wasn't hoping to bring down the drop ship—in fact, he was trying to get it up. The vessel was the most vulnerable on the ground, and taking fire was enough to get it moving again.

*It's running,* Nyx said.

The Zen Tech ship took off with a roar, but Alex didn't care. He worked his jaw, trying to get the words out of his mouth.

"Newt?"

There was no answer, and his eyes filled with tears. He felt them spill over and run down his face.

*His MBS is down. I don't know if he's okay.*

Grief was even more debilitating than fear. Alex knew that for the moment he had to set it aside, but knowing what needed to be done and having the strength to do it were two completely separate things. Alex circled back toward his friend and teammate. Coming under missile fire at close range was exceedingly dangerous, and if not for Nyx's fast reaction, Alex might have been killed. He could only hope that Newt survived.

*Alex, the drop ship is getting away.*

He could see wreckage on the ground. The Titan seemed mostly intact, but Alex could see charred and twisted metal. One of the gun placements was missing, and smoke was rising from the fallen MBS.

*Alex?*

"Okay," he said, his grief suddenly boiling into total rage.

He turned again and gave the Titan full power. He shot ahead like a bullet. The drop ship was screaming through the night, trying to get enough distance from him to set down somewhere on the planet. Alex could hear the chatter from the spaceport. Echo and Romeo Companies were in a pitched battle with the Vipers that had escaped from the fourth Zen Tech ship that crashed but didn't blow up. He could only imagine how difficult the smoking hulls of the ruined drop ships made the battle. With fires burning, not to mention the roiling, black smoke, night vision would be impaired.

The fleeing drop ship was nearly ten kilometers ahead of him and once more descending for a rapid landing and deployment. Alex had heard of ground-based forces training to disembark as rapidly as possible, but being a Titan operator, he hadn't done that type of drill himself. He was flying with both of his arms extended over his head so that the weapons he controlled were pointing forward, ready to fire. The drop ship was hard to see in the distance, but it wasn't out of range of his missiles.

"Firing missiles," Alex said, as much to himself at to Nyx.

*Target locked.*

Alex knew what was about to happen. The drop ship was low to the ground. As soon as he launched the missiles, a warning would go off in the cockpit of the drop ship and the pilot would evade. The mini rockets propelling the Titan's missiles were designed for short flights and didn't have a lot of maneuvering capability. Alex knew the pilot would have just enough time to fire his counter measures and evade the missiles. He waited a full second, then fired his auto cannon into the air, above the drop ship. There was no warning about the rain of projectiles, and the pilot flew straight into them. Most were stopped by the ship's armor, but the pilot was giving the vessel full power to escape the missiles, which opened up the ship's armored exhaust ports. Several of the high-caliber projectiles found the ship's weakest area and tore through the exhaust and into the engines.

"Yes," Alex said, as black smoke went flooding from the ship's exhaust.

*It's running. Looks like perhaps it's being recalled.*

The ship was wounded, but not disabled. It was climbing hard and fast. Alex followed. It made sense that the Zen Tech officers would try to salvage what they could from the trap they had stumbled into. But Alex wasn't through. He followed the ship upward, biding his time for the perfect shot.

*Six thousand meters. I don't think it's going to try and land again, Alex.*

He didn't respond. He didn't care that the ship was running away, or that technically he had fulfilled his orders.

*Romeo and Echo Company need our help.*

Alex still didn't respond.

*I know you hear me, Alex. Destroying that ship won't help Newt.*

"I have to," Alex snarled.

*Every second you waste here is putting the other operators at risk.*

The drop ship was faster than Alex's FA Titan. Even with the damage his bullets inflicted, the ship rocketed upward faster than Alex could follow. He wanted to destroy them. He wanted to make sure they could never hurt his friends again. He had his finger on the missile trigger. He could fire everything at them—but Nyx was right. There was a possibility that he might need the missiles to help the ground-based operators at the spaceport.

He growled in anger and grief as he turned away from the drop ship.

"Keep an eye on them," Alex said, his voice half a sob. "If they come back, I want to know."

*I will,* Nyx replied softly.

Alex turned back toward the colony. He had flown nearly two hundred kilometers away during the brief fight. Getting back took several minutes, and he used the time to check in on his team.

"Titan Three, what's your sit rep?" Alex asked over the team channel of his com-link.

"We got it!" Sly said. "Nailed the bastard."

"Titan four?" Alex asked.

"I read you," Ash said. "We're two hundred klicks north of Tunis. Returning that way. All systems green, but my power cells are down to one quarter and I'm out of missiles."

"Roger that," Alex said. "Be advised. Titan two is down."

The words were painful, like acid in his mouth. There was no immediate response from Sly or Ash—not that Alex expected any. He wanted desperately for someone to make him feel better, but he knew nothing would.

"I'm returning to lend aid to Echo Company," Alex said. "You should do the same."

"Roger that, Titan leader," Sly said stiffly.

"Copy," was all Ash said.

"Nyx," Alex said over their private link. "What's the situation at the spaceport?"

*From what I can tell, our operators are trapped inside the warehouses. They have decent cover but can't maneuver. The Vipers have taken cover behind the wreckage of their drop ships. There's too much interference to get accurate readings on radar. Both sides are doing a lot of shooting, but not much actual damage.*

"Makes sense," Alex said. He switched over to the command channel.

"Echo Company, this is Titan One, on approach."

"Roger that, Titan One," Master Sergeant Gellar said. She was as calm as if she were running a controlled exercise where no one was in actual danger. "See if you can hit the Zen Tech operators from the far side, but be aware of their ground-to-air missiles."

"Copy, Master Sergeant," Alex said. "Stand by."

*Alex, if you can get above the area and mark coordinates, Sly and Ash can fire missiles from a distance. That would make you all harder to target with counterfire.*

"Good idea, except Ash doesn't have missiles. I'll have her do it," Alex said, before opening his team channel. "Ash, get above the spaceport and mark the Zen Tech MBS's for us. Sly and I will fire at them from just inside our effective range."

"Got it," Ash said.

Alex brought his Titan to a hover twenty-five kilometers from the colony. He could see flashes of light in the distance from the battle, but only because he was over a thousand meters in the air. From the ground, he knew the colony wouldn't be visible. Fortunately, his missiles had an effective range of thirty kilometers. Once Ash sent coordinates, Nyx could program his missiles, and all Alex had to do was fire them. If there were survivors, it would take them too long to locate Alex and Sly to fire back. And hopefully in all the chaos, they wouldn't notice Ash up above them.

"Sending targeting data," Ash said.

*Got it, Alex. Are you ready?*

"When you are."

*Fire four missiles.*

"Roger that, firing four."

He pulled the trigger slowly, counting off the shots in his mind. It took the missiles several seconds to cover the distance, and then explosions were visible. Alex flew his Titan toward the colony, maintaining his altitude and using the battle suit's enhanced optics to zoom in on the fight.

"Solid hits," Ash said. "But I've lost all visibility."

Alex heard Master Sergeant Brooks give an order over the command channel. "Destroyer team, move in and search for survivors."

The chatter turned from battle orders to calls for help. Several operators had sustained damage. Some were wounded, others silent. Alex turned from the battle and found the wreckage where Newt had gone down. He landed nearby, hoping against all odds that his friend had somehow survived.

"Titan team, locate my position and join me," Alex said. "Nyx, I'm going offline."

*That's not a good idea, Alex. There could be more Vipers out there, and the temperature is falling.*

Alex knew she was right, but he had to know. Newt was his friend, and he had trusted Alex to lead him in battle. If he was dead, Alex was responsible.

"I have to, Nyx. Stand by," Alex said.

He pressed the button to power down the Titan battle suit and open the armored shell so that he could climb out. He was struck by the cold air when the suit opened, and climbing down was difficult without assistance. He had to dangle from the opening, with a full meter drop, but he did it. Getting back in would be even more of a challenge, but Alex decided he would worry about that once he had seen to Newt.

He jogged over to the wreckage. It was more extensive up close than it had seemed from the air. Alex pulled off the cover of the emergency manual controls. The battle suit had no power, and Alex had to use a small ratchet fastened to the armored cover of the control hatch to slowly crank the suit open. He was working the ratchet back and forth as quickly as he could when Ash and Sly landed nearby.

"Is he alive?" Ash asked, her voice booming from the suit's speakers.

"I don't know," Alex shouted back.

The cold air burned his lungs, and his eyes stung with tears as he cranked away on the ratchet.

"Newt?" Alex shouted. "Can you hear me?"

There was no response. It took Alex several minutes to get the armor open enough that he could see inside. Ash and Sly turned on their suits' exterior lights. Alex could see Newt's pale form inside the battle suit. His eyes were open, but there was no movement. He wasn't breathing.

Alex turned up his head and screamed in rage. His friend was dead, and nothing he could do would bring him back.

# Chapter 30

Sly helped Alex back into his Titan suit. It wasn't graceful, but it was effective. Alex took the time to wipe his face off on the sleeve of his dark gray compression shirt. Despite the cold, he was sweating, his nose ran, and tears burned down his cold cheeks. Newt was dead. He couldn't believe it, but neither could he deny it. His friend had been less than a meter away and yet completely out of reach. Alex had taken the time to close the damaged Titan battle suit back up in an effort to protect his friend from the elements, even though he knew that Newt couldn't feel anything anymore.

"What happened?" Ash asked once Alex had pressed the button to reactivate his suit and the big MBS had come online.

"Missile attack," Alex said. "Almost got us both. The drop ship was trying to land, and we came in hot."

"Damn," Sly said. "I can't believe he's gone."

There was a catch in his voice, and Alex knew Sly was weeping.

*I'm sorry, Alex.*

"Me too," Alex said, using their private link. "He was a good friend."

*It's not your fault.*

"Of course it is. I should have sent him into a backup position. There was no need for both of us to attack the drop ship."

*You didn't fire that missile.*

"No, but I should have known it was coming," Alex said.

He switched to the team channel and ordered them to return to the colony. Nyx marked the spot where Newt had fallen. A Valkyrie would have to be deployed to retrieve it, or perhaps some of the heavy equipment from Tunis could bring it back. The Titan battle suits had gun-arms and no hands; they weren't built for picking things up, just for killing the enemy—and Alex knew that he hadn't even done that.

Nyx was silent on the flight back, as were Ash and Sly. The battle had gone pretty much as they had expected. Seven Zen Tech drop ships were destroyed, along with an equal number of operator groups—but all Alex could see was his failure.

When they reached Tunis, one of the warehouses was on fire. The rest had taken heavy fire. Some of the laser blasts had even burned their way all the way to the second row of buildings. The landing pads were all completely destroyed. Of Romeo and Echo company, half of the mechanized battle suits were out of commission. Flood lights were being set up, and medical personnel from the colony were working on the wounded. Alex saw a row of bodies in CDF fatigues. They had won the battle but taken their share of casualties.

"Master Sergeant Gellar," Alex used his com-link to contact his superior, "where do you want us to land?"

"She's out of commission," Master Sergeant Brooks replied. "A laser blast sparked a nearby power unit, and the EM wave short-circuited her Interceptor. Land your team near the burning warehouse and then walk toward the lights. We're occupying one of the other buildings for the night. You're to stay in your battle suit, both for warmth and in case there's another attack from the Zen Tech ships."

"Yes, Master Sergeant," Alex said. "But we're low on power."

"The techs will get you charged up," Brooks said. "Your air strike turned the tide. We'll salvage what we can and make sure you're ready if Zen Tech sends another strike force."

"Thank you, Master Sergeant," Alex said.

They came down in a small clearing. The ground between the buildings was hard-packed soil with no grass, but no rocks, either. Alex had lived most of his life on a planet that was essentially one big rock. He couldn't help but hope that Carthage Prime became something significant. Newt gave his life for his friends and for Ahzco. Maybe he wouldn't be remembered by the people who lived on Carthage in the centuries to come, but his sacrifice couldn't be in vain.

"You ready to talk about it?" Ash asked as they walked toward the building the CDF had taken over.

They were walking past smoking mounds of twisted metal, melted wiring, and wasted munitions. There were bodies inside, too, but they weren't visible. Alex had been horrified at the carnage of their first battle, but all he could think at that moment was that every fighter for Zen Tech deserved to die.

"There isn't much to talk about," Alex said. "We went after one ship, you went after the other. My focus was on the target when Newt went down. I should have done a better job leading him."

"It's not your fault, Ace," Sly said. "Newt was a good guy. You have to remember we were under attack. Bad things can happen even under good circumstances."

"Maybe you should have held him back," Ash said.

Alex wanted to scream at her—to say of course he should have held Newt back—but getting angry at her wouldn't help.

"Hindsight is always perfect," Sly said. "We just have to learn from it."

They lined up inside the warehouse. They were out of the way, letting the technicians work. It didn't take long for power lines to be laid out and plugged into the Titan battle suits.

"Are you going to contact his family?" Ash said.

Alex hadn't thought that far ahead, but he knew as soon as she said it that he would. He could find Newt's family information from the company network once he was off Carthage Prime. Contacting them would be one of the very first things he did.

"Yeah," Alex said. "I will."

"And then you have to let it go," Sly said. "Newt was proud to be a Titan operator, and nothing we did would have changed his mind about it."

Alex didn't know if he agreed, but it made him feel a little better. After a few minutes of silence, he could feel sleep pulling at his eyes. There wasn't really anything to look at in the warehouse. The wounded had been moved into the colony's medical facility. The dead were outside and out of sight. All operators were still in their MBS's, and most of the activity in the warehouse was from technicians. Alex was thinking he should try to sleep when a row of FA Minotaurs came rolling by in front of him. The last one stopped, and Alex heard Oggy's voice over the command channel.

"One, two, three," he said slowly. "Lose somebody, Ace?" He said Alex's nickname with such derision that it sounded like an insult.

"Beat it, Oggy, before I smash your face in," Alex said.

"Stay off this channel!" Master Sergeant Brooks snapped. "You Minotaurs get parked and start recharging. Move!"

The four Minotaurs scooted away, their tires squealing on the slick floor of the warehouse. Alex watched them go, knowing it was only a matter of time before Alex got his hands on Oggy. He couldn't wait to show that arrogant jerk a thing or two.

*Alex?* Nyx shook Alex from his daydream.

"Yeah, I'm here," Alex said.

*Captain Chastain wants a report. Would you like me to tell her about Newt?*

Alex thought before he answered. It didn't seem right to let anyone else share the news—not when he was responsible for it.

"Can you patch me through to her, on a private link?"

*Yes, stand by.*

A moment later the captain's voice crackled through Alex's com-link.

"What do you have to report, Sergeant?"

"We lost a team member, Captain. Corporal Kyle Newton. He was flying with me. The drop ship fired missiles at us and he was..."

"I'm aware of the loss, Sergeant," Captain Chastain said.

"Well, Captain, it was my fault. We were too close. I should have ordered Newt to back me up."

"And then he'd be having this conversation about you," Captain Chastain said. "You can't say what might have happened if you'd done things differently, Evans. That's the burden of leadership. We are warriors, this was a battle, and people died. You did your part. Corporal Newton did his. Today we won. Tomorrow, who can say? This is part of being in the Corporate Defense Force, so get used to it, Sergeant. We need you."

"I was just going to say that maybe I shouldn't be a sergeant," Alex replied.

"Every leader faces that dilemma at some point," Chastain said. "Of course it would be easier for us if we let someone else take the lead. But things wouldn't be better —not by a long shot. If you want to mope around and feel sorry for yourself, I can't stop you, but you better understand that your team is counting on you to get them through this difficult time, and the next one after this. Part of being a leader is standing between the horror of what has happened and shielding those who follow us from the bitter taste of it. Learn from this, Evans. Otherwise your friend died for nothing. I didn't promote you to be perfect. I promoted you to lead, and odds are high that this conflict isn't over. So find a way to deal with it, and be strong."

"Yes, Captain," Alex said.

"I'm sorry for your loss, and believe me, I've been there," she said. "How do things look on the ground?"

"The landing port is in shambles," Alex said. "But Master Sergeant Brooks has things well in hand."

"Very good. Your plan worked. We took out the majority of their invasion force with minimum losses. Your team gave us the time and the ability to hold this planet. You should be proud of that."

"Yes, Captain," Alex said, even though all he could think about at that moment was revenge.

A voice carried through the transmission. Alex couldn't make out the words, but suddenly Captain Chastain was gone.

*Alex, stand by. Something's going on.*

"Okay," Alex said.

A minute passed, then another. Alex was beginning to feel worried. He imagined more drop ships descending to the planet. For all he knew, the eight ships that initially came down from the Zen Tech carrier in orbit were merely the first wave. Then again, the CDF had more forces than the remnants of Echo and Romeo Companies; there were at least twice as many MBS's at the base camp. If the Zen Tech ship sent more fighters, Captain Chastain would be ready.

*Alex, there's a problem. A company transport has entered the system.*

"Why is that a problem?"

*Because the* Republic *is no longer here to protect them. And it looks like the Zen Tech battleships are moving to intercept the transport. Your team's MBS's are the only assets capable of stopping them.*

"Are you saying you want us to fight battleships?" Alex asked.

*Captain Chastain has the drop ship powering up right now. We're going to carry you into orbit.*

"What? That's insane."

*You need to meet us halfway.*

"We can't—we're almost out of power."

*You're just below half a charge. The drop ship will do the heavy lifting. Once you're in zero-gravity, you'll expend much less power.*

"Ace, is this for real?" Ash asked.

"We're going to orbit?" Sly added.

"We do what they tell us," Alex said. "Let's get someone to disconnect these power cables. There isn't a moment to waste."

# Chapter 31

Nyx walked out of the multipurpose building with the group. The cold outside had turned from bitter to painful as day turned to night. She wondered how anything could survive in the harsh environment. She had grown up on a space station with climate control where it stayed a perfect seventy-two degrees year-round.

Captain Chastain was in a hurry. They were leaving all their equipment except for the PCCs. Lieutenant Cooper was staying behind, as well. Only the Captain, Nyx, and the two controllers for Ash and Sly would take the drop ship back to orbit. There was still no word on why the mission was so important. The rational thing to do was to order the transport to turn around and return through the space tunnel it had arrived through before the battleships destroyed it in retaliation for the loss of their operators and ships on Carthage Prime.

The little group hurried onto the ship, which was powered up and ready to go. More importantly to Nyx, the life support was on, and the temperature inside was much warmer than outside. She sat in a seat in the shuttle's first row and whispered into her headset mic.

"Alex, what's your status?"

"Still waiting for the techs to unhook us from the power lines," he responded.

"We're about to take off," Nyx explained. "I'll send our flight plan to you once we're in the air. Just head south once you're able."

"We can do that. Any word on why this transport is so important?"

"None," Nyx admitted. "Once you reach the ship, you'll need to match our speed, then use your magnetic clamping abilities to stick yourself to the hull."

"Okay," Alex said.

"I'll be right here the whole time."

She hoped her presence was reassuring to him. Alex had been through a lot in the past twenty-four hours, and things didn't seem to be slowing down at all. The toll for holding Carthage Prime had proven costly. Thirteen operators were dead, and four more were seriously wounded and wouldn't be able to continue as operators. That left just a handful to protect the colony. Lima Company, which consisted of twelve AT Interceptors, was already on their way north to join the group protecting the citizens in case the Zen Tech forces tried another attack. The presence of the FA Titans made the Zen Tech forces wary, but if they got wind that the Titans had left the planet, which they surely would, they might risk another drop ship full of Vipers or Hunters. If so, things in Tunis were bound to get ugly fast.

The drop ship lifted off and began flying north. Nyx tapped into the ship's network, got a heading from the navigation computer, and sent the info to Alex. If he could get moving, they would need less than an hour to meet in the air.

Captain Chastain appeared from the cockpit, where Nyx guessed she was giving the pilot orders or perhaps using the ship's communication system. Chastain looked tired, which made Nyx feel tired. She missed the comforts of being on board a ship where she could work in shifts and get regular rest and meals. She hadn't eaten in a while and was tired of wearing the PCC. Still, she wouldn't leave

Alex in the lurch, not even for a soft bed and a gourmet meal.

"Do you have a status on the Titan team?" Captain Chastain asked.

It was courtesy to ask, but the truth was, if Nyx didn't know their status, she wasn't doing her job.

"Yes, Captain. Unfortunately, they're still at the colony, waiting to be cleared by the technicians."

"I've sent word that we need them ASAP."

"Captain, may I ask why the transport doesn't just leave the system?" Nyx asked.

Chastain settled into the seat next to Nyx and fastened her safety harness. She even closed her eyes for a few seconds before replying.

"The transport is malfunctioning," the captain said. "Comms are down, so we can't warn them of the danger. And either their radar is down and they don't see the danger, or for some reason they can't turn back."

"Why would a company transport be coming all the way out here?" asked one of the other controllers.

"That's a very good question," Chastain said. "We don't know for certain. Nothing is scheduled that we know of. My guess is that Vice President Haley is coming to check on our efforts."

"The Vice President of Ahzco security?" Nyx said. "But why would he come out here?"

"He has a propensity for checking on projects personally," Captain Chastain said. "I've always admired that about him. He was an operator once upon a time. But in this instance, I wish he weren't coming."

"We don't know for sure that it's him, do we?" Nyx asked.

"No, we don't know...we can't know. But neither can we risk letting him get captured or killed. Do you know what a rival corporation would do with a powerful executive from Ahzco?"

"Ransom, maybe," said one of the other controllers.

"We could hope to be so lucky," Captain Chastain said. "If Vice President Haley is on that shuttle, he carries with him the knowledge of all our CDF assets, deployment numbers, and the secrets to our INC technology—and that's just in the security division. He's also privy to other proprietary information that would give a competitor an edge over Ahzco. We can't take the chance that they whisk him away to torture him for information."

"But if he gets captured, won't the company just make changes?" asked the third controller.

"Yes, but think of the time and money that will be wasted," Chastain said. "Not to mention, we'll be seen as vulnerable. Vice President Haley is more than just an executive; he's the face of the CDF to the galaxy at large. Losing him would hurt us in ways we can't even imagine."

The weight of urgency was just settling in for Nyx when Alex spoke through her headset.

"We're on the move," he said.

"The Titan team is in transit, Captain," Nyx said.

"Excellent. Time until contact?"

"Forty-seven minutes," Nyx said, checking Alex's airspeed against the drop ship's. It was a complicated formula—two objects moving toward each other at different speeds over a vast distance—but Nyx had always been good with numbers. Her mind fixed on the answer without wrestling with the data. She had no trouble trusting that her estimate was accurate.

"Catching the Zen Tech battleships won't be easy," Captain Chastain said. "But what else can we do but try?"

# Chapter 32

"There it is," Ash said, referring to the drop ship that was flying toward them.

"I see it," Alex replied. "Let's swing around and start working to match their speed."

It felt strange for only three Titans to be flying. There had only been three training suits at the facility on Helena Prime, and they had often trained in trios, but since the mission on Carthage Prime began, they had done most things as a group of four. Alex had to shake off his thoughts and feelings about Newt's death. It was counterproductive, and while he didn't know much about the mission they were being sent on, he knew it would require his full focus.

"Nyx, we see you," Alex said via the link he shared with his controller.

*Roger that. Prepare to make contact with the hull. When you do, I'll activate the electromagnetic portions of your armor that will adhere you to the hull.*

"Do you have readings on my power levels?"

*Yes, I have full system readings. You've got more than a quarter of your available power. Once we reach orbit and break out of gravity, that should be enough to power your Titan for eight to twelve hours.*

"All right, keep an eye on it for me. The idea of going into a mission with only a fraction of our usual power makes me nervous. Any word on the transport?"

*We don't have contact with the ship, and it isn't turning back. Odds are, there's a malfunction that's keeping it here. Captain Chastain believes that VP Haley may be on board, so we've got to do something to try and help.*

Alex thought VP Haley must have dreadful luck. By the time the Titan Team reached outer space, the Zen Tech battleships would have a huge lead on them. Just catching up would be difficult. Perhaps, he thought, they could distract the heavily armed battleships, but he didn't really think there was a lot more they could do. Anything was possible in a fight, but Alex didn't relish being attacked by a ship with dozens of laser cannons and missile launchers. One wrong move and he would be dead, just like Newt.

"All right team, let's match the drop ship's speed," Alex said as they closed in above the ship. "Sly, you come in on the ship's port side. Ash, you take starboard. I'll make contact on top."

"You got it, team leader," Sly said.

"How come you get to ride on top?" Ash teased.

Alex knew the drop ship was faster than they were and could outrun them if it tried. Instead, it cruised at a relatively slow speed, and Alex had little difficulty coming in from above and making a gentle landing on top. He inverted the Titan suit so that he was flying in the same direction but with his back to the ship's roof. Meter by meter he closed in on the ship.

"I'm close, Nyx," Alex said. "With my back to the ship's roof."

*Activating the electromagnets now.*

Alex felt the powerful magnets pull him against the hull of the ship with a thump.

*Wow, that was loud.*

Alex didn't respond. He could hear a strange keening sound, and his mind seemed to be scrambling. It felt like there was a storm raging in his mind, with hot rain bouncing around in his skull. The ship, now with Alex and his friends on the hull, engaged the main engines and shot upward like a rocket. The wind was howling around him, but Alex didn't feel it. He couldn't hear the roar of the engines or their passage through the upper atmosphere—yet he somehow *felt* the surge of the engines, not through the hull but through his INC. He could sense the power of the vessel, and almost without thinking he began to transfer power from the drop ship's fusion reactor to his Titan MBS. The energy flowed through the ship's hull and into his battle suit.

*Hold on, what's happening?*

Alex didn't answer. He could read the drop ship's instrument readings; they were passing thirty thousand meters. He could feel the pings from a distant radar and even sense the passengers and crew on board. It was a radical feeling, as if his mind had suddenly grown, doubling or even tripling in size. He thought about Ash and suddenly knew everything about her Titan. He began to transfer energy to her Titan battle suit the same as his own.

*This is boring.*

Alex was shocked. It was as if Ash had spoken directly into his brain.

*Passing forty thousand meters,* her controller said. *All systems are...*

*Are what?* Ash asked.

*That is so strange. Your battle suit's power is increasing at an exponential rate.*

Alex grinned. He reached out through his mental link to Sly's Titan and fed power to it as well.

*Alex,* Nyx asked, *what is happening? Can you hear me?*

"Yes, I hear you, Nyx. I hear everything."

*What do you mean?*

"I don't know what you did, but I'm picking up the drop ship through my INC."

*That's not possible.*

"Actually, it is. We just passed fifty thousand meters. The ship is at seventy percent power, even while recharging all three Titans."

*Alex, are you okay?*

"Check the altitude."

There was a pause, and Alex knew Nyx was trying to figure out what was happening, but he already knew. He couldn't help but laugh.

*Why are you laughing?*

"I can almost hear you thinking," Alex said. "Trying to figure this out."

*It's not possible. The drop ship doesn't have an INC-compatible system.*

"And yet I can feel it. The information is pouring into my mind like a fire hydrant, I'm diverting power to our suits, and that isn't all."

*What isn't all?*

"I can hear Ash talking to her controller."

Alex focused on Sly and heard him too. He did a quick weapons' check and saw that he had eighteen missiles left, his suit's power was at three quarters, and Sly was humming a song completely out of tune.

*That's...*

"Impossible? I know it, but somehow I'm doing it."

The strange keening sound had transformed to an almost musical pitch, weaving in and out of the lower tones of his connection with his Titan MBS. The two sounds weren't dissonant, but rather worked together like two parts of the same melody. He closed his eyes and focused on the information flowing into him. It felt like a surge of intoxicating power, and not just from the energy recharging his suit; it was a feeling of total control. He knew in that instant that if he lost his connection with Nyx, he could still operate the Titan MBS.

*You're connecting via your INC to the drop ship and both other Titans?*

"Yes."

*I have to tell the captain.*

# Chapter 33

"Captain!" Nyx said.

"Yes, Sergeant West?" Captain Chastain was listening to the communication coming from the cockpit, the base camp, and Tunis on a small headset. She could give orders as needed, but as the drop ship continued climbing through the planet's atmosphere, the only thing she had to do was wait for more information.

Nyx couldn't keep the worry from her voice. She had her headset muted, but would that matter if Alex could really sense the drop ship through his INC? There was no way of knowing.

"I'm not sure if this is a problem or not, but my operator is experiencing an increase in his INC connectivity," Nyx said.

"I don't understand," Captain Chastain said.

"Since connecting to the drop ship via his suit's electromagnets, he can sense the ship itself as if it were his own battle suit."

"That's impossible, Sergeant."

"I know," Nyx said. "But he's doing it. He even transferred power to the Titan battle suits through the ship's hull. His MBS went from just over a quarter to ninety percent power, and it's still climbing."

"My operator's suit is powering up, also," said Ash's controller.

"Mine as well," said Sly's controller.

"He claims he can hear the private links between the other operators and their controllers," Nyx continued, "as well as the communications from the pilots and all the ship's systems."

"If that's possible, then he'll be able to control something we can measure," Captain Chastain said. "Although it sounds like maybe he's experiencing a stress-induced episode."

"Such as turning on and off the cabin lights?" Sly's controller suggested.

"Yes," the captain replied. "That's a measurable outcome. Have your con—"

She stopped speaking in mid-sentence as the lights in the cabin went off and came back on again. They flashed several times, and Captain Chastain looked as if she'd just seen a ghost.

"He can hear us," Nyx said.

"Is my mic transmitting?" Captain Chastain said, pulling the headset off and looking at it as if it held the answers.

"No, he's picking something up," Nyx said. "I think perhaps his INC is malfunctioning."

"That's one way of looking at it," said Sly's controller.

"What's another way?" Chastain asked.

"That he's so sensitive to the EM waves produced by the drop ship and the other Titans that he's picking them up on his INC," the controller explained.

"He's touching the ship via electromagnets," Nyx said. "And the other Titans are, as well. Perhaps it's forming a super-conductive environment."

"There may be elements in the atmosphere or from the planet that could be enhancing the connectivity," Ash's controller said.

Nyx knew they were thinking of the issue like scientists trying to understand a strange phenomenon. Nyx just wanted to make sure Alex was okay, but there was nothing she could do.

"Can the other operators read the drop ship?" Captain Chastain asked.

The other controllers whispered into the mics and then shook their heads.

"Where is Sergeant Evans located on this ship?" Chastain asked.

Nyx pointed up. "The roof."

"Maybe there's something about being on the roof that's enhancing his INC's capabilities. How close are we to orbit?"

"We just passed eighty thousand meters, Captain." Alex's voice boomed through the cabin speakers. "We'll reach zero-gravity in eighteen seconds."

Captain Chastain nodded. "Once we are free of Carthage Prime's gravity, I want all three Titans to launch. We'll worry about your operator's INC once we've dealt with the matter at hand."

"Yes, Captain," Nyx replied.

She sat back in her seat, worrying. Alex's Titan was fully charged and no longer drawing power from the drop ship's reactor. All his systems were green. He only had eleven missiles and half of his soft-alloy projectiles, but that didn't really concern her. She was more afraid that his INC was malfunctioning and might lead to permanent brain injury. She unmuted her headset mic and whispered the captain's orders to Alex.

"Roger that. But I don't think going after the battleships is a good idea," he responded.

"Why not?" Nyx asked.

"They're too far away. Odds are, we won't catch them before they damage or destroy the transport."

"If VP Haley is on board, we have to do something."

"Better to let them capture the transport than risk it getting destroyed," Alex said. "But don't worry, I've got a plan that I think should draw them away from whoever is in that shuttle."

"A plan? Do you want to run it by me or perhaps inform the captain?"

"Sure," Alex said. "The best way to save the transport is to attack the carrier."

Nyx realized that Alex was losing his mind. He was having delusions, and that meant he was a danger to himself, his team, and the mission. She knew what she had to do, but no controller ever wanted to do it. On her PCC, she had a master kill switch. It wouldn't harm Alex, but it would terminate his control of his Titan. It was a simple computer program that slammed the door on the connection between his Implanted Neural Controller and the Titan's advanced computer interface. She could leave him attached to the ship until the mission was over and he could get the help he needed.

Tears welled up in her eyes as her hand hovered over the kill switch. She knew he would hate her for putting him on the sidelines. Yet she felt she had no choice.

"I'm sorry, Alex," she said.

"Sorry for wh—"

His voice was cut off from her headset as soon as she pressed the kill switch. Her heart was racing with worry and fear. Would he hate her? Was he cursing her name at that very moment? Nyx didn't know and wasn't sure she wanted to know. She still had to tell Captain Chastain what had happened.

But before she could, Alex's voice came over the drop ship's speakers again. He was laughing.

"I'm not crazy," he said.

The cabin of the drop ship was silent. Captain Chastain was looking directly at Nyx, who was trembling in her seat.

"Titan team, launch."

# Chapter 34

In space, movement was hard to determine. It had to be relative to another astral body, be that a planet, star, or space vessel. Alex jumped from the drop ship and immediately gave his thrusters a boost. It reminded him in many ways of jumping into the zero-gravity bubble on the *Republic*.

"So what's the plan?" Ash asked. "I've got my controller telling me you've gone insane."

"Yeah, mine mentioned that," Sly said. "What gives?"

"Something happened," Alex said.

He could still feel the drop ship, but he had severed his link with it. A quick check showed that his newfound abilities to sync with other devices via his INC chip was still effective with his team. He could get readings on their MBS's with a mere thought.

"I'm not sure how, but I can sync to your battle suits now," Alex explained.

"How's that?" Sly asked.

Alex activated his friend's stern thruster, sending him head over heels in a slow spin.

"Like that," Alex said.

"Hey man, that's not cool!" Sly shouted.

Alex tapped into the link between Ash and her controller.

*...return to the drop ship immediately.*

"I wouldn't return to the drop ship immediately, Ash, no matter what that controller is telling you," Alex told her.

"You can hear that?" Ash asked.

"If I try," Alex said.

"You mean you can take over our Titans at will?" Sly asked.

"I don't know," Alex said. "I don't think I can wrest control away from you, but I can sync with it. I was connected to both of you and even the drop ship when we were on it."

"You connected to the drop ship?" Ash asked. "It's not even INC-compatible, is it?"

"It isn't supposed to be," Alex said. "But every electronic device emits EM waves. I just found a way to sync up and influence things. Check your power charge."

"Holy crap, I'm at a hundred percent," Sly said.

"I'm fully charged, too," Ash said. "How's that possible?"

"I transferred power from the ship to our suits," Alex said.

"But we weren't connected to the ship's power supply," Ash argued.

"Not in the traditional sense," Alex said. "But the electromagnets that we used to clamp onto the hull created a bond, and I moved the ship's excess power through her hull and into our battle suits. The Titan has a recharge capability. When we entered atmo, our suits converted the heat to energy, so I was able to do the same."

"And you're not crazy?" Sly said.

"I'm not imagining I can do these things, Sly. You can see your power levels. I activated your thrusters. It's real, and I think if I can get close enough, I might be able to tap into the Zen Tech carrier as well."

"You mean, take control of an entire ship?" Ash said.

"Possibly," Alex said. "Let's face it. We aren't going to catch those battleships before they capture or destroy the inbound transport. And even if we could, taking them out isn't likely. But if we present a threat to the carrier, maybe they'll call the battleships back to help."

"Ambitious," Ash said. "But neither plan is likely to work. I say one is as good as the other."

"Fine by me," Sly said. "But taking on that carrier ship is a big risk."

"Which is why you aren't going to do it," Alex said. "I want the two of you to do a fly by, just close enough to be a threat, but not so close that you're in danger of their weapons."

"And what are you going to do?" Ash said.

"Get close enough to test my theory," Alex said. "You distract them, and I'll run in and see what I can do."

"If you get killed, can I be team leader?" Sly asked.

"You can be team leader now," Alex said. "I've got no problems with that."

"Nah," Sly replied. "I like things the way they are. So don't die."

"And don't make us have to come rescue you, either," Ash said. "There's no need to be a hero."

"Roger that," Alex said. "Just follow my lead, then. Turn to heading two-one-seven and watch for that carrier to open fire. If it does, you get out of there as fast as possible."

The trio split up. Alex moved as close to the planet as he could get while staying in orbit. The Zen Tech carrier ship was in sight but too far away to be a threat. Alex hoped that by staying close to the planet, he might not be seen until he was close enough to avoid the carrier's weapons.

The connection to Nyx was still severed, and while Alex's new abilities allowed him to control his Titan on his own, he couldn't replace Nyx's instincts or the ability to have someone watching his back. He reached out with his mind and engaged the PCC using the Titan's controls in reverse. It was a bit like jogging backwards. He had no trouble doing it, but the process felt a little bit risky.

*Alex, did you just reestablish a connection?*

He could hear her in his head and felt a little better for it. They were a team, and he didn't like that she had tried to cut off his control of the Titan battle suit. But he couldn't hold it against her, either. She was following orders, and his abilities were unprecedented. Still, that wasn't going to stop him from using his newfound power to accomplish the mission at hand.

"Hi Nyx," Alex said. "Sorry to usurp control, but a lot is changing, and there isn't time to explain it all."

*What's that mean, Alex? We're very worried about you.*

"Don't be," Alex said. "We've got a plan. I'm going to get as close as I can to the Zen Tech carrier and see if I can connect with their ship the way I did with the drop ship."

*That's not possible, Alex. Their technology isn't the same as ours.*

"Maybe not, but I can hear it. Their ship is blasting EM waves, and if I can sync with them, I can disrupt their plans."

*Or get vaporized. It's too risky.*

"Sly and Ash are going to create a diversion. It might be enough for the carrier to call back their escort ships," Alex went on, undeterred by Nyx's concern. "It's the best chance we have. You know we'll never catch those battleships in time."

There was a moment of silence. Alex didn't know if Nyx was thinking about things or if she was discussing his plan with Captain Chastain. Either way, he wasn't going to change his mind. Even if he was successful, he might be ruining his career by disobeying orders, yet it was the only chance they had of saving the transport and perhaps truly defeating the Zen Tech forces in the Carthage system.

*Okay, Alex. We can't stop you. Can you at least stay in contact with us?*

"Of course," he said. "I'm not trying to be a problem, Nyx. Please convey that to Captain Chastain. I just know this is the right course of action."

*How can I help?*

"Turn the drop ship this way."

*We don't have weapons on this vessel, Alex. It's more of a passenger shuttle than a military-grade drop ship.*

"Yeah, I know. But the Zen Tech people don't. We need to make them feel threatened so that they call the battleships back to defend them."

*I'll see what I can do.*

He wished they could all understand that he was trying to do the same thing; he wanted to see what he could do and how far his new abilities would take him. It wasn't pride or insanity, but merely the discovery of a new weapon. His mind had become more powerful than his Titan battle suit or the weapons on the battleship. If he could disrupt an enemy ship using his Implanted Neural

Controller, he could save lives by ending a dispute before shots were even fired.

The Zen Tech carrier ship was still nearly a hundred kilometers away, but the EM waves were strong. Alex reached out with his mind, trying to find a way to connect with the rival vessel. Since getting his INC, he had trained himself not to hear every EM wave that he came into contact with. The cacophony of noise from every electrical device around him would drive anyone insane. It was like listening to an orchestra with a thousand instruments all playing different music at the same time. The waves coming from the Zen Tech carrier were loud but had a completely different cadence than the Ahzco devices. They sounded like out-of-tune pianos, and it took him several minutes to find the pattern in the noise and adjust his mind to it.

*Alex, are you okay?*

"Yeah, just trying to adapt," he said.

He was less than fifty kilometers from the carrier and well within range of their weapons when things finally started to make sense in his mind.

*Ash and Sly are drawing some interest. The carrier is tracking them, but I don't think they've noticed you yet.*

"Good," Alex said through clenched teeth.

It felt like he was trying to plug into a recharge line from fifty kilometers away. It was too difficult, and he knew he needed to get closer.

"I just need a little more time."

*You're in the danger zone. If they pick you up on their radar, you'll be an easy target.*

"I know, but I've got to get closer."

*You're forty klicks from their position. Captain Chastain is moving the drop ship toward you. The battleships are still moving toward the transport. They're not feeling threatened by us.*

Alex wanted to curse his bad luck, but he knew it wouldn't help. He had to set his emotions aside. Fear would only cloud his mind, and anger wouldn't get him connected to the carrier any faster.

He felt a thrill as he began to pick up snatches of identifiable data from the Zen Tech ship. It was like seeing a city through a dense fog that was slowly breaking up.

"I think it's working," Alex said.

*You're thirty klicks away. Ash and Sly are turning back.*

Alex remembered the first time he had successfully synced his INC chip to a device. The feeling had been small but solid, like bringing two magnets together, one in each hand, and feeling them jump together with a snap. The connection with the Zen Tech ship was just as solid, only on a much larger scale. His mind seemed to expand when he connected with the drop ship and his fellow Titan operators, but the carrier was a huge vessel with more systems than Alex was prepared for. It was like trying to catch a thousand balls that had all been thrown toward him at the same moment. For a few seconds, he felt like his mind might rip apart. It was too much information and too many things to decipher at once, but with each second he felt the pressure back off. His mind was reeling with new information. He could feel the Zen Tech carrier's weapons systems tracking Ash and Sly. The radar was locked on the drop ship. Threat assessments were being run. The ship was on high alert.

"Nyx, take flight controls," Alex said.

*Are you okay, Alex? You sound stressed.*

"It's a lot of information," he replied. "But I'm in."

The Zen Tech battleships were standing by to turn back and help. There were two more companies of operators on board, ready to launch toward the planet. He could feel the entire vessel's massive array of systems, from propulsion to life support. Better still, he could control them. He sent word to the battleships to turn back and return to orbit.

"Take me right to their hull," Alex told Nyx.

*Won't they see you?*

"It doesn't matter now," he said. "I have complete control."

# Chapter 35

They did see him. Radar picked up the Titan suit immediately. He was still twenty kilometers away, a direct threat. Alex felt the ship's computers tracking him, formulating a firing solution for the starboard bow laser cannon. He even felt the big gun accumulating power. At short range, even with the Titan suit's armor, he would simply vanish. The big laser blast would reduce him and the MBS to atoms.

*Alex, they're preparing to fire on you,* Nyx warned him.

The warning wasn't necessary. Alex shut down the entire weapons system on the Zen Tech carrier as easily as blinking his eyes. It was almost involuntary. What Alex couldn't hear were the panicked voices on board the ship, unless they were picked by the communication officer's microphone. He heard indecipherable shouting in the background as the comms officer questioned the battleship commanders who had changed course and were returning to the carrier in orbit.

"It's all good," Alex said. "Prepare to connect me to their hull the same way you did with the drop ship."

*Okay.*

"Titan team, return to the drop ship," Alex ordered.

"Yes, team leader," Sly said.

"You okay, Alex?" Ash asked.

"Never better. Nyx, can you connect me with Captain Chastain?"

*She's on the command channel of your com-link. I'm activating it now.*

Alex couldn't deny the fact that he needed help. The Zen Tech carrier's systems were so vast that it took all his focus to control them and to keep track of what the crew was doing to discover what had happened to their weapons. He was grateful for Nyx and excited at the same time by the incredible power he was suddenly able to control.

"Sergeant Evans, what is your sit rep?" Captain Chastain asked. He could hear her through the Titan's tiny but well-designed helmet speakers. It sounded different to him than the flow of information being poured directly into his brain.

"I'm closing on the Zen Tech carrier *Yomi*. I have full control of the ship's systems, Captain. I've shut down their weapons and recalled the battleships."

"You're sure?" Captain Chastain asked.

"Positive, Captain. I can shut down their artificial gravity or even their life support systems," Alex said. "I can overload their fusion reactor, deactivate their escape pods, flood the ship with carbon dioxide, or send them on a course straight toward the system star."

There was a moment of silence. Alex knew that over the command channel, everyone could hear him—even the operators and controllers on the planet below if the signal was strong enough.

"And you're controlling their ship with your INC?" Chastain asked.

"The same way we control our battle suits," Alex said.

"Can you patch me through to their commander?"

"Yes, Captain."

The connection was easy enough. Communications from ships to planets all utilized the same technology. It was only the frequencies that were different. Alex adjusted the *Yomi's* com frequency so that they picked up the Ahzco command channel.

"You're patched into the *Yomi's* bridge, Captain," Alex said. "They can hear everything on the command channel."

"Zen Tech carrier, *Yomi*, you are under Ahzco control. Please state your name and rank, commander."

There was a pause, then a new voice spoke up.

"This is Admiral Li, to whom am I speaking?"

Li's voice was full of trepidation. Alex couldn't feel the tension on the bridge of the *Yomi*, but he could imagine it.

"This is Captain Chastain of the Ahzco CDF. You are in violation of the Free Trade Association's guidelines for planetary operations. Your invasion forces have been destroyed, and we now have control of your ship. You are hereby ordered to leave this system forthwith and cease all attempts to thwart Ahzco operations."

Another pause. Alex couldn't hear anything over the ship's communication channel, which the officer had wisely muted. From the *Yomi's* radar, which was much more powerful than anything Ahzco had in the system, Alex noticed the Zen Tech freighter creeping around from the dark side of the planet. It was coming toward the Ahzco drop ship from behind.

Alex switched his own com channel so that he could speak to Ash and Sly without being heard by the officers on the bridge of the *Yomi*. Dividing his concentration between his own battle suit and the huge array of systems on the rival ship was difficult, but not impossible, as long as he didn't do anything too complicated.

"Titans, the Zen Tech freighter is approaching the drop ship from her blind side," Alex said.

"I see it," Ash said.

"It shouldn't be armed, but I wouldn't count on that," Alex said. "I'm guessing Nyx is already warning the captain. Stand by for orders."

"Roger," Sly said.

The *Yomi* was a huge ship. Alex had closed in to within a few hundred meters. He wasn't monitoring his battle suit's systems, but he could tell that Nyx had slowed his progress. She needed to get him close, but not so close that he would crash into the ship. He switched over to his private channel that he shared only with Nyx.

"You get that?"

*I did. The Captain is giving Ash and Sly orders to fend off the freighter, but she wants Admiral Li to call the ship off first. She's waiting for them to respond.*

"How close are we to their ship?"

*About a hundred meters. This is extremely hard without visuals.*

"You don't have visual feed on your PCC?"

*No, and I'm using the drop ship's radar.*

"I have faith in you, Nyx. Get me on that ship."

Before she could reply, Admiral Li came back online.

"We do not recognize your claim to Carthage Prime or the system's space," Li said. "Your forces are outnumbered and outclassed. Surrender now and your operators will be spared."

Captain Chastain responded immediately.

"You will recognize it when we shut down your life support systems," she snapped. "Call off your freighter or my Titans will open fire."

"Your aggression is well-noted and will not be tolerated," Admiral Li replied. "We have control of the system, and that includes your ground forces. If you choose to fight, we will have no choice but to terminate all Ahzco personnel."

"Titan One, show them the measure of our resolve," Captain Chastain said.

Alex immediately shut down the *Yomi's* artificial gravity. He heard shouting over the com channel before it was muted. Next, he cut the power to the ship's lights.

"As you can see, Admiral, we are not bluffing. This is your last chance. Call off the freighter, set an immediate course out of the system, and do not molest our incoming transport. Acknowledge this command, and I will restore your vessel to your control."

After several tense seconds, Admiral Li replied. "As you wish."

"Thank you," Captain Chastain said. "Titan One, restore control to Admiral Li and his crew."

"Affirmative, Captain," Alex said.

He brought the gravity back online and turned the lights on, but he kept the ship's weapons powered off. He felt the crew's attempts to fire the weapons, but it was an exercise in futility. Every system on the ship was his to control, at the speed of thought. Even if they could bring the weapons up on a different computing system, he would sense it and intervene.

*Twenty meters,* Nyx informed him. *Do you still want to be attached to the* Yomi*'s hull?*

"Yes," Alex said. "Tell Captain Chastain that I'll ride out with the carrier and make sure they don't harm the transport."

*Okay, but my PCC won't reach that far. It's not made for long-range contact.*

"I'll be okay on my own."

*You're sure?*

"Yeah, I don't think the battleships will fire on their own ship, even if they spot me on the hull. And if they try, I've got control of the *Yomi*'s weapons."

*You know this changes everything, Alex. Nothing will be the same.*

He knew she was right. Odds were good that the medical technicians would want to study his brain, while the RDT department would want to find a way to replicate his abilities. He might end up spending the next twenty years in a laboratory running tests and being bored silly. If that were the case, he hoped they didn't separate him from Nyx.

"I didn't ask for this power," Alex said.

*I know.*

"And I'm not crazy."

*We know that now. I'm just glad you're okay.*

For the time being he was okay, but he couldn't help but wonder if that would last. He had taken a huge leap forward, but there might be some people who would feel threatened by his ability. And for all Alex knew, it was temporary. He might climb out of the Titan and never be able to sync with anything outside his battle suit again.

# Chapter 36

Loman Haley was standing in the passage between the cockpit and the crew cabin. It was actually a prep area for the attendants whose job was to make sure the passengers had all they needed. The seats in the long-range transport were spread apart from the others with privacy enclosures. They could also recline from a sitting position to a flat sleeping surface.

For seven days, Loman had lived and worked from the cabin. He was the lone passenger, traveling along the FTA open route toward the newest planet in their chain of free worlds. But something had gone wrong just before they'd made the final jump through the space tunnels that linked the star systems. Communications were down, and power levels were fluctuating. The ship needed help, and the closest planet was Carthage Prime, although it seemed that his CDF forces had been overrun.

"They're leaving orbit," the pilot said.

"What are those battleships doing?" Loman asked.

"They haven't changed course," the pilot said. "We're safe for now."

"For now—that's not very reassuring," Loman said. "Where the hell is the *Republic*?"

"Still no sign of her, Mr. Haley. They could be on the dark side of the planet, but I kind of doubt it."

"Trajectory of that carrier isn't favorable," the co-pilot said. "It's heading straight toward us."

"Toward us or toward the space tunnel?" asked the pilot.

"What are those tiny blips?" Loman asked, pointing at some specks on the radar near the planet.

"Could be a satellite," said the pilot. "But they haven't been approved for this planet yet."

"Could be a surveillance ship," the co-pilot guessed.

"Or a drop ship, we really can't tell," the pilot continued. "Without our communications, we're dead in the water. It could be anything. And we can't even request help."

"We could make a run for the space tunnel," Loman said.

"I'll do that only if you order me to, sir," the pilot said. "With our power acting up, we could get stuck in that tunnel and lost. It isn't worth the risk."

"That's because you don't know what those Zen Tech bastards will do to me if we're captured," Loman said.

He knew all too well. His forces had captured enemy combatants, but a high-level executive was different matter altogether. And they were in a new system. No one would be able to prove that Zen Tech had captured his transport. They could sneak him away to one of their own worlds and torture him for company secrets. It was barbaric, but they were well beyond the civilized systems. Anything could happen on the frontier, and often did. Loman already suspected that his entire security force, six companies of operators and controllers, had been wiped out by the Zen Tech force—not to mention the *Republic*. It was a devastating loss, probably the worst in company history since he'd taken control of the CDF. But he didn't think he'd be alive long enough to face the consequences. Everything seemed to be going wrong all at once.

"The battleships have stopped," the co-pilot warned. "Looks like they're waiting on the carrier."

"It's probably coming to gloat over us," Loman said.

"They can't know that you're on board," the pilot pointed out. "Our own forces didn't even know we were coming."

None of it made sense. Upon arriving in the system, Loman had found enemy forces in orbit. Two Zen Tech battleships had been sent to intercept them. Loman had been hoping to see the *Republic* appear and come to their rescue, but that hadn't happened. Instead, for some reason that no one could fathom, the battleships turned back, and now the carrier was heading toward them. All Loman knew for sure was that he couldn't let himself be captured. He was a strong man, but even the strongest would reveal their deepest secrets under the strain of torture. The only way for Loman to ensure that he didn't betray Ahzco and spend the rest of his life in complete agony was to end it before the enemy got their hands on him.

He reached down to his coat pocket, as he had so many times since entering the system. There was a small laser pistol tucked inside. He had retrieved it from his personal belongings once he realized there might be a need to ensure he didn't fall into a rival corporation's hands. It was both terrifying and reassuring to feel the weight of the small weapon, knowing that while he didn't have many choices left, ultimately his fate was in his own hands.

"How long do we have?" Loman asked.

"We're four hours out of orbit," the pilot said. "The carrier is still building speed, but my best guess would be an hour before they reach us."

An hour left to live. It wasn't much, and Loman felt the bitter sense of futility over the hopelessness of his situation. Of course, circumstances could change. An hour wasn't much time, but it was some time. He walked back to his seat and picked up his PIL. It was encrypted, but he couldn't let it fall into enemy hands. The device was his only link to his computer and all the information on Ahzco's Corporate Defense Force. He would have to destroy it as well, if worse came to worst. He would jettison the Personal Information Link out the trash chute once it was clear that no help was coming. Then he would savor one last drink before putting the little gun to his head and making sure that he was beyond the reach of his enemies forever.

# Chapter 37

Alex couldn't help but smile. He knew the transport was on the Zen Tech carrier's radar, even though he couldn't see the small ship from his place affixed to the hull. It was the sound of the transport's EM waves that made Alex smile. The ship was over a hundred kilometers away, and yet Alex could feel it. Perhaps it was due to the emptiness of space. On Helena Prime there had been hundreds, perhaps thousands of different signals all pounding at him from different sides. He had learned to ignore them, to turn their uproar into an indistinguishable background noise until his brain completely tuned it out, and he had to focus just to hear it again. But in space, there was no roar, especially as they moved away from the planet and far from the drop ship where his own people were transmitting.

Alex had pulled his mind back from all the carrier's systems save their weapons controls. He kept them shut down, the way one might keep a single eye closed or breathe only through their mouth to avoid a bad smell. It was a bit like freeing up memory on a computer so that there was room for different programs to run at the same time. He synced his Implanted Neural Controller with the battleships, focusing on their weapons systems long enough to knock them offline in several places. The technicians on board were undoubtedly working to fix the problems, but Alex knew it would take time. All he really needed was the insurance that none of the Zen Tech ships would harm the transport. If that happened, he would destroy them all.

The freighter was actually a military ship in disguise. There were hidden weapons behind faux panels. The ship could eject the panels and bring the weapons to bear—except that Alex had disabled those systems as well. He planned to ride the carrier long enough to reach the transport, identify what was wrong with the small passenger ship, and use the carrier's communication array to send word back to the planet. Then he could detach himself from the Zen Tech ship and fly back. He had plenty of power, and with the rival ships running scared, he had nothing left to fear in the Carthage system.

The transport had altered course slightly, trying to put a little more distance between themselves and the approaching Zen Tech vessels. But they were still moving toward each other, and Alex had no difficulties syncing with the transport. The sound in his mind, like music, sounded off-key, as if the systems producing the EM waves were out of tune. It took Alex several moments to discover a malfunction in the reactor. Something was causing the power to surge. It was a problem in the balance of the fusion, and the safety systems had shorted out. He realized the entire ship's power was on the verge of failing, and the other systems were dropping off one by one. Communications were down, as were the ship's sanitation systems. Artificial gravity would be next to go, then the engines. Life support would remain even when the reactor went down completely, using the auxiliary batteries to keep the occupants alive long enough for rescue.

A quick check of the ship's occupants, itinerary, and log, showed that Captain Chastain was right. The ship, Ahzco's *AH08*, had a single occupant, Executive Vice President of Security, Loman Haley. Alex thought it slightly odd that their paths kept crossing, but he didn't dwell on it. Repairing the ship wasn't possible, but he could connect to it and from there act as a go-between. But first he needed to send word that the ship would most likely lose propulsion and navigation capacity before reaching orbit.

He tapped into the carrier's communication array. It was a vast system with multiple techs operating at dozens of stations. Alex found an empty channel, dialed into the Ahzco frequency, and transmitted his message. They were already thousands of kilometers from the planet, and he didn't expect a response. In fact, once he sent his message, he would change the frequency to ensure it wasn't copied by anyone else on the carrier.

"Ahzco drop ship, this is Titan One with an update on the transport inbound. They are losing power. Communications are down. I repeat, the transport is losing power and communications are down. I will transfer to the ship and attempt to make contact. It is my belief that they will lose the ability to pilot the ship and request help to keep the vessel from crashing. Titan One out."

The ships were about to cross paths. Alex detached himself from the carrier and jumped free, engaging his thrusters to fly away from the massive ship. As it passed him, the transport came clearly into view. It was less than three kilometers away, and he could see the running lights on the hull flickering like old incandescent bulbs on the verge of burning out. The transport was a sleek ship, but it looked old and dingy with the running lights flickering. Alex was about to maneuver that way as the battleships followed the carrier past him, but the freighter—which was still several klicks behind the other ships—began to alter course. Alex didn't need to sync with the disguised warship's systems to know it planned to clip the transport. The larger freighter could take a hit, especially on the parts of its hull that were merely cosmetic, without sustaining any real damage, but the transport would be destroyed by the freighter's mass.

Alex focused on the freighter, letting his mind sync with the large ship. It only took a second, and he felt the familiar snap in his mind, the ship's thrumming EM waves becoming a melodic throb. Alex immediately fired all the ship's thrusters on the side nearest the transport. The large ship swung around in a lopsided flop away from the transport—but unfortunately right toward Alex.

His first instinct was to call for help. With his mind burdened by the freighter's multiple systems, he had to wrench his mind back to the controls of his Titan battle suit. He was drifting through space and tried to fire the thrusters to push him out of the freighter's path, but he was too late. The big ship hit the very bottom edge of the Titan's foot, crushing the limb in the process. Alex felt the sudden jarring sensation followed by a searing pain as his shin bone snapped. The blow not only damaged the battle suit, it sent Alex spinning through space.

Pain and fear paralyzed Alex, and he was helpless for several moments. Then the pain settled into a terrible, aching throb that was just manageable. If he'd had to move his leg—or worse yet, put his weight on it—he would have been done for. But the suit's padding compressed around the wound, holding it fast, the counter-pressure easing the pain just a bit. He focused on regaining control of his battle suit. His experience in the zero-gravity bubble onboard the *Republic* once more came to his aid. There were no walls to bounce off of or grab onto, but he used the thrusters to correct his spin and regain control of the direction he was moving. He sent the battle suit racing after the transport, which had gotten ahead of him. At the same time, he reconnected with the freighter's computer system. The other Zen Tech ships were out of Alex's range, and he considered for a moment using the freighter's weapons to fire on them. But he couldn't be certain that they wouldn't shoot back and perhaps hit the transport with Vice President Haley inside. He couldn't risk the VP's life for his revenge. Instead, he shut down the ship's systems. The artificial gravity would send the crew reeling. They would have no life support, not even any light to see to fix things. There was a small chance they could get the freighter's systems running again, but Alex was doubtful. The ship was in the process of correcting its spin when the engines shut down, and the bulky vessel was left drifting in the wake of the other Zen Tech ships.

Turning his attention back to the transport, Alex synced with the ship's computer system. He couldn't fix the reactor or even the communication array, but he could speak to the occupants inside using their own internal speakers. It would be a one-way communication, but for the moment that was okay. He only had a single message for them, and he announced it suddenly.

"Ahzco transport, this is Titan One," he said. "Slow down, immediately."

# Chapter 38

Stopping a ship in space was not an easy matter. Inertia was not on their side. The transport's normally powerful engines were malfunctioning, and all they could manage was to fire their weak bow thrusters.

"What's happening?" Loman said as he clung desperately to the opening that led to the cockpit.

The transport's artificial gravity was down, and anything not secured was floating freely in the spaceship, including Loman Haley. The two attendants had managed to get to their safety seats and strap in. The pilots were already strapped into their seats in the cockpit. Only Loman was left floating, along with most of his belongings. The lights were flickering inside the ship, and it was clear that the ship was about to lose all power.

"We just got a message," the pilot said.

"The comms are working?" Loman demanded.

"Negative, sir," the co-pilot said. "We have no idea where the message came from."

Suddenly the ship's engine shut down and the lights went off, along with all the instrument panel readings. The only light was from the system star and the reflection of the light off of Carthage Prime. It looked like a spark far, far away. Loman felt fear squeezing his heart, as if it were being encased in ice.

"Power's out," the pilot said.

Suddenly the lights came back on, and the heated air circulators began to hum.

"We have life support," the co-pilot announced. "We'll be okay as long as the auxiliary batteries have power."

"Except we're headed right for the planet and moving too fast," the pilot said. "We'll bounce off the atmosphere and go spinning off into space."

"Unless there's help," Loman said. "Surely someone on Carthage Prime can help us."

"I don't see how," the pilot said.

For a moment, no one spoke. The horror of their predicament was difficult to come to terms with. Loman heard one of the attendants sniffling behind him.

"You all heard the transmission," Loman said. "Someone knows about our problem."

"I don't know how they sent that message, but you heard it," the pilot said. "They need us to slow down, and we can't. They wouldn't have told us that if they had a plan to stop us."

"The *Republic* isn't even in the system anymore," the co-pilot said. "We'd be fools to think there's hel—"

*Thump!*

The sound reverberated through the ship.

"What was that?" Loman asked.

"Something hit us," the pilot said.

Another thump was heard, followed by a grinding sound. At first Loman thought that something was trying to get inside the ship, but then the sound repeated. He thought it was louder, maybe closer.

"We've got something on the ship," Loman said. "Probably an FA Titan with one of our guys inside."

Another thump, scrape, repeat. Then, after a moment of silence, the upper body of a Titan MBS slid down from the roof of the cockpit to the transparent viewport. Loman would have fallen on his backside if there had been any gravity to pull him down when he saw the operator's call sign painted on the chest portion of the battle suit. Even upside down he could read the initials "ACE" in bold, white paint.

"My God," Loman said. "That's Evans."

# Chapter 39

Despite the pain in his leg, Alex had managed to catch the transport. It had slowed slightly just before losing all power. Unfortunately, with most of the ship's systems down, Alex couldn't sync with it. His ability to communicate with the ship was lost, but that didn't mean he couldn't help. He was beginning to hear the distant EM waves from the drop ships and his team members. Soon, he'd be able to call for help, but until then he was determined to do all he could to save the ship.

Once he reached the viewport, he could see the shocked faces inside. Two pilots and Vice President Loman Haley looked at him with surprise. He would have waved if his battle suit had arms, but all Alex had were his weapons. Without losing his magnetic grip on the transport, he twisted around, flinging his one good leg and one damaged leg out in front of the ship. Then he fired his thrusters. The sudden power pushed him along the hull a short way, but he quickly increased the power to the electromagnet, securing him to the transport's hull. The force of his main thruster, which was attached to the lower part of the battle suit's legs, began to slow the ship. Alone, it was futile effort, but it didn't take long before he heard friendly voices.

"Ace, you are crazy, man," Sly said. "Are you really trying to stop that ship?"

"Don't have a choice," Alex replied. "They've lost power."

"Hold on, we're coming to help," Ash said.

Ash and Sly had traveled a good distance to be in transmission range again. The drop ship was still too far away for Alex to make contact.

"What happened with the freighter?" Ash asked.

"They tried to take a passing shot at the transport," Alex said. "I had their guns shut down, but they tried to clip the ship."

"We saw it go tumbling, but we couldn't tell why," Sly said.

"I fired all the port thrusters at once," Alex said. "But they managed to hit me before I could get clear. I think I broke my leg."

"Is your suit intact?" Ash said.

"By some miracle," Alex said.

"You're lucky," Sly said.

"Tell me about it," Alex replied.

The other two Titans joined Alex and added their own thrusters to help slow the transport. It took almost half an hour, but the ship finally slowed to a manageable drift almost a hundred kilometers from orbit.

"What's the sit rep, Titan leader?" Captain Chastain asked over the command channel once the drop ship was in range.

"The transport has been stopped, but it lost all power, Captain," Alex reported. "We managed to get it stopped, but we still need to get the passengers off."

"Any idea who's inside?"

"Exactly who you suspected," Alex said. "Executive VP Loman Haley is listed as the only occupant."

"Very good work, Titan One. It's time to get everyone safely on the ground. We'll take over from here. Have your team stand by for planetary insertion."

"Roger that," Alex said. "Titan team is standing by."

The drop ship performed an emergency ship-to-ship docking maneuver. VP Haley and the transport's crew were transferred to the drop ship, which then disconnected from the transport and made its way down to the surface of the planet. Alex and his team of Titans followed. Fatigue was setting in. None of them had slept more than an hour or two at a time since the first CDF forces made their way onto Carthage Prime. Alex was looking forward to getting out of his battle suit and into a bed.

But that would prove more difficult that he anticipated. His left leg was broken, and the Titan's foot was damaged. A conventional landing was impossible. Instead, Alex had to land the battle suit on its back—a feat he managed, just not gracefully. The real trouble came when he opened the suit. Once the system shut down, the padding that had increased and held his leg tight released, and the pain increased exponentially. Moving was even worse. He had to be pulled from his suit, and he passed out in the process.

When he woke up several hours later, he was in a medical facility bed. His leg was elevated and encased in a light therapy device. He felt sick, his mouth was incredibly dry, and his eyes were gummy.

"Hello," he managed to croak.

There was no one in the room. He found the bed's controls and elevated his head so that he could look around. There was a water bottle on a table beside him. He opened it, drank some, and splashed a little on a towel to wipe his face with.

"Who's out there? Where am I?"

There was still no answer. Alex was beginning to feel perplexed and angry. Had he just been discarded and forgotten?

"Hello!" he shouted.

Finally, the door to his room opened. Nyx walked in, carrying a cup of coffee. She looked surprised.

"You're awake?"

Alex's bad attitude softened immediately.

"Yeah, what's going on? Did the Zen Tech ships come back?"

"No, everything is fine. How do you feel?"

"Okay, I guess. A little sluggish."

"You're on pain meds."

"I can tell," he said. "How long was I out?"

"Ten hours or so," Nyx explained. "The med bot surgically repaired your leg, but it's going to take a while before you're walking around again."

Alex sat back in his bed, grateful that he could actually relax. The threats were gone, and he had reason to be off his feet. It still felt a little selfish, but as long as his leg was in the therapy device, he really had no choice.

"Do you feel like talking about things?" Nyx asked.

"Sure," Alex said.

"Colonel Chastain and Vice President Haley want to debrief you," Nyx said.

"Colonel Chastain?"

"She was promoted, which was the reason for VP Haley's visit. Of course, all anyone can talk about is you."

"Us," Alex said. "We're a team."

"Are we?" Nyx asked. "You did things you shouldn't have been able to do, Alex. I had no part in it."

"That's not true. You flew for me when I couldn't," Alex said.

"Yes, and you flew even when I used the kill switch," Nyx said.

"Are you angry about that?"

"No, but I'm worried about you."

"About this," he waved at his leg. "It's nothing. I'll be fine."

"No, Alex. I'm worried about you. What you can do, it isn't..."

"Natural?" he tried finishing for her, but she shook her head.

"There's nothing really natural about the INC, is there?"

"I guess not."

"What you did was impossible," Nyx said. "The INC chip is supposed to enhance your mind's ability to interact with technology, but your mind actually enhanced the INC's ability to connect with other devices."

"I didn't mean for it to happen, it just did," Alex said.

"Don't get me wrong," she said with a small smile that made him feel light all over, as if he might float off the bed, "it's a good thing. But you've been cut off from everyone who wasn't part of the rescue mission. From what I gather, the vice president wants to keep your newfound abilities a secret. Ash, Sly, their controllers, and I are all sharing a couple of adjoining rooms. They haven't let us out of the med facility since we landed."

"Because of me?"

She nodded again. "Not that we needed to. We all got some rest. The others are finishing up breakfast. I told you things would change."

"But not between us, right?" Alex said. "You still want to be my controller, don't you?"

"Do you even need one?"

"Yes, I need you," he said, hoping he didn't sound too desperate.

She rewarded him with another smile. "Of course I'll be your controller, if they'll let me. We're in unchartered territory. I wouldn't be surprised if they sent you to a lab somewhere and ran tests to find out what happened."

"No, that's not what I want," Alex said.

"I don't think what we want factors in," Nyx said. "You've just become the most powerful weapon in Ahzco's arsenal, and I don't think they're going to be content with just one of you."

# Chapter 40

Loman stood watching a monitor that showed Alex's room. A computer showed the rejuvenation work on his leg was seventy percent complete, although he would need several days to regain his strength and ensure that the blood flow to his broken leg was adequate. And then what? That was the question plaguing Loman.

"How's the hero?" Colonel Chastain asked as she walked into the small office carrying two cups of coffee.

Loman wished he could add a generous dose of strong alcohol to his, but he took the cup she offered and said thank you.

"Healing," Loman said.

"What's next for Evans?"

"That's what I'm trying to decide."

"It could have been a fluke, you know," she offered, although they both knew it wasn't a fluke.

Perhaps Alex could have gained an unforeseen ability while being magnetically attached to the drop ship, but what he did was much more significant than that. Somehow he had synced his tiny INC chip with rival corporation vessels and manipulated their systems. That was no fluke. Loman had taken the opportunity to run scans of Alex's brain while he was being worked on in the little medical center on Carthage Prime's sole colony. Tunis was a rough place, still in its infancy, but the medical facility was more than adequate. It had a brand-new, full-body diagnostic scanner and a top-of-the-line surgical bot. Yet the scans had found nothing abnormal about Alex's brain. Loman knew he should send Alex to Helena Prime to have his INC checked, but he doubted that there was anything wrong with the technology. Alex's Implanted Neural Controller was the same as that in every operator in the CDF.

"No, I'm not sweeping this under the rug," Loman said. "He really saved us out here. The company has a lot invested in this planet, and the CDF is stretched thin. If the Zen Tech raiders had wiped us out here, we'd have been forced to hire an outside defense firm."

"We took our losses, but it could have been a lot worse," Chastain said. "And if I'm being honest, everything we did once the Zen Tech operators hit the ground came from Alex and his controller, Nyx West."

"What do you mean?"

"I worked up the strategic plans, but they came up with the ideas," she admitted. "I like to think I would have thought of them too, but they beat me to it, just as Alex took control of the rescue in space. He's got a talent for strategy and tactics."

"This kid is mystifying to me," Loman said. "The last thing I want is to stick him in a lab and let the eggheads poke and prod him, hoping they'll learn something. He's the future."

"Some people won't see it that way," Chastain said. "Some people will think he's too powerful."

"I know," Loman said. "I'm one of them. But he's also loyal and smart. I've known in my gut that this kid was the future of the CDF since I met him."

"So you're keeping him in the field?"

"I'm going to try, yes. But we're going to need to keep a close eye on him."

Colonel Chastain's Flex PIL beeped and she glanced at it.

"Good news, I hope?" Loman asked.

"The *Republic* is back in the system," she said. "They must have just come through the space tunnel. Tunis Space Control just received word. They're inbound. ETA is seven hours."

Loman nodded, grateful they wouldn't be stuck on Carthage Prime for weeks waiting for a transport. The ship that brought him to the system was slowly orbiting the planet. If left alone, it would eventually fall into the atmosphere and break apart. It was a space vessel and wasn't built for atmo.

"Excellent. I want a garrison built here," Loman said. "As long as we have a presence on this planet, the locals should know we have their back."

"Not everyone was thrilled by our actions at the spaceport," Chastain said. "I'm hearing word of nasty comments being pointed our way for the damage to their warehouses and goods."

"I'll get it all replaced," Loman said. "We'll rebuild the port and make reparations. But for now, our priority is the people in that room."

He pointed at the small security monitor. Ash and Sly were joking around, and their controllers looked around nervously as they sat together in the corner. Nyx was by Alex's bedside. The boy looked hale enough to Loman. Once the *Republic* was in orbit, he would have them moved to the carrier ship.

Then the true test would begin. If Alex could sync to an enemy ship, he could certainly sync to one of their own. Whether Loman wanted to face it or not, if Alex tried to take control of a military ship, he would have to be stopped, one way or another.

"Get me his controller," Loman said. "I want to talk to her face to face."

# Chapter 41

Nyx's Flex PIL vibrated on her forearm. She glanced at the message: *Report to the administrative office ASAP.*

"I've got to go," she said.

Alex had been talking to Ash and Sly but turned his head toward her.

"What's up?"

"Orders, I suppose," Nyx said. "A debrief. It's probably just the first of many."

"Okay, let us know when you're done," Alex said. "And if you get sent out, just shoot me a quick message. I want to know."

"Sure," she said, hoping she would have the opportunity.

They had been isolated since returning from orbit, and Nyx didn't think that was a good sign. It had been a successful mission, but that didn't mean the brass wouldn't hit them with gag orders and ship them off to isolated planets so insignificant that they didn't even warrant a name.

Nyx was torn between her ambition and her desire to stay with Alex. She had strong feelings for him and was tempted to stay with him no matter what. They might even have a future as more than merely partners—but there was a risk that he might ruin her career. If the senior officers saw Alex as a replicable phenomenon, merely a happy accident, they would ship him off to the RDT division, and she would spend her days in mind-numbingly boring tests. If they saw him as a threat, which in many ways he was,

Alex might get quietly dealt with, and perhaps anyone associated with him as well.

Ahzco was aboveboard, from what Nyx could tell. She had done her research before signing with the CDF, but what Alex could do was a game-changer. An operator in a battle suit was a force to be reckoned with, which was why they were paired with controllers. Her job was to be a second set of eyes and hands when needed, to help run the advanced features of the battle suit while the operator focused on combat. But a controller also had an obligation to make sure their operator didn't go off the rails. If he or she refused orders or showed signs of mental breakdown, their controller was obligated to use the kill switch, which should sever the link between the operator and the battle suit. Alex had shrugged off the kill switch as easily as one might flick a bit of lint from their clothing. She had been locked out, and he had retained total control of his battle suit and the surrounding vehicles. She couldn't deny that it scared her a little bit.

Colonel Chastain was waiting at the door to the administration office, which was directly down the hall from the medical center. She stepped aside and waved Nyx inside. Executive Vice President of Security Loman Haley was waiting inside. He even extended a hand to her. Nyx shook it to be polite, but she couldn't hide her nervousness.

"Don't worry—this is an informal debrief, Sergeant," Loman said as he waved her toward a rolling desk chair. "As I'm sure you're aware, we have a lot of questions about what Alex did up there. But first, I need to know if anything happened before that, which might explain his newfound abilities."

"No," Nyx said. "We were running regular missions. Surveillance, mostly."

"And nothing unusual happened? It could be anything. A sun flare, gamma radiation, a dissociative episode, anything? I know we're getting into comic book territory here, but you have to admit what Alex did up there was supernatural."

"I won't disagree," Nyx said, "but there's nothing that happened that I'm aware of that would have led to his increased abilities."

"What about during the fighting?" Colonel Chastain asked.

"No, Colonel, nothing unusual happened. We came under fire and lost Corporal Kyle Newton, but that wasn't out of the ordinary in any way."

"So when did he first exhibit the enhanced powers?" Haley asked.

"Right after I used the Titan's electromagnets to clamp him to the ship."

They continued questioning her for over an hour, but there was nothing Nyx could do to shed light on Alex's newfound abilities.

"I don't have to tell you that this is highly sensitive information," Loman finally said as he was wrapping up the interview. "All the Zen Tech people know is that we were able to hack into their ships' operating systems and shut them down. They'll be trying to find out exactly how, and if word gets out, you'll all be in danger."

Nyx nodded. She understood that things had forever changed. If people knew what Alex could do, they might be inclined to force answers from anyone connected to him. The truth was, Nyx worried that VP Haley and the newly promoted Colonel Chastain might do exactly that.

"I have a soft spot for Alex," Haley continued. "As you know, he saved my life. What you might not know is that before joining the CDF, his colony on NP8261 was attacked. He saw one of our operators struck down and took it upon himself to take the operator's place in an MP Defender."

"He told me that story," Nyx admitted.

"Yes, I figured as much," Haley continued. "I picked you especially for him. My hopes for his career were high, and I wanted to pair him with the best controller we had available."

"You set up the 'accidental' meeting in the administrative offices?" Nyx asked.

Haley nodded. "I needed to know you'd be compatible before making the assignment official."

She didn't like being manipulated, but she also understood what was at stake.

"He really operated the Defender alone?" Nyx asked.

"The unit had been hit with an electric blast that fried many of the unit's systems," Haley explained. "There was no connection with the controller. But he saved one of our own, got the unit working, and took out four disrupter drones all on his own. The funny thing is, he didn't pass our entrance exams. I even had him retested. He shouldn't be fit for the CDF, much less able to operate the most advanced MBS in our fleet." The VP shook his head at the mystery.

"What are you going to do to him?" Nyx asked.

"That depends on Alex and yourself," Haley went on. "Step one is to get him up to the *Republic*."

Nyx looked at Colonel Chastain, who answered her unspoken question. "It's back in the system, as per orders."

"For all we know," Haley continued. "Being surrounded by the powerful computer systems and multiple battle suits might drive him insane."

"And if it doesn't?"

"We'll have to run a few more tests," Haley said. "But we have the most powerful secret weapon ever devised by man. History will judge us for our actions, Sergeant West. If we misuse him, we'll be seen as tyrants, but I think we have an obligation to the company to keep him in the field."

"Doing what?" Nyx asked.

"Doing what no one else in the galaxy can do," Haley said with a straight face. "He's a hero at heart. He's proven that time and again. I say we let him do what he can do. Our job is to stand by him, guiding him at times, following his lead at others, and to protect him from those who would hurt him or take advantage of his abilities for their own gain."

"Isn't that what we're doing?" Nyx asked.

VP Haley stood up, rubbed his face, and looked over at the monitor that showed Alex in his bed, talking with his friends.

"I can't deny it," Haley said. "But he signed up to be an asset of the CDF. If he's still willing, I think we can put him to use."

Nyx nodded. She knew there was no morally correct choice, but she could help him. She made up her mind in that moment: no matter what happened with Alex in the days ahead, she would stand by his side no matter what.

# Chapter 42

A day after waking up in the medical center, Alex was helped into a wheelchair and taken to a transport outside. It was a large vehicle on oversized wheels. His team was with him, along with their controllers. Nyx stayed close, and he liked that most of all.

After Alex was on board, Colonel Chastain and Vice President Haley boarded, and the vehicle carried them out of the small colony and into the flat plain. The plain was covered in fresh snow and looked peaceful and pristine, as if battle had never been fought there.

Alex had been expecting VP Haley to speak to him. He had saved the man's life twice, and all of his friends had been called in for a briefing—but not Alex. Neither the colonel nor VP Haley had spoken to him yet. They approached a shuttlecraft, and everyone hurried from the ground transport to the ship. Alex had instructions not to put weight on his leg. The bone was mended but still brittle. He needed rest and additional light therapy to make the bone strong. Twice a day he was taking calcium supplements, and he had been given old-fashioned crutches to help him move about without putting weight on his leg.

He hobbled from the ground transport to the spaceship. There were rows of comfortable chairs in the ship. Ash and Sly were sitting side by side, and Nyx was only one seat over from them across a small aisle. Alex moved to join them, but VP Haley had other plans.

"Sergeant Evans," he said without getting up from his own wide seat. "Why don't you join me?"

The cabin was small enough that everyone heard the VP's request, which wasn't really a request at all. Alex sat down, stretching out his bad leg and propping the crutches against the next seat over.

"Comfortable?" Haley asked.

"Sure," Alex said.

"Good."

They fell into a strange silence as the ship lifted off Carthage Prime. Alex wasn't sure what the VP wanted from him, and Haley was in no hurry to talk. The ship rose higher and higher through the planet's atmosphere, and still Haley didn't speak. They were almost in orbit when he finally spoke up.

"I want to know if and when you notice the *Republic's* EM waves," Haley said.

"Yes, sir," Alex replied.

"You would tell me if there was some reasonable explanation for your abilities, wouldn't you, Alex?"

"Sir?" Alex asked, sincerely confused.

"I'm on your side," Haley explained. "I always have been. I guess I see a bit of myself in you."

"Thank you," Alex said.

"That being said, you've done things that no one else has ever done," Haley continued in a soft voice.

Everyone else was chatting or absorbed in an app on their PIL. Alex guessed that the VP had been waiting for everyone else on board to get busy doing other things so that he could have a private chat.

"Sir, I promise you I have no idea how I'm doing these things," Alex said.

Haley nodded. "So you're an anomaly—that's okay. But we're entering uncharted territory here, Alex. No one knows what you're fully capable of, and we can't let other people know about you. We've got a lot of decisions ahead of us. But the most important right now is: what do you want to do, Alex? Do you want to stay in the CDF?"

"Yes, sir," Alex said without hesitation.

"Hang on, don't be so hasty," Loman Haley said. "You need to think about this. It's possible for us to remove your INC and give you a reasonable cover story for the discharge. You could join your parents on Skandia Seven. I hear that your father is proving himself to be a real asset to the work being done there. You don't have to worry about repercussions from the company if you choose to leave, I guarantee you that."

"But I don't want to leave," Alex said. He felt a little confused. Did the VP want him to quit? Alex didn't know, but leaving his team and going on to some boring job somewhere wasn't appealing at all. "You took me from a place with no hope and showed me that I could be something," Alex said. "I love the CDF. I love being an operator. I don't want to give that up, no matter what."

"Even if your entire career is viewed under a microscope?" Haley went on. "I won't lie, your abilities are incredibly exciting. But the power you possess makes you a target. Everything you do will be scrutinized by committee. You'll have to give an account for every action you take and every decision you make. I won't lock you up in a lab, Alex, but we'll have to run tests on a regular basis. And once the other senior execs find out what we can do with an operator that possesses your abilities, well...I can't promise that you'll like it."

"So don't tell them," Alex said. "Don't tell anyone."

"It's not that easy," the vice president said.

"Sure it is," Alex said. "I don't have to do anything above what's expected of a regular operator."

Loman Haley frowned. "You mean, we just pretend it never happened?"

"Why not?" Alex asked. "Keep me with my team and task them with keeping tabs on me. You have people that watch for impropriety. Have them keep me under surveillance—I don't mind. I have nothing to hide."

Haley cleared his throat. It was exaggerated, and Colonel Chastain was clearly listening for it. She moved from her seat to join them, and Alex could tell they had the entire onboard interview planned out. What wasn't clear was the result. Haley seemed surprised, and Alex wasn't sure if it was genuine or not.

"How many people know about Alex's abilities?" Haley asked.

"Outside this cabin," Chastain said, "no one. The pilots know something happened, but they don't really know what. And they certainly don't know it was Alex using his INC to sync with their ship."

"So hypothetically," Haley said, "we could keep it all a secret."

The colonel shrugged her shoulders, "I don't see why not."

Alex heard a gentle hum. He wasn't sure if he was just hearing it for the first time, or if it had been in the background of his mind for a while and he was just noticing it. What he knew for certain was that it had the deep, low thrum of powerful systems that were transmitting large EM waves.

"Sir," Alex said. "I can hear it."

Haley nodded, picked up his PIL and spoke directly into it.

"Pilot, how far are we from the *Republic*?"

"Just shy of a hundred kilometers sir," the pilot responded. "We'll make orbit in the next few minutes. ETA at the *Republic* is forty-two minutes."

"Very good, thank you," Haley replied. He powered the PIL off and set it aside.

"Could you sync with the ship from here?" Chastain asked.

"No," Alex said. "I'm just aware of it. I'd have to be closer."

"Okay, here's what we're going to do," Haley said. "When you feel like you can sync, you do it, but don't change anything. I don't want the officers on board to know you're doing it."

"Roger that."

"We'll get everyone else off the shuttle," Haley went on. "You stay put and wait for medical to come and get you. What we need to know is how you're going to respond being on the ship, surrounded by their systems. We need to know if you can handle it when you're not synced."

"But you want me to sync?" Alex asked.

"I want to know if and when you can," Haley said. "The one thing you're wrong about, Alex, is that we can just pretend you're like everyone else. I know what you're capable of, and right or wrong, I need someone with your skills. The only question is: what's the best way to use you? Colonel, as soon as we get on board, I want you to begin scrubbing the information on Evans and the Titan Team."

"Controllers too?" Chastain asked.

"That's right. We'll classify them as black ops. I don't want anyone being able to find them in our system."

"Yes sir, Mr. Haley."

"This could work," he went on, but he was merely thinking out loud. "A secret team of operators. No one knows about them but the two of us. Opportunities like this don't come along very often...let's do it."

# Coming This Summer:
## Titan One
## (Ace Evans Book 3)

www.ingramcontent.com/pod-product-compliance
Lightning Source LLC
Chambersburg PA
CBHW052030240626
47153CB00006B/2030